one

ACCEPTANCE.

I repeated that word over and over again in my mind, trying to clear my head.

I squeezed my knees into the horse's flank, pushing him to race faster, then faster still. I crouched low in the stirrups, my legs screaming as I hovered over the saddle. The reins were sandpaper on my blistered palms, and each gasp of air burned my throat.

For two beautiful minutes, I was *there*, free from every thought beyond the fight to stay astride.

But the horse could run that fast for only so

long. Already he had slowed to a trot. I had to relax, and the second I did, the world crashed down on me.

Was it really only two months ago that Rayna and I were in France? That felt like another lifetime, and in a way it was. I was a different person before Sage.

Not that there *was* a "before Sage."

I pulled back on the reins and eased to a stop, then swung myself down. I pulled a small, hand-tied bouquet of wildflowers from a saddlebag. Resting my palms on the horse's heaving flank, I took a deep breath. I'd been doing this for weeks, but I still needed that moment. Facing the grave of someone you love never gets easier. I turned and smiled.

"Hi, Dad," I said. "I brought you flowers."

I knelt and placed the flowers on the memorial I'd put together. The large rocks looked like they were in the form of a cross, but I meant them as a caduceus, the symbol of my father's medical profession. I laid the bouquet by the largest stone, just under the silver iris necklace he'd given me when I was young. I'd worn that necklace every day, but now I preferred to keep it here.

The "real" grave for my father was in upstate

devoted

ALSO BY
HILARY DUFF

elixir

AN ELIXIR NOVEL

devoted

HILARY DUFF

with ELISE ALLEN

SIMON & SCHUSTER BFYR

NEW YORK LONDON TORONTO SYDNEY NEW DELHI

An imprint of Simon & Schuster Children's Publishing Division
1230 Avenue of the Americas, New York, New York 10020
SIMON & SCHUSTER BFYR is a trademark of Simon & Schuster, Inc.
For information about special discounts for bulk purchases,
please contact Simon & Schuster Special Sales at 1-866-506-1949
or business@simonandschuster.com.
The Simon & Schuster Speakers Bureau can bring authors to your live
event. For more information or to book an event, contact the Simon &
Schuster Speakers Bureau at 1-866-248-3049 or visit our website
at www.simonspeakers.com.
Also available in a SIMON & SCHUSTER BFYR hardcover edition
Book design by Lizzy Bromley
The text for this book is set in Cochin.
Manufactured in the United States of America
First SIMON & SCHUSTER BFYR paperback edition November 2012
2 4 6 8 10 9 7 5 3 1
The Library of Congress has cataloged the hardcover edition as follows:
Duff, Hilary 1987–
Devoted : an Elixir novel / Hilary Duff with Elise Allen. —1st ed.
p. cm.
Summary: When her recently discovered soulmate Sage is kidnapped,
photojournalist Clea Raymond makes an uneasy alliance with his enemies,
not knowing if he is dead or alive, in a desperate attempt to be reunited with
him.
ISBN 978-1-4424-0855-5 (hardcover)
[1. Mystery and detective stories. 2. Kidnapping—Fiction.
3. Supernatural—Fiction. 4. Photojournalism—Fiction. 5. Celebrities—
Fiction. 6. Youths' writings.] I. Allen, Elise. II. Title.
PZ7.D8713De 2011
[Fic]—dc23
2011022096
ISBN 978-1-4424-0856-2 (pbk)
ISBN 978-1-4424-0860-9 (eBook)

love

DOES NOT CONSIST IN

GAZING AT EACH OTHER,

BUT IN

LOOKING OUTWARD

together

IN

THE SAME

DIRECTION.

—Antoine de Saint-Exupéry

New York, in the sweeping plot of land devoted to generations of Westons. Dad was a Weston by marriage, so when he was declared dead last year, he immediately earned a place of honor among the family's power brokers and politicians. I could picture the tombstone, long enough to fit two names. Throughout the graveside service, I kept stealing glances at my mother. Did she realize she was staring at her own grave, just waiting for her?

The funeral made it onto CNN, or so I was told. Didn't make a lot of sense to me at the time. It wasn't a real funeral. There wasn't even a body. My dad had disappeared from Brazil while on a humanitarian mission. He was a world-renowned heart surgeon, almost as famous as my mother, whom the media dubbed American royalty thanks to her political career and storied family. There was a worldwide manhunt when my dad disappeared. A United Nations of countries did their part to help, and the Westons were one of many wealthy families throwing money by the boatload into private investigations. Every single person involved eventually agreed: Grant Raymond was dead. His body was missing, and he was gone.

You'd think that would have been enough for me. It wasn't. I couldn't accept it.

Mom did. She threw herself into her career, which soared, and avoided the topic of Grant Raymond, even among her closest friends. Even with me. Tabloids called her the Ice Queen. They said her marriage had been a disaster, and the worst muckrakers wondered if Victoria Weston had planned her husband's disappearance, so she could both get rid of him and also use the ensuing public sympathy to propel her career.

It wasn't true. Mom loved Dad, so much that she couldn't live with her grief. Instead, she dropped a steel wall between his death and the rest of her life.

I was different. I became obsessed with the idea that there was more to the story, and that my dad was alive.

I was partially right. There *was* more to the story . . . but was my father alive? I had no idea. He had disappeared the day he was supposed to meet Sage for a journey. When I first met Sage, he said he believed my father had been kidnapped by one of two groups, either of which would want to hold my father for what he knew.

Sage *also* told me his journey with Dad was a mission to retrieve the Elixir of Life. This was a lie. Sage and my father knew where the Elixir of

Life was—it coursed through Sage's veins. The two of them were on a mission, but it was a mission to end Sage's centuries-long life . . . because they both wanted to protect *me* from an endless circle of tragedy.

Sage was my soulmate. Our hearts were tied together so securely that we found each other in every lifetime . . . and every lifetime ended early, in my own violent death.

Sage told me he believed my father was alive, but I'd had a lot of time to think over the past six weeks, and I understood now that Sage would have said anything to keep me around. Not because he loved me—he was fighting against that from the second we met—but because he was determined to destroy himself, and with my father missing, I was the only person who could get him the information he needed in order to do it.

So did my father's disappearance really have anything to do with Sage or the Elixir? Or had Dad simply wandered into the wrong place at the wrong time? The investigators had found no shortage of possibilities. They proposed everything from Dad getting caught in the cross fire between rival gangs in the *favelas* of Rio to Dad being mauled to death by wild animals.

devoted

I didn't know. What I *did* know was that Sage himself *was* alive. Gone, but alive. And I had to give him my full concentration if I ever wanted to get him back.

I fingered the iris charm hanging off my father's memorial. "I miss you. . . . I love you . . . and I'm sorry."

I had to apologize. Every time I came here, I felt like I was killing him all over again, but for me it was the only way. I had to let go of pipe dreams if I wanted to hold on to Sage. What-ifs only got in my way; I needed to close off everything but what I knew for certain.

Acceptance.

In one fluid motion, I rose, turned away from the memorial, pulled my camera from its shoulder case, and started shooting. Once, I'd have taken my time, lining up every snap for the perfect angle and layout, but now I didn't care—I wanted quantity. This was my fact gathering; it was how I knew for sure Sage wasn't dead. For weeks now I'd take pictures every day, and at night I'd download them and scour them for Sage. It always reminded me of the first time I'd discovered him, tucked impossibly into the backgrounds of Rayna's and my vacation snapshots. It terrified me then, even more so when

6

I learned Sage had been lurking in pictures from all parts of my life—the same ageless face, whether I was six or sixteen. Back then I'd thought I was going crazy, and I'd have given anything for the whole thing to go away.

Now I ached for his image. It was the sign of our soul connection, and it wouldn't be there if his soul had been destroyed.

I clicked off countless pictures, turning in a slow circle to get every angle. Not that the view mattered—I could just as effectively have taken a hundred pictures of my shoe. But I *felt* like I was doing more if I changed the view. I needed to do things to try to find Sage, or I'd start to feel helpless, and I did *not* do helpless well.

I slipped my camera back into the saddlebag and swung onto the horse . . . which screamed and bucked under me.

"Whoa!" I yelled. "Roosevelt, stop!"

I pulled the reins as Roosevelt's front, then back, legs kicked into the air. I had a feeling pulling was the exact opposite of what I was supposed to do, but the reins were the only thing keeping me attached to Roosevelt. I tried to squeeze his flank with my legs, but he was too strong—each buck flung me higher off the saddle.

"ROOSEVELT!" My screams were as frantic as the horse's, which had grown louder and more shrill. With a final buck, he launched me off his back, then raced into the surrounding woods. My last thought before I thumped to the ground was about my camera. I hoped it wouldn't break, bouncing around like that in the saddlebag.

I landed flat on my rear end. I screamed as the pain shot through me, and every horror story about horse-throwing injuries flashed through my head. I squeezed my eyes shut and took deep breaths, waiting for the worst to pass.

"I think we scared your horse," a small voice said. "I'm sorry."

My whole body whipped around to face the voice. Apparently I wasn't damaged from the fall, but what I saw paralyzed me just as effectively: four people, standing just a few feet away. Three adults and a young girl. The adults held themselves upright and motionless, but the girl smiled and waved. All four of them had shockingly blue eyes.

They hadn't been there a minute ago, when I was snapping pictures, and there was no way they could have raced to their current spots without me noticing.

"*You're* not scared of us though, Clea, are you?" the girl asked.

"No," I said.

The crazy thing was, it was true. Once, I'd have been as terrified as Roosevelt by four people appearing out of nowhere, especially four people with glowing blue eyes, three of whom looked like living statues, and who somehow knew my name. Now I was a veteran of far eerier sights (A decimated mummy rising from the dead and chatting with me? Been there, done that.), and I knew better than to think just because something was impossible, it wasn't real.

Acceptance.

"Oh, good," the girl said. "My name's Amelia. It's nice to meet you." She seemed about to say more, but the man next to her cleared his throat, and instead she closed her mouth and lowered her head. She kept her eyes on me though, and they danced with excitement.

"You're so sad, Clea," the man said. "Too sad. It weighs on you, I can feel it."

His voice was so deep, I felt more than heard it. It was soothing, like sinking into a warm bath. His big voice matched his size. He was more than six feet tall. He looked young: His tan skin was smooth and glowed with health, and his thick, golden-blond hair fell just above his shoulders. There was a depth and knowledge in his eyes that gave him the gravity of someone older.

"It doesn't have to be this way," he continued. "You can have so much more. You can have peace. True peace. Don't you want that?"

His voice wrapped itself around me, cradling and supporting me. I'd never thought about wanting peace, but hearing him say it . . .

"Yes," I said, "I do."

"Of course you do," he said. "And you can have it. Let Sage go."

The name jolted me more than my fall. "Sage? Where is he? Do you know?"

"Sage is not your destiny," another voice said. "It's time to move on." This man had white hair and deep wrinkles, but he stood tall and strong.

"Please," I said, "if you know where Sage is, you have to tell me how to find him. He has the dagger; they could kill him. They could destroy his soul!"

It was more than I should have said. I didn't know who these people were—if they were part of the Saviors of Eternal Life, who had taken Sage from me in Japan; or if they were with Cursed Vengeance, the other group out to destroy him. I only knew that for the first time in weeks I was on the verge of real information, and I'd do anything to get every bit of it I could.

"Men," came a sigh. It was from the last member of the group, a chestnut-haired woman who stood on Amelia's other side. She was short, maybe five feet tall, and she had a honey-sweet voice that seemed to smirk even though her mouth did not. "It's all about the ones we can't have, isn't it?"

"Please," I said. "You have to help me find him. *Please!*"

The girl winced in sympathy, but it was the woman who spoke. "We won't do that. Quite the opposite: We're here to help you *break* your tie to Sage. For your own good. Think of us as your guardian angels. Do you believe in guardian angels, Clea?"

"I believe in Sage," I said. "I believe in us together."

My eyes flicked to Amelia, the girl. She'd furrowed her brow. She looked upset. Like she didn't agree with the others? She was the only one who hadn't told me to give up on Sage. Maybe she could help. I'd never spent much time around kids, but I put on a big smile and sweet voice and did my best to charm her.

"Amelia? Have you ever had a best friend?" I didn't wait for her answer. "Because Sage is my best friend, and it's really, *really* important that I find him. So if there's anything you know about where he is, can you please tell me?"

"You heard Mommy. She said we won't." Amelia's voice was small and meek, but her gaze was steady, and her eyes bore holes in me. She was trying to tell me something, but I didn't know what. I pressed further.

"I know what your mommy said, but I don't think she understands. I bet you will, though. See, Sage needs my help, and—"

"We said NO!" Amelia shouted. She gave a tantrummy stomp, but again her eyes were disconnected from her words and actions. I only got to look at them for a moment before she turned and looked plaintively to the woman next to her. "Mommy, she's not listening."

"She will," the woman said. "Good-bye for now, Clea. We'll talk soon."

And then they were gone. They didn't dissolve or fade away like a special effect in a movie; they were just gone. Blinked away in an instant.

"Wait!" I cried, but I was screaming to the air. I turned, looking everywhere, but I knew it was useless. It's not like they'd ducked behind a rock; they'd vanished right in front of me. Instinctively I reached for my camera case. The people . . . or whatever they were . . . seemed to know a lot about me. Were we connected somehow? Was there a chance they'd show up in my pictures?

But of course my camera case was still in Roosevelt's saddlebag. I called out his name and wandered through the woods until I found him, calm now and munching on brush.

"You didn't have to run, you know," I said, patting his neck. "They were perfectly harmless."

Roosevelt blew air through his lips. Apparently he didn't agree. I wasn't sure I did either, so I couldn't hold it against him. I rescued my camera and took a few test snaps. The bouncing hadn't hurt it at all. I climbed back into the saddle and rode back to the clearing, pausing to click through several more shots I could pore over later, just in case.

On the ride back I tried to process what I'd seen. Four people. Amelia had called the woman "Mommy." Were they a family? Was the younger man Amelia's father, the older one her grandfather? Was there a reason the older ones didn't move, while Amelia did? How exactly did they know about Sage and me, and why would they want to pull me away from him? Why did it matter to them? Why would they care?

One image kept flashing into my head—Amelia's face at the end, when she yelled. Everything about her was typical frustrated kid . . . except her eyes. In my mind, I could see the look she gave me. It was kind and patient, the look of a loving parent trying to explain something her child doesn't have the experience to understand. It was a strangely sophisticated expression for a girl who couldn't have been more than eight years old, and even stranger for one who seemed like she was about to have a meltdown.

It was similar to what I noticed in her grandfather, who looked old but gave off a vibe of youth and energy.

Knowledge beyond one's years . . . vitality beyond one's age . . . I knew that. I had seen it in Sage. He'd been twenty when he drank the Elixir of Life. Now, five hundred years later, he was as strong and vibrant as ever. Stronger, even. And his mind was sharp from centuries of experience.

I didn't even realize how tense I'd become until I heard the boom of Roosevelt's galloping hooves. We were moving quickly, faster than I'd ever gone, but I couldn't release my grip on Roosevelt's flanks. If anything, I pushed harder as everything fell into place.

An old man more vital than his age; a child sophisticated beyond her years.

Did Amelia and her family drink the Elixir? It seemed to fit, but it didn't explain everything. The Elixir kept people young, but it didn't give them superpowers. Unlike this family, Sage couldn't pop in and out of existence. If he could, I'd have seen it happen — it's a power he'd have found helpful many times between when I found him in Brazil and lost him in Japan.

Yet there was no doubt these people were connected to Sage somehow. They knew all about him . . . or they wanted me to believe they did.

Amelia's mother had said I should think of them as guardian angels. She wanted me to believe they were on my side. If they were, why would they want to keep me away from Sage? What did they know that I didn't?

Roosevelt slowed to a walk. We were back at the stables. He took a slight stagger-step, and I put my hand on his neck, hot and coated in sweat. I felt terrible; I hadn't meant to push him so hard.

"Wow," Nico marveled as he and Rayna walked

toward me, "you sure put Roosevelt through his paces."

Nico was my mother's latest hire, one of a battalion of staff members who had converged on our home in the past several weeks. I hated the extra scrutiny of so many fresh pairs of eyes, but I suppose I'd brought it on myself. Part of the deal with Mom and Dad letting me pursue a photojournalism career at a young age was that I'd let them know where I was at all times . . . something I neglected to do when I took off for Japan with Ben and Sage. Mom found out when she heard some of her young staffers gossiping about pictures of Ben and me that had been snapped by gawkers in Shibuya and posted on the web.

That was bad enough. It only got worse when she received a frantic call from Piri, our housekeeper, screaming that I'd come home with a gunshot wound to the leg. Mom raced home in a panic, and nearly lost her mind when neither Ben nor I could offer her a decent explanation for what happened.

Mom decided the whole incident was a direct result of my continuing struggle with Dad's death. Though she'd thought therapy would help me, she was now positive that I was acting out because she hadn't been available to me. I swore that wasn't it, but she went ahead and relocated her entire office from Capitol Hill to our home. As the junior senator from the great state of Connecticut, she had to spend a certain amount of time in D.C., but the Weston family fortune made chartered flights a simple solution.

Once, I'd have been thrilled to have my mom change her life for me, but right now I wanted time alone to think. Instead I was surrounded by chaos. And even though Mom was in the same house, she was so busy, I barely got to see her . . . just her huge, constantly moving and buzzing staff, including Nico. He was brought in to help Rayna's mom, Wanda, a.k.a. our "Equine Professional." Wanda was unstoppable, but with Mom home and riding more, she needed the extra help.

Rayna couldn't be happier. She was my best friend from birth, and I was used to her falling head over heels within seconds of meeting someone, but her instant obsession with buff, blond Nico might have set a record even for her. Despite her mom's job, Rayna had never been particularly horse-oriented, but the day she saw Nico, she put together an entire wardrobe of jeans, button-down plaid shirts, cowboy boots, and hats so she could "blend in" at the stables.

It took Rayna no time to work her way into Nico's confidence, and everything he told her, she then passed on to me. As a result, I knew far more about him than I was interested in knowing, including his age (twenty-one), home state (Montana), family structure (four younger siblings and a deceased father), economic status (poor — especially since he sent 90 percent of each paycheck home to his family), and plans for the future (continue his mom-mandated furlough to see the country and expand his horizons before going back home to the ranch).

As I dismounted from Roosevelt, Nico took the reins and led him into the stable. I felt like I owed him an explanation for returning the horse in such a state, so I followed. "Sorry," I said. "I think he's a little overheated."

"He's not the only one," Rayna lilted in my ear. When I turned to her, she pointed to Nico and threw her head back, then fanned herself as she mouthed "OMG."

I smiled and rolled my eyes. Rayna had been in near despair because after weeks of her most concentrated flirting, Nico hadn't touched her except to help her up after she tripped and fell. A fall that, of course, was orchestrated for that very outcome.

"He's okay," Nico said. He had already untacked Roosevelt and was reaching for the hose. "He likes to go long and hard."

From anyone else this would be a blatant — and pretty cheesy — double entendre, but Nico looked oblivious. That fit with what Rayna said about him, that he was "adorably innocent." I didn't buy it, but Rayna said I was letting recent events make me overly suspicious, and cloud my otherwise open nature. I reminded her I didn't *have* an otherwise open nature, but she liked the theory and was sticking with it, so I let it go.

"Clea, did you get that Camila Dexter song I e-mailed you?" Rayna asked loudly enough to be heard over the running water. "It's been going through my head like crazy."

"The new one?" Nico asked. "I love that song."

Of course he did. And of course Rayna knew it before she asked. Camila Dexter was a country singer, and neither Rayna nor I ever listened to country music, nor e-mailed songs to each other, but already she and Nico were in a deep discussion about the track, so this was my perfect exit.

Alone again, I was free to think about Amelia and her family.

Family.

Was there even a chance they could be *Sage's* family?

I had never seen his family in my dreams of Olivia, the woman I was when Sage and I first met. I supposed it was possible they could be ghosts of family members. If so, it would explain the blinking in and out of existence. But then why did they claim to be looking out for *me*? Why would they tell me to give up on Sage?

I put my hand on the doorknob of my house and cringed as I prepared to enter. I couldn't believe I was pining for the days when Piri's bizarre Hungarian superstitions were the only things I dreaded. They used to make me crazy, but at least I could slip past her and have the house to myself. These days I barely had the space to breathe. I was lucky to even have this quiet moment outside—when dignitaries were in town, we had Secret Service members flanking the front door.

The wall of sound smacked me the second I walked in. As I made my way to the kitchen to grab a snack, I passed several aides walking with great purpose, carrying who-knew-what to who-knew-where as they talked a mile a minute into their earpiece phones.

One in particular stopped in her tracks when she saw me. Suzanne.

"Clea!" she cried, and wrapped me in a huge Chanel-scented hug. She was several inches taller than me to begin with—add in her five-inch heels, and the hug had the effect of pushing me face-first into her C-cups.

Just when I thought I might smother, she pulled away and held me at arm's length, scrutinizing me with her makeup-counter, lacquered face. I'm a healthy person—I eat right, I exercise. . . . I'm in good shape. But Suzanne's long frame, tucked into her button-front, silk fitted shirt and pencil skirt, made me feel three people wide.

"We've missed you this morning!" she said.

"We" meant Suzanne and my mother, and it made me crazy that this woman felt perfectly at ease speaking for the both of them. Like Nico, Suzanne was one of Mom's recent hires—a right-hand aide here in the "Connecticut office." Mom liked the idea of someone local taking the job, and Suzanne had been an aide for Hartford's Mayor Josephson since graduating Yale with an honors degree in poli-sci the year before. Ed Josephson was in his eighties and an inveterate lecher. The buzz was she'd walked into the interview and "accidentally" spilled a sip of her bottled water down her cleavage. By the time she'd finished blotting it dry, the interview was over. She had the job.

In a strange way, I'd have been less disgusted by that story if Suzanne was unqualified, and using the mayor's sleaziness to her advantage. But she *was* qualified. Mom raved about her, and when I watched her in action, I understood why. Suzanne was brilliant at handling people, and she could go toe-to-toe with anyone on any hot-button issue and leave them reeling. She didn't need to act like a Playmate to win a job. The fact that she did it anyway turned my stomach.

Suzanne, however, felt no such shame about her former job. It had been a prime position for someone her age, and she worked both it and her Ivy League education (summa cum laude!) into conversations as often as possible.

"The senator thought you might be around after breakfast, but now she's on a string of calls that'll go all day. She's hoping her one-thirty will end in time for her to have a proper lunch, but it's with Mayor Josephson, so it won't happen.

Believe me, I would know—I was there when he spoke to the *president,* and even *he* couldn't get the mayor to hang up."

The senator. One more galling thing about Suzanne—she wouldn't say "your mother." It was always "the senator." The title that tied my mom to her top aide, not to me.

I realized Suzanne was staring at me, expecting some kind of reaction to her close encounter with the leader of the free world.

"Wow. Well, I won't count on her for lunch then. Thanks."

I slipped past Suzanne and made my way into the kitchen, where Piri was struggling to stir a wooden spoon around a giant pot—one of several that steamed and bubbled over every burner on the stove. I peeked in.

"That smells amazing, Piri. What is it, oatmeal?"

"Horse food," Piri groused.

"I read on the Internet that horses respond exceptionally well to homemade treats," Suzanne said, following me into the kitchen, "and the senator *adored* the idea. This recipe has oats, apples, carrots, salt, sugar, molasses, and water: Easy as pie!"

"Easy for *you*," Piri muttered.

"What?" Suzanne asked.

Piri smiled and nodded. "Easy."

But when Suzanne turned away again, Piri made a face and did something with her hands. I couldn't be positive, but I was almost certain she'd just flipped Suzanne the Hungarian bird.

I walked into the pantry and rummaged around for a snack I could easily take to my room. I was eager to get to my computer and scrutinize the pictures I'd taken.

"So," Suzanne called inside, "do you have dinner plans?"

"Depends," said a voice I recognized immediately. "What are you offering?"

From deep inside the pantry I couldn't see Ben, but I knew it was him. For a moment I considered staying where I was. We used to be close, but Ben and I had been avoiding each other for a long time, and right now I didn't have the patience to handle the awkward stares and stammers I knew I'd get if he had to deal with me.

"Ben!" Suzanne said. "Hi! I was just, um— well—"

Was she stammering? Suzanne didn't stammer; she was far too on her game for that. I came out of the pantry to see. I took a deep breath first, rallying patience for the moment Ben saw me.

I needn't have bothered. Ben was slouched in the doorway, gazing at Suzanne with a teasing smile on his face. I was in his field of vision, but he didn't even glance my way. I might have expected that—that he'd make a point of trying to avoid my eyes, all the while sweating and stammering and making it clear that the whole thing was a world of effort—but this wasn't like that at all. He wasn't *working* at not looking at me; he just wasn't. For a second I suspected it wasn't even Ben. The sweater he wore was much more casual than his usual button-down oxford, and his hair . . . I swear it was tamed with product.

Stranger than anything superficial was his body language. Even leaning against the doorjamb he seemed to hold himself taller than he had before, and his smile radiated confidence. And was it possible he had gotten stronger and more filled out over the past several weeks?

I pushed farther out of the pantry for a better view.

"Ah, I misunderstood," Ben said to Suzanne. He pushed off the door and glided to the kitchen island, where he grabbed an apple from a fruit bowl. He was close enough that I could stretch out my arm and touch him if I wanted to, but I wasn't even on his radar. "Tell you what," he continued, "*I'll* offer then: Dinner tonight?"

Suzanne's grin spread wider than her skinny face. "I'd love it. I don't know how late I'm working, though. . . ."

"Call me when you're done. I'll pick you up."

"Great!" Suzanne chirped. "Should I bring the cribbage board?"

Really? They were playing cribbage? Until that moment I thought I was Ben's sole cribbage partner. He'd taught me the game, and the two of us played marathon sessions.

Of course, that was back when we were close. Before he realized he had feelings for me. Before I nearly felt the same way. Before I met Sage and the entire center of my world shifted. And before I learned that in our own way, Ben and I were just as connected as Sage and me. Our connection wasn't based on love but on death. In lifetime after lifetime, Ben's jealousy destroyed me. It happened in this lifetime too—it was Ben's fault Sage had been captured.

Was Ben interested in Suzanne now? And if they fell for each other, would that be enough to break the crazy cycle of tragedy he, Sage, and I had been playing out again and again?

"He's special, isn't he?"

The honey-sweet voice whispered into my ear, but when I whipped around there was no one there.

"Is something different about him?"

The lilting voice was in my other ear now. It was familiar, I realized, as the blood drained from my face. It was the woman I'd seen at the memorial—Amelia's mother.

"He'd be good to you. Not like Sage." She gave a long sigh—a rush of sweet air I seemed to feel inside my head. "Poor Clea. If only you knew. . . ."

Was the chestnut-haired woman really there with me? Could I talk to her?

If I could, it wasn't going to happen in a room full of people. I darted up to my room and shut the door behind me.

"It's a terrible shame," the voice continued, "but the sad truth is just because someone says he loves you, you can't trust it's the case. You don't want to believe me, but you'll see."

"Tell me where he is," I said to the empty room. "That's all I want to know."

"I'll show you," she said. "You'll see. Good-bye for now, Clea."

"Wait!"

But I could feel the difference in the room; the woman was gone.

What was she? Why was she just a voice in my head, when before I had seen her in front of me? Why had she come alone this time, and not with her family? And what kind of creature could both blink in and out of existence, and speak inside someone's mind?

I smiled and paced as adrenaline surged through me. It was a strange reaction to my bizarre day—I supposed a saner response would be fear. But for the first time since Sage was ripped away from me, I had a lead, no matter how inexplicable.

Now I just had to follow it.

two

I spied on Mother while she was talking inside Clea's head.

I had to. Keeping Clea and Sage together was the only way I could stop my family from doing something so horrible, it could destroy the whole entire world.

It sounded dramatic, I knew—it was the kind of thing I used to say when I was mortal, and Mother would laugh and tell me to stop exaggerating.

I wasn't exaggerating now. What Mother, Father, and Grandfather planned to do was unthinkable. If they'd been in their right minds, they never would have considered it.

But they weren't in their right minds. Not anymore.

"I'll show you," Mother said to Clea. "You'll see. Good-bye for now, Clea."

I had a feeling I knew exactly what Mother would show Clea, but I'd have to watch and make sure. More spying. In the meantime, I had to run away quickly. If Mother knew I was watching her, she'd be furious. She was already suspicious of me, and it didn't help that when we were all in the field, Clea acted like I might be on her side. It was my own fault, but now I'd have to be extra careful.

I ran away before Mother realized I'd been watching.

I guess that's not really accurate. You can't run when you don't have legs. And you can't watch when you don't have eyes. The problem is, there aren't really words to describe how we live, and how we do what we do, since there's never been anyone else like us. We're pure consciousness . . . or pure psychic ability, I suppose you could call it.

We weren't always that way, though. Thousands of years ago we lived a normal life—back in what today is called ancient Greece, though there was nothing "ancient" about it to us at the time. We all lived together: me, Mother, Father, and Grandfather. I loved Grandfather, but I didn't see him very often. He was a well-respected teacher and philosopher, and he traveled a lot, speaking to groups or just learning about the world. I had never been outside our village, and I thought his life sounded magical. I wanted to join him on his trips, but he said they were no place for children.

Since I couldn't go with him, I was even more excited to hear his stories whenever he came back. He told his best story after a trip to Ethiopia. He had gone with a group of explorers but got separated from them after they arrived. Completely lost in an uninhabited no-man's-land, he watched the sky, hoping to find direction in the flight pattern of passing birds. He eventually saw a small lark and followed it for a while . . . until it was attacked by a hawk. Grandfather had become attached to the lark after following it for so long. When the hawk dropped it, Grandfather kept his eye on the little bird, and ran to see where it would drop. He had a crazy idea he might be able to save it.

The lark fell into a small puddle of strange-looking liquid. Grandfather got a good look before it hit the water and knew there was no way he'd ever be able to do anything for it. The bird was mangled beyond recognition. It splashed into the puddle, and Grandfather bowed his head in a moment of respect.

A moment later the little lark flapped furiously and rose out of the water . . . perfectly healed. It flew away, but Grandfather was too stunned to follow it.

The bird had been dead when it hit the water. How could it have flown away?

Grandfather knew only one answer: the storied Elixir of Life, a potion created by the gods but hidden away when they decided humans were unworthy of its immortal gift. Grandfather didn't dare drink it, but he also couldn't leave it behind. He dumped out the last of his water and filled his flask with fluid from the puddle. He was risking dehydration, but Grandfather felt that if the gods saw fit to show him their Elixir, they would certainly see fit to bring him back home alive. Sure enough, he found his group less than an hour later.

Grandfather eagerly shared his discovery, but no one believed him. They laughed at him. They said he was crazy. Grandfather tried to prove otherwise. He'd smash insects with his bare hand then bring them back to life with drops of the fluid. It didn't help. He went from being a respected member of society to being a village joke.

I was the only one who believed Grandfather. I wanted to know all about the Elixir, but Grandfather was usually too upset to talk about it with me . . . which only intrigued me more. I'd spend ages staring into the small bowl in which Grandfather kept the thick, silvery fluid. Colors and shapes swirled inside it. I imagined its flavor on my tongue — like clear, crisp honey. Once I had the image in my mind, I couldn't shake it. Grandfather wouldn't have to know, would he? It would just be a taste. What harm could one taste do?

I held back as long as I could.

Then I drank it — a long swallow that sent shivers through my throat.

It wasn't honeylike at all. It tasted both fruity and metallic, and made my tongue tingle like I'd sucked on a peppermint leaf too long.

I'd never tasted anything like it. I knew I'd be in trouble, but I couldn't help it—I drank the rest of the bowl.

"Amelia!" Grandfather screamed. "What are you doing?!"

I dropped the bowl in shock and turned. His face was white and pale, and his voice so high and loud that I burst into tears.

Grandfather pulled me close and I buried my face in his robes. "Oh, Amelia . . . Amelia . . . ," he said gently, "what are we going to do?"

He held me, rocking gently back and forth, until I stopped crying. He settled me at the table with a cup of water, then called my parents to the room.

"Amelia has ingested the Elixir of Life," he said. "The entire bowl."

Mother and Father had seemed dubious about the Elixir before, but now they paled.

"What are we going to do?" Mother asked.

"As I see it, we have two options," Grandfather said. "We can do nothing, and live normal, mortal lives, eventually leaving Amelia alone; or we can go back to the Elixir's source and join her in eternal life."

Only then did I understand the enormity of what I'd done.

I imagined myself all alone, forever. I started to cry again.

Mother wrapped her arms around me. Father took my hand.

"We'll go," Mother said.

Almost immediately, we started the long trip to Ethiopia, and somehow Grandfather found his way back to the pool of silvery water. He said it was much smaller than when he'd left it, but there was plenty left for the three of them to have a dose as large as mine, if not larger.

Grandfather lowered a cup into the pool, and filled it with Elixir. The liquid looked alive, swirling in dizzying circles.

"You need to understand," he said to my parents, "I believe in my bones this is the Elixir of Life, and it will keep us alive and healthy for eternity. But there is much I don't know. There is a chance it could wear off one day. There's a chance we could react poorly to it. There's a chance it will work differently in each one of us. I simply don't know. There is no shame if you don't wish to drink."

"I won't leave Amelia alone in the world," Mother said. She wrapped her arm around my shoulders and pulled me close. "Not when we can be together."

Father agreed and held out his hand for the cup.

"One moment," Grandfather said. "We need to consider something. Eternal life is a rare and dangerous gift. Many would abuse such a privilege, and use their longevity for personal power. If we take this step and join Amelia on this

adventure, let us do it the right way. Let us be custodians of the earth, and those people and creatures who cross our path. Let us furnish ourselves with everything we need, but not overindulge. Most important, let us do no harm to another living creature. Are we agreed?"

"We are," they intoned.

Grandfather didn't know how much or how little we needed to drink. Mother, Grandfather, and Father drank first, to catch up with me, but we kept refilling the cup and passing it around until we'd emptied the pool.

Afterward Grandfather took a spade from his satchel and dug into the dirt of the now-dry puddle. He wanted to see if the liquid would bubble back up, if it came naturally from the ground.

But the land beneath was arid and sandy. No sign of any fluid. And Grandfather kept digging, deeper and deeper, searching . . . which is how we knew the Elixir was working. Grandfather had never been a strong man, yet he dug into the ground under the beating heat of the sun for an hour and barely broke a sweat. We didn't know back then that we'd achieved eternal life, but something was very different.

I was remembering all that when Mother's voice broke into my thoughts. It wasn't the voice I remembered from back then. It was cold, with an edge that could cut steel.

"I am very disappointed in you, Amelia," she said. She shook her head and her long chestnut curls swayed side to side.

I could see this, could hear her as if she were right next to me, but she wasn't. Our real bodies were far away and seemingly lifeless. The woman and girl who faced each other were just psychic projections of our minds.

"I heard the way you spoke to Clea," Mother said. "You were trying to get her to trust you over the rest of us."

"I wasn't," I lied. "I was only trying to help you, Mommy, just like I told you I would."

She narrowed her eyes, then smiled and spoke in a low voice, the soft one she'd once used to tell me stories before bed.

"You may have fooled your father and grandfather, but you don't fool me. I don't trust you, and I'm watching you."

Then she was gone.

Hot tears pricked at the back of my eyes, but I ignored them. I had to stay alert and attuned to Mother's mind. She'd told Clea she'd tell her more. I had to know what she'd say.

three

ALONE IN MY ROOM, I went to work.

I clicked on the computer and checked my e-mail. There was one from Dr. Prichard, the coworker of my dad's whom Ben and I had met in Brazil. He was brief and to the point. He said my father had never spoken with him about his great hobby, the Elixir of Life, so there was nothing he could tell me about it.

It was what I expected, but I was covering all my bases. Sage had been taken by the Saviors of Eternal Life. If I wanted to find him, I had to find out everything I could about them, including grilling Dad's friends and colleagues for any information he might have shared with them. I'd sent out dozens of e-mails, made tons of phone calls, and had all kinds of follow-up conversations. Some people had heard quite a bit about the subject from Dad, and my file on the Saviors was growing every day, though I had nothing concrete to go on. I did, however, get to hear all kinds of stories about my dad; laughing and reminiscing with his friends brought him back to me in a way nothing else had.

It made me sad all over again that he was gone, but it gave me peace, too.

I had a few other e-mails along with Dr. Prichard's, but I scanned them quickly. I was far more interested in downloading and enlarging my pictures, looking for Sage . . . and maybe Amelia and her family?

I scanned every image, aching for a glimpse of Sage's profile, his silhouette, the sharp angle of his cheek. I bit back panic as I searched. I had no idea if Sage had kept the dagger hidden from the Saviors, but if they had it, they could destroy him any night at midnight without my even knowing. His absence from my pictures would be the sign he was gone forever. No soul . . . no soul connection . . . no pictures.

Hours after I began, I found him. He was far in the background of the shot; I'd had to zoom in to see him. His figure leaned against a distant tree. His body was turned, his brown eyes staring off into the distance. I gazed into them, searching for the soul of the man I loved in the pixilated grain. If I concentrated, if I thought of everything I knew and remembered and felt about Sage and poured it into the image, I could see it.

I reached out to touch the screen . . . and started sobbing.

I'm not someone who falls apart. I didn't do it when my dad disappeared, I didn't do it when everything I believed changed around me, I didn't do it when I lost Sage—at least not for long. I wasn't raised to be a weak person. Weak people fail, and I couldn't afford to fail right now . . . not when so much was at stake.

But I missed him so much.

Sage saw the parts of me I didn't share with anyone . . . the weak parts I scratched and clawed at every day . . . and he loved me anyway. The world felt right when we were together. Our past was epic, but when I was with him, I didn't think of those times: Sage and Olivia, Sage and

Catherine, Sage and Anneline, Sage and Delia. I thought about *Sage*.

It was the ultimate irony, I knew. In ninth grade, when everyone wrote reports on the romantic significance of *Romeo and Juliet*, my essay began, "*Romeo and Juliet* is the story of two unbelievably immature fools. Their story isn't tragedy; it's idiocy. If they lived today, they'd win a Darwin Award."

I went on from there. Romeo and Juliet were all of fourteen, and they knew each other for exactly a minute before they decided they were so in love they couldn't live without each other. Adding to the idiocy was Romeo, who two seconds before he met Juliet was convinced some girl named Rosalind was his soulmate. Then, when Romeo finds Juliet in her tomb, he's so overcome by "romantic" despair that he kills himself . . . *two seconds* before she wakes up!

The moral of *Romeo and Juliet*, I concluded, was that the romantic notion of true love at first sight was bunk, and those stupid enough to succumb to it were doomed to misery.

Four years after that I met a man on the beach in Rio, and felt immediately that he was the love of my life.

To be fair, I had a *little* more to back me up

than Juliet did. Sage had been mortal once, and engaged to a woman named Olivia—me, in a past life. The two of us had that long courtship that Romeo and Juliet skipped. Sage had that with my other incarnations too: Catherine, Anneline, and Delia. And while I didn't consciously think of those times, they were part of what made our bond so strong so quickly. Except in dreams and visions, I couldn't remember my past lives. And from what I saw, I was outwardly very different from each of those earlier versions of me.

But inside we were the same. And Sage knew and loved us all.

When I first met Sage in this life, I fought against what I felt. I didn't want to be a fool like Juliet. But the truth is, he and I fit. Even in the middle of the worst chaos, he had the power to make me feel safe and protected. Romeo and Juliet may have thought they had been waiting for each other their entire short lives, but I had photographic proof. From the day I was born, my soul was biding time, waiting for Sage to come claim it.

Sage made me complete. He made me happy. He was as much a part of me as my own body.

How could anyone lose that and still exist?

I wasn't sure I could.

I wasn't sure I wanted to.

But every day I saw Sage in a picture, I knew he was alive. There was hope for us, but I couldn't fall apart each time I saw him on the screen. I might be in pain, but I couldn't let myself feel it, not entirely. I'd drown if I did.

I waited for the sobs to die down, then printed the enlarged picture. I pulled out my overstuffed file where I placed each grainy image. I'd wanted to put them up on my walls so I could feel him surrounding me, but a room wallpapered with Sage would raise questions from my mom I didn't want to answer. I contented myself with the file of pictures, which I laid out each day in an ever-growing circle on the floor around me.

It was comforting for a moment, but then I had to get back to work.

None of the pictures had featured Amelia or her family. They knew me, but they weren't tied to me the way Sage was.

The Elixir. I kept going back to it. Every time I thought about the little girl and the old man, especially. It didn't explain the blinking away, the statue stance of the adults, the speaking inside my head . . . but I couldn't shake the feeling that it was the Elixir that tied them to Sage.

And if they were involved with the Elixir, my dad might have known about them.

My father's career was medicine, but his passion was the Elixir of Life. He'd been obsessed with it since before I was born. It would seem like the greatest coincidence in the world, that Grant Raymond would be transfixed by the one myth that would play such a huge role in his daughter's life, but of course it wasn't. It was all part of fate, working overtime to bring Sage and me back together.

Thanks to his single-minded pursuit of the Elixir, Dad was the one who found its ancient, long-buried containers. He also found Sage long before I did, and he knew about the groups that were out to get him: the Saviors of Eternal Life and Cursed Vengeance. Dad found out about everything before I did, including the doom that seemed to await me in every life. He disappeared trying to protect me from all of it, and hoping he could stop the cycle before it began again.

Dad hadn't succeeded in keeping me from Sage, but he *had* succeeded in gathering an entire downstairs studio full of information about the Elixir of Life, the Saviors of Eternal Life, Cursed

Vengeance, and anything else even remotely associated with his obsession. I hadn't even begun to sift through it all, even though I pored over it every day.

Yet now I went down to my father's studio with a different goal than usual. I wanted to search for anything he might have known about Amelia and her family, or creatures like them. I spent hours down there but finished with nothing but bleary eyes. It was late; even Mom's aides had called it a night, and the house was blissfully quiet.

When I got to my room, I found a tray outside the door with a pot of tea and a cup. For just a second I thought about Ben. After we got back from Japan, he'd made trays like this for me. He'd fussed constantly—an urgent, pleading look on his face as he fluffed my pillows, brought me snacks, and kept my favorite movies running on the TV. I knew he meant well, but I couldn't take it. Every time I replayed those last moments on the beach, I thought about Ben, ignoring what he'd been told, racing onto the beach, getting the Saviors' attention, giving them a hostage they could trade for Sage. Ben was the reason I'd lost the love of my life . . . *again*. And this time it could be forever.

Ben's was the last face I wanted to see, and I

finally had to tell him I needed time apart. A clean break. No contact.

Ben tried to quit after that. His actual position was adviser to Alissa Grande, the pseudonym I used as a photojournalist. It wasn't something he could do if he and I weren't speaking. Add to that the fact that I had no interest in working or doing anything else until I'd found Sage, and it made even more sense for Ben to go his own way.

Mom was the one who kept him on. Even if I couldn't use Ben's services, *she* could. Ever since Dad's death, we'd been deluged with requests to turn his work on cardiac disease and surgical procedures over to researchers. Mom had decided it was time to do just that. It wasn't a choice I'd have made, but it was her call, so I didn't give her a hard time about it. Mom asked Ben to sift through Dad's office—a separate room from his studio—sort through his notes and papers, and organize everything until it was ready for donation. I understood her choice. Ben and my dad had been close, and Mom trusted Ben more than anyone else outside the family . . . but I wish she had just let him go.

With the new job, Ben had been in the house every weekday, just down the hall from my room, but he respected my wishes. I hadn't seen him until today in the kitchen.

I looked down at the tea tray again. I'd been so sure he was flirting with Suzanne. Was he just trying to make me jealous? Was the tray his way of reaching out?

Then I saw the note. My mom's handwriting. *"Hoped to see you for dinner. Talk to Suzanne—let's make time tomorrow. Love you!"*

I brought the tray inside and set it on my nightstand. I was so tired, I barely had the energy to get undressed. I preferred it that way. Sleep had once been my salvation. I would dream of Sage—memories of the times we'd spent together throughout our history. But since the night I lost him, I didn't dream. Not of Sage, not of anything. It hurt so much, I could barely take it. I'd stay awake until sleep forced itself on me. I'd wake up empty and devastated . . . but I'd be rested enough to search another day.

In that last second, as I closed my eyes and felt the world recede, I heard a voice.

"Get ready, Clea. . . . It's time. . . ."

The blackness fell . . . and for the first time in weeks, I dreamed.

Sage.

He was there, right in front of me, sprawled out on a bed. His eyes were closed, and a growth of beard spread over the chiseled bones of his face.

My heart leaped into my throat, and tears welled in my eyes. I raced to him and tried to throw my arms around him . . . but I couldn't. I couldn't see my arms as I reached out. I wasn't even visible to myself. I wasn't a part of this dream; I was just watching it.

I stepped back to take in my surroundings. The room was . . . flouncy. The white four-poster bed in which Sage lay was bathed in sunlight from a large window flanked by gauzy blue-and-white-flowered drapes. A night table skirted in the same fabric sat by the bed, and on it sat a tall glass of water and a pot of white carnations, my least favorite flower. An upholstered, white wicker chair draped in a baby-blue afghan sat across the room, and a matching armoire filled out the space. The floors were hardwood, the wallpaper a maze of thin green vines bursting with tiny pink flowers, and gold-framed black-and-white pictures of baby animals hung on the walls.

It was like Sage was in a girl's dollhouse. Splayed out on the lacy pillows and flowered comforter that exactly matched the drapes and skirted night table, he couldn't have possibly looked more out of place. If this was a dream, it was the oddest dream I'd ever had.

And yet . . . it didn't feel like a dream.

Laughter tinkled beside me, and I turned to see the chestnut-curled woman. Her blue eyes flashed with life, and she wasn't frozen anymore. She was so vibrant she practically glowed, and she grabbed my hand to pull me close, like we'd been girlfriends all our lives.

"Poor Clea, you look so confused!" she said. "Let me help you. This is not a dream. You're seeing what's really happening, right now. No dream, no projection, no fantasy. Sage is here, at this very moment, and thanks to me, you can see him."

"Sage is . . . here? Where? Where are we?"

"Not telling. And honestly, we're not here. He is. I am, in a way. But you're not. I'm gathering the things I see here, and simultaneously taking them to your sleeping mind at home."

"I don't understand. . . . How?"

"The mind can do amazing things when you work with it long enough."

She must have seen that I had no idea what she

meant, because she rolled her eyes and flopped back into a chair, twirling one of her curls around her finger. "Okay, sweetheart, I can see your brain is having a hard time with this. Let me be clear. You are right now fast asleep in bed. *I* am . . . nowhere of concern to you. I do, however, have the power to see what's happening here, and to bring the images into your mind. The result is that you *feel* like you're here, but you're not. You're a fly on the wall—unseen and unheard—witnessing what's happening with your darling Sage at this very moment."

"But . . . how can you make that happen? What are you?"

"I'm Petra."

Sage groaned. I knelt by his side and ran my hand over the contours of his face. In my mind I could feel the heat of his body, the stubble of his cheek on my palm. Slowly his eyes opened, and I concentrated every bit of my energy into him.

See me, I urged. *See me.*

"Clea?" Sage croaked. His voice was rough and scratchy, and he rolled his head on the pillow until his eyes locked with mine. "Clea . . ."

"Yes! Yes, I'm here!" I leaned in, staring into his eyes. Despite what Petra had said, I *was* here somehow. Sage could tell. The tie between us was strong enough that he could feel my presence. I was certain that even though it was physically impossible, if we both just concentrated hard enough, I wouldn't be simply a ghost in his presence. He'd pull me through the dream somehow and I'd be here, truly be here, with him. I'd feel his arms around me, and once that happened, everything else would fall into place. . . .

"Shhh," a woman's voice cooed as it entered the room. "Don't strain yourself. You've been through so much."

My view of Sage was blocked by someone who walked right through me. At least she would have had I *been* there. As it was, I felt nothing, but I was instantly several feet farther back from Sage, watching as the woman set down a small basket, then bent over him. She had a white washcloth in her other hand and dabbed it gently over his cheeks and brow.

The woman looked young. She wore ballet flats and a simple cotton dress that tied in the back to accentuate the curve of her waist. She had no makeup on, and light freckles dotted the graceful curves of her cheeks. There was something so naturally beautiful and innocent about her that I couldn't stop staring, and when she smiled down at Sage, I felt myself start to smile in return.

I had no doubt she was lethal as poison.

"It's always the sweet ones, isn't it?" Petra sighed. "Come sit. This might be a lot to handle."

She tried to pull me to the chair, but I tugged away and moved closer to the bed. I willed Sage to recognize me again, but his eyes were fixed on the woman's. They looked wild, though, as if he were struggling to hold on to his own sanity.

"I need to change your dressings again. I'm sorry. . . . It's going to hurt."

"Lila . . . ," Sage said. "I saw Clea. She was here."

"Your girlfriend," Lila said, as if even the words pained her. "But there's no way. They'd know." She reached under Sage's arms, pulling him close to her. I wanted to scream.

"Try to sit up," she said.

Sage obeyed, though it was Lila who pulled him upright.

"I saw her," Sage insisted, but with less certainty this time. "I thought. . . ."

"You're so weak. It makes your mind play crazy tricks on you." Lila hissed in the air as she rolled his gray T-shirt along his back, revealing sheets of gauze soaked through with blood and stuck to Sage's skin.

I felt nauseous. "What are they doing to you?" I asked, even though I knew he wouldn't answer.

"It's worse than I thought," Lila said. "I'm so, so sorry."

Closing her eyes against the pain she was about to inflict, she pulled at a corner of the gauze. Sage gritted his teeth and sucked in air as she tore it away in a giant sticky layer of gore. Lila looked like she might cry, but she reached into her basket and pulled out a bottle of water, liquid soap, and some fresh gauze. Sage's voice wavered as she cleaned the wounds.

"You don't have to do this," he said through gritted teeth. "You know it will heal by itself."

"Eventually," Lila agreed. "But the more they hurt you, the longer it takes. It goes faster if I help." She scrubbed at a deep slice, and Sage growled with pain, yanking away from her. Lila looked like she'd been slapped. "I'm sorry," she said. "I just want to make you feel better."

Sage's face softened. "You do. You make me feel better . . . and then they do something worse."

"I know." Lila put down the gauze and poured water onto a fresh cloth to rinse Sage's tortured back. As she did, I looked more closely at Sage. I'd been so happy to see him, I hadn't even realized the changes in his body: the crisscrossing of somewhat-to-nearly-healed scars covering his skin. Even the scruff of his beard was interrupted by scar-shaped slashes where the hair wouldn't grow.

"They say if you give up on her, they'll stop. That's what they tell me."

"I can't. Clea is my soulmate."

"You've never loved anyone else?" She couldn't meet his eyes as she asked. "Not at all?"

"Not like with Clea."

They were silent for a moment, Lila working on Sage's back as he thought.

"Lila . . . ," he said, "have you ever been in love?"

Lila blushed. "Not so much."

"Then you don't know. You can't know what it feels like to meet a person and suddenly know without a doubt that the whole purpose of your life so far—every choice you made, every twist of fate along the way—was just a journey to get you to that person. My life started when I met Clea. Every minute without her is just killing time until we can be together again."

"That's beautiful. But . . ."

She let the thought drift away. Sage prodded her.

"What?"

"It's just . . . I've heard the story . . . from you and the others . . . and it's tragic. Too tragic."

"Too tragic?"

"I'm sorry. It's not my place to say. It's just that . . . if you're meant to be together . . . why doesn't it ever work out?"

Sage was silent. Of course he was. My soul had spent four previous lifetimes in love with Sage, and while we'd had moments of happiness beyond anything I'd ever known, without fail we'd ended in tragedy. My tragedy, to be specific. I've had the rare privilege of watching my own murder, four times over. I've been told a fifth is inevitable.

"I shouldn't have said anything. I don't want to upset you. It just seems like whatever holds you together . . . it keeps you both in so much pain. And if I loved someone . . . I wouldn't want to see them in pain. I'd try to stop it . . . even if it meant hurting myself." She squeezed antiseptic cream into her hand and cringed in sympathy before slathering it over Sage's wounds.

Without disturbing Lila, Sage, or the bed, Petra flounced down on the bed's edge with a dramatic sigh. "I think someone has a crush. And you know the whole Florence Nightingale thing—it's just a matter of time before he succumbs."

Her voice snapped me to action. I rose and made my way to the night table. I'd start there. If this place existed, there had to be something around that would identify it. But before I was halfway to the table, I felt myself getting sucked away, like a cord was pulling me backward from my center.

"No!" I cried, but it was too late. I opened my eyes in my own room, curled under my covers. The sun's first light crept through the window, but I leaped out of bed, wide awake. I was energized. Sage was alive, and I knew where he was and who he was with. Every detail of Lila and the room was vivid in my mind, and even though I didn't yet know how I'd use that to track him down, there had to be a way.

"I don't know, Clea," Petra's voice whispered faintly in my ear. "I thought our girl Lila asked a very good question. If you love someone, *shouldn't* you try to stop their pain, even if it hurts you?"

four

I whisked my consciousness away as Mother left Clea's room. I felt reasonably safe. If Mother was communicating with Clea, it was unlikely she'd have the energy to notice me.

Unlikely, but not certain. That was the thing with our psychic powers. It was hard to say what we could and couldn't do. It changed. Something we could easily do one day might be impossible the next. Or something one of us had never been able to do would suddenly be simple. I had a pretty good idea of what I could do at any given moment, but my family's skills were more mysterious to me. That wasn't a big deal when we were all on the same side, but now that I was secretly fighting against them . . . it could be a problem.

There were, at least, a few things I could count on, like our relationship with the physical world. Since we were pure consciousness, we didn't really exist in any specific place. We just kind of . . . were. In a free-floating limbo that none of us liked. It made us feel like ghosts.

To feel more normal, we liked to tie ourselves somewhere specific. It wasn't hard. We just had to think of a place—like the New York Public Library. If I thought about it, I'd go. And even though I'd be invisible to any mortals around me, I'd be there, anchored to the spot for as long as I wanted to be. I could spend a whole day feeling almost normal, taking books off shelves and flipping through them at my leisure. Granted, I'd be using my psychic energy and not my hands to do that, and unlike most kids, I could move entire racks of books if I concentrated hard enough. But still, I'd have a sense of place, and I liked that. We all did.

Another thing I knew is how the four of us communicated. If we ever wanted to find one another, we only had to concentrate, and we'd go to that person. So if I was in the library and Mother wanted to see me, she'd think of me, then she'd be there with me. If I wasn't tied to someplace at the time, she'd meet me in that limbo place where we otherwise existed. Being together had that same almost-normal feeling as being in a specific place: We saw, heard, and felt one another as if we were back inside our bodies.

Talking to mortals could make us feel normal too, if we

devoted

did it in their dreams. That was a skill we all had, though Mother and I were best at it. We could pop into a dreamer's head and be a real part of their imaginary world. Sometimes I'd do it just for fun, and not even talk to the dreamer. I'd hang out in the background—a child on a swing set at the playground, maybe. I liked blending in.

Mother and I could also do all kinds of tricks in dreams. We could bring dreaming minds together, or take a dreaming mind with us to see something happening in the real world, like what Mother had done with Clea.

My family and I didn't have to pop into dreams to speak with mortals, but it was definitely the easiest way. The alternative was splashier, I guess, even though it was tougher and kind of awful. If we concentrated very hard, we could astrally project what looked like living versions of ourselves into the mortal world, like when all four of us appeared in front of Clea. It had been mother's idea. She thought we'd have more impact on Clea if she saw us "in the flesh."

Mother was right—Clea had seemed very spooked by my family. I couldn't blame her. The projection was so hard for them and took so much energy that they had to stand stiff as statues. I could move and seem effortlessly human, but doing so felt like swimming through tar. For all of us, being visible was so overwhelming that we usually couldn't do much else—we couldn't move things with our minds, or any of the other mental tricks that usually came so easily to us.

I tried not to put a label on what exactly we were. If I thought about it too much, it bothered me. Were we even human at this point? Were we really alive?

It hadn't always been this way. For years—for millennia *after we drank the Elixir, we were regular people. Yes, regular people who never aged or got sick, and who could heal themselves when they got injured, but we never stayed in one place long enough for anyone else to realize. We traveled the whole world. We experienced everything in every city, every small town, every stretch of uncharted territory. We knew eternal life was the greatest gift in the world, and we took full advantage. We did things we never would have dared try without the Elixir: We swam the English Channel, we climbed Mount Everest, we BASE jumped into the Grand Canyon. We sought out the greatest minds of the modern age: We'd had conversations with da Vinci, Shakespeare, Picasso, Einstein. We saw movies, we went to amusement parks, we read and watched TV and raised pets. . . .*

We did it all. And we were happy. Blissfully happy. Before everything went wrong, we'd been alive for twenty-five hundred years, and expected to live joyfully for at least twenty-five hundred more.

But everything did *go wrong. More horribly than I ever could have imagined.*

The sickness hit Mother first. It didn't seem like a big deal in the beginning. She got clumsier, that's it. She dropped things a lot, and she'd trip. She made light of it, but I could tell something was seriously wrong.

"Mommy?" I asked. "Are you sick?"

Her eyes looked scared, as if I'd trapped her into revealing a horrible secret, but then she laughed. "We don't get sick, remember?"

She was right, of course . . . but her clumsiness got worse and worse. Even Father and Grandfather started to worry, though Mother swore it was nothing. She even said she'd prove how fine she was by making the kind of feast she used to prepare back in Greece. She spent a whole day cooking, and wouldn't let anyone help her or even peek in to see.

The smells were unreal. By the time we sat at the table, all set with our best china, linens, and candles, our mouths were watering so much we weren't worried about anything except how much longer we'd have to wait before sinking our teeth into the meal. Finally, Mother emerged from the kitchen with a huge platter of roasted pork, crowded with a mix of figs and apples and chickpeas. We burst into applause, and Mother glowed with happiness as she walked the platter to the table.

Then her legs stopped working.

One minute she was walking toward us, that huge smile on her face, and the next she was tumbling to the floor. She screamed, and threw the platter so she could catch herself. Father jumped out of his seat and raced to her. He tried to help her up, but she couldn't move, just screamed and sobbed.

"What happened?" I cried. "Mommy, are you okay?"

She ignored me. So did Father. He scooped Mother into his arms and carried her to their room. I tried to follow, but he shut the door on me without a word.

I went back to the dining room. The spilled platter had toppled the candles, and the tablecloth was on fire. Grandfather was sitting a foot away from the flames, but he didn't even notice. He stared straight ahead.

"Grandfather!" I yelled, shaking him. "Do something!"

He didn't budge. I ran and grabbed the fire extinguisher myself. It took the whole canister to put out the flames. The dining room looked like a war zone.

I cleaned it up by myself. I wanted to check on Mother and make sure she was okay, but I knew she wasn't.

Could she die? We had the Elixir in our veins. How could she die?

I concentrated on cleaning.

Grandfather didn't help. He didn't even acknowledge me. He just sat there, lost in his own thoughts. I wanted to scream at him. Sure, I'd been alive for thousands of years and I knew more than any other seven-year-old in the universe, but I hadn't ever grown up. I was still a kid, and it wasn't fair for me to deal with this on my own.

I cleaned until I was so tired I fell asleep on the floor. I hoped things would be better in the morning, but they weren't. Mother got weaker by the day. She was depressed, too. She kept pushing herself to walk, and when her legs buckled under her—like they always did—she screamed like an infant having a tantrum. She also hurt herself. A lot. She kept trying to walk down the stairs, and she fell every time. She broke her leg and her arm, and got horrible gashes all over her body. It was almost like she was trying to kill herself, but with the Elixir in her, that wasn't an option. She always healed, and when she did, she'd try walking again and it would start all over.

Father finally got her a wheelchair and convinced her to use it. She powered it with a joystick, but even that became difficult for her as the weakness spread through her arms and hands.

Mother never laughed anymore. I tried to make her feel better. I'd dance for her, or tell jokes, or put on little shows . . . all the things I always did to make her happy, but now they infuriated her. Father said Mother was jealous that I could move and she couldn't. He said I should spend some time away from her.

So I did.

I tried spending time with Grandfather, but he didn't want me around either. He was too busy on the computer or the phone, trying to figure out what was going on with Mother . . . and now with him.

Grandfather was shaking. Not all over, but in his hands. I could see it when he drank his tea—the liquid would slosh around and spill out long before he got the glass to his lips.

He didn't say anything about it, just stopped eating and drinking in front of anyone.

Soon Father started having problems too. He'd drop the remote or stumble on his way up the stairs. Little things . . . but scary.

At night I'd cower under the covers, trembling. My home was a house of horrors. We were all being stalked by some nameless, faceless thing. I ached to talk about it, but every time I tried, my family shut me out. It was like they were afraid if we said anything out loud, the bogeyman would come and get us even faster.

And if it was coming after everyone else in my family, I knew it would come for me, too.

I checked myself every night before I went to sleep. I clenched and unclenched every muscle; I did fitness tests I found on the Internet: squats, push-ups, sit-ups. I made crazy faces in the mirror. I taught myself to juggle. I did anything to prove I could control my body.

Grandfather eventually figured out what was happening.

"It's the Elixir," he told us. "It gives us eternal life, but it is not incorruptible. It loses potency over time — vast, vast swaths of time — and while it will keep us alive forever, it can only power our mortal bodies for so long."

"How do you know?" Father asked.

Grandfather filled us in. He got his first clues on the Internet. He'd had to sift through misinformation, but eventually he found transcriptions of ancient writings about the Elixir, plus modern theories and research. It was stuff we could have learned before, I suppose, but despite our love of learning, we'd never researched the Elixir. It seems silly now, but once we'd outlived our normal life spans without incident, we just assumed Grandfather had been right about the Elixir, and we'd be fine forever. Maybe if we'd been more cynical, we'd have seen all our problems coming, but maybe not. Grandfather said the pieces weren't easy to put together. If he hadn't known what to look for, he probably wouldn't have found it.

Once Grandfather read everything he could find online, he went further. He tracked down and contacted the historians, archaeologists, and other researchers who wrote the articles that impressed him most. He never told anyone our real story—he didn't have to. He just presented himself as another Elixir enthusiast. His biggest question for everyone was always this: What, if any, were the Elixir's limits?

The answer? Over thousands and thousands of years, it lost its strength and its ability to keep our bodies working properly.

"That doesn't make sense," Father said. "The Elixir is still working. Even now, if Petra gets cut, she heals."

"For the moment," Grandfather said. "Healing cuts might be one of the last things to go, but it will . . . it will. . . ."

"You mean," I said in a voice so high and tiny I didn't even recognize it, "we're going to die?"

"No," Grandfather said. "The Elixir won't let us die. Ever. But it will stop affecting our bodies. What's happening to your mother . . . what's happening to every one of us . . . is the Elixir is conserving its energy to simply keep us alive, as opposed to alive and well."

Father had his hand on Mother's, and I could see his knuckles go white as he squeezed. His voice stayed calm.

"So what exactly will happen to us?"

"I don't know for certain, but I believe our physical weakness will get progressively worse, until finally our bodies will go completely limp and lifeless. Even our organs will stop working—our eyes, our lungs, our hearts. To anyone who saw us, we would look like long-dead corpses, having gone in and out of rigor mortis."

"But we'd be alive?" Father said.

"No . . . ," Mother murmured. Her eyes were wild, and she looked like she wanted to scream but no longer had the power. "No . . ."

"Yes," Grandfather continued. "The Elixir will keep us alive. It will keep our brains intact and functioning, even as our bodies become immobile husks."

What he was describing was hell. It was coming for me next, and there was nothing I could do to stop it. Tears started rolling down my face and my breath hitched.

"Mommy?"

I wanted to climb into her lap. She couldn't hold me anymore, but if I could climb into her lap, it would be a tiny bit okay.

She hissed at me before I could even get close.

"Stay away from me! This is all your fault!"

I fell back on the floor, then started sobbing for real because this was it; my legs were going just like Mother's, and soon I wouldn't be able to move or speak or do anything but sit inside my head for the rest of eternity all by myself forever.

But this wasn't it. Mother had startled me, and I'd tripped. That was all. Grandfather reached out a shaky hand to help me up, and I leaned against him, but it didn't help. I wanted to catch Mother's eye, but she wouldn't look at me.

"This is not hopeless," Grandfather said. "There are things we can do."

The human brain, Grandfather explained, can make new synaptic connections for its entire life span. The more you challenge your brain—stimulate it with puzzles, reading, and constant attempts to master new tasks, both mental and physical—the more it grows in its capacity.

This wasn't news to us. Grandfather had suspected as much from the start, long before he knew the science behind it. He had always made sure we stretched and exercised our brains. Not that we needed much urging. We enjoyed trying new things. It's one of the reasons we had so much fun together for so many years.

Yet what Grandfather was saying now was different. He said the things people usually called "psychic" skills—moving things with pure mental power, communicating psychically with other people, going on out-of-body journeys—were just further capacities of a well-honed human brain. Anyone could do them, provided they trained their minds.

If anyone had brains developed enough to tackle psychic ability, Grandfather said, it was our family. In a way, we'd spent the past twenty-five hundred years limbering up for the feat. That would help us. While mortals could spend a lifetime working on their mental skills and never master them, our minds should be so primed that it wouldn't take much study at all. We'd have to work very hard, but we could do it. And if we succeeded, our brains could keep us active in the world even if our bodies went dormant.

Mother was skeptical. She thought we should spend the rest of our active time seeking a cure for the paralysis — perhaps a way to strengthen the Elixir. Grandfather said no. If we wasted our time searching, we might not gain the skills we'd need, and then we'd absolutely end up prisoners in our own frozen skins. Yet if we followed his suggestion and it worked, we'd have an eternity to look for a cure that would one day restore our mobility and physical health.

"I think we should do what Grandfather says!" I blurted.

Mother glared at me, but I looked away, and she seemed to calm down when Father took my side too.

Once we'd agreed, we had to prepare. If we were going to end up immobile, we needed a place for our bodies to remain safe until we restored our movement. It took precious weeks, but Grandfather eventually found a house in Switzerland that was acceptably remote. We moved there together, then Grandfather talked Father and me—the ones with the most use of our bodies—through the process of renovating it so it would be both highly secure and impervious to the elements. An inner, climate-controlled room I couldn't help but think of as "the mausoleum" would be our resting place. Per Grandfather's specifications, Father set up the glass-enclosed beds, rigged with muscle stimulators that would help avoid atrophy while our bodies hibernated. If and when we came back, the Elixir would eventually heal any atrophy, but Grandfather imagined we wouldn't want to wait any longer than we had to before we were totally back to normal.

Once we were set up, we began training our brains to reach their full psychic capacity. We spent eighteen-hour days in deep meditative states, listening to hypnosis tapes, working to channel every bit of our energy into these new skills.

Though she had been doubtful at first, Mother was the most dedicated, since her paralysis was the furthest along. When they didn't know I was listening, I heard Grandfather murmuring to Father that he made a mistake taking so long to set up the house. He started our training too late, and now we'd lose Mother forever, entombed inside her own skin. Grandfather sounded distraught—he kept murmuring about Mother as a little girl, and how much he loved her. He cried a little when he said he couldn't live with himself if he let her down. My father said it wasn't his fault—Mother brought this on herself by being so stubborn and hiding her problem for so long. If she hadn't, Grandfather could have figured out what was happening much sooner, and we'd have a better shot at training our minds. He said Mother's pride would be the death of us.

Grandfather gasped, but he couldn't have been as shocked as I was. I had never heard my father say a harsh word to or about Mother. That, more than anything, was what made me start sobbing out loud, even though I was trying to hide. Father and Grandfather must have heard me, but neither of them came to comfort me. They had more to worry about than my feelings, I guess. Besides, Grandfather couldn't exactly rush to my side — he wasn't moving much anymore.

My father may have thought Mother's stubbornness was our downfall, but it was also her salvation. She was the first to accomplish something in one of our meditations. I heard the scratching sounds from my clearly-not-so-deep trance, and opened my eyes. A seashell coaster inched across the coffee table. I gasped and looked around at my family — who was doing this?

Mother's entire body was coated in sweat, and she trembled violently.

It seemed like a lot of effort to slide a coaster a few centimeters, but at least it was something.

We had to hope it was enough. Mother came out of her trance weaker than ever, and the next morning it happened. She stopped. No pulse, no breathing.

I knew because early in the morning I heard Father

wailing. A horrible, animal howl. I tiptoed to their room and cracked the door open to see them on the bed together, his body draped over hers as he wept.

She's not dead, *I repeated over and over to myself as I tiptoed back to my room.* She's not dead.

But if her mind wasn't strong enough to leave her body, her continued life wasn't a comfort—it was torture.

*Later that day we laid Mother's body to rest in her glass-enclosed bed—*not a coffin, *I kept reminding myself,* it's not a coffin because she's not dead. *I thought it was the worst moment of my life, but I was wrong. Worse than that was the wait . . . the wait for her to communicate with us, so we knew she wasn't stuck inside herself.*

Grandfather said he had confidence. Mother had learned a lot, and since her brain was alive and well inside her body, she could keep working on her psychic skills. She wasn't necessarily gone from us forever, but there was no way to know for sure.

It took two weeks . . . then I woke to find a mug of steaming hot water mixed with honey on my nightstand.

I ran through the house screaming. I had to know if anyone else had done it, or if the gift had truly come from her. But of course it had. My room was the farthest from the kitchen . . . and by then no one else in the family could walk that far.

And the day before I had started tripping over my own two feet.

That night Mother came to me in my dreams. She held me close and apologized for blaming me, and for getting so mean and cold once the weakness hit. She said she'd been scared and angry, and regretted lashing out at me. She kissed my head, and my nose, and told me again and again how much she loved me. For the first time since it all started, I believed that everything would be okay.

Just as Grandfather had hoped, Mother's mental abilities grew and grew. She spoke to us in our heads, made things move around the house, and visited us in our dreams. In many ways, she was more present after her "death" than she'd been when she was "sick."

Things moved quickly in the next weeks. Grandfather fell the day after Mother left me the tea, then finally Father. Since I was the youngest and strongest, it was my job to get my family settled in their beds, one at a time. I didn't do it alone. Each time, those already on the other side of consciousness helped me, lifting things I couldn't lift, double-checking to make sure I left no important steps undone.

As the last one standing, I also had a list of chores from Grandfather to follow—things that would keep our bodies protected during what could be a long hibernation. There were alarms and thermostats to set, and backup generators to put in place. There were also final calls to a banking establishment Grandfather trusted. Our family had apparently been a major source of revenue for them for many years, but they never asked questions, and Grandfather liked that. The company wouldn't have access to our "mausoleum," but they would receive a large salary for keeping the house safely guarded. They were the ones who'd get the call if anything happened to the electricity and would make sure it was back on as soon as possible.

With everything in place, I had nothing to do but wait for my own turn to succumb to the weakness. It was terrifying, especially when I considered how helpless I was, alone in the house, my ability to move fading day by day. I would have lost my mind if my family hadn't worked so hard to make sure I didn't feel my solitude. The whole house danced with their invisible hands cooking, cleaning, and bringing me everything I needed. Mother sang my favorite songs in my ear, and Father hoisted me onto his shoulders in my dreams. In the last seconds of my body's functional life, my ghostlike family hoisted me into bed and closed the glass case around me.

Like Snow White, was my final thought . . . and then everything changed.

After Mother, Grandfather, and Father crossed over, I'd asked them what it was like. How was it to exist as nothing but a conscious mind? How did it feel? I'd get so frustrated when they wouldn't answer me, but now I understood. It wasn't that they wouldn't answer me, but that they couldn't. Being a mind . . . pure, untethered consciousness . . . it felt like nothing I could possibly describe.

Even saying it "felt" wasn't right, because it didn't feel—not the way I'd felt before.

Life was suddenly timeless. I didn't sleep or eat, which doesn't sound like a huge deal, but sleeping and eating had been part of what defined each day. To be honest, none of us had needed to eat or sleep since we took the Elixir—we'd have survived without—but we'd have been awfully uncomfortable. Now eating and sleeping weren't options. There was no mealtime, no day, no night. . . . There wasn't even a sense of place. Our bodies were in their beds, but we weren't there. We had far more freedom than that. We could be anywhere.

Yet no matter how strong we got, our mental powers weren't limitless. And though we constantly found new things we could do, we also found unexpected blocks. A mind we could speak to one day would be deaf to us the next, and for seemingly no reason. And while we didn't need actual sleep, if we exerted ourselves too much we'd get . . . "tired," I suppose, but it wasn't as human as that. We'd just . . . lose steam. Our consciousness would go away. Then, out of nowhere, we'd be back. It wasn't like sleeping. . . . It was more like dying, and then reviving.

It was scary. But we couldn't avoid it, because the threshold of "too much" changed constantly.

For twenty-five hundred years we hadn't exactly been normal, but we'd been human.

Now we existed, but it was different. We had one another, and that was good, but we were more ghost than human.

devoted

The hardest part was losing our senses. Anything we touched, saw, smelled, heard . . . it wasn't real, just a memory of the sensation. It was like living inside a foot of cotton batting.

I handled it better than my family. Maybe it was because I was younger. Maybe that made me more adaptable, I don't know. The rest of my family had a harder time — they missed everything they'd lost too much. I'd hear them screaming in frustration sometimes, especially when years went by and our senses dulled further and further as our memories of the sensations faded. I'd think about my mother and find her sobbing as she tried to sniff a flower, or pet a dog . . . the simplest things, but they were impossible the way we were now.

I concentrated on things I enjoyed, like visiting dreams, and joining my family just by thinking about them. I also loved my freedom of movement. If I wanted to visit a person or a place, I just had to know exactly *where that person or place was, concentrate on it, and I'd be there. The Great Pyramids? I could just think hard about their location, and there I was. I just needed to be specific. If I wanted to see the* Mona Lisa *but had no idea where it was, I couldn't think about the painting and be there. Yet if I knew it was in a certain gallery at the Louvre in Paris, I could think myself right there.*

It was the same way with mortals. We couldn't think about a mortal and go to them, but if we knew where he or she was, we could think ourselves there.

I discovered my most amazing skill a couple years into our new state of being. I was still getting over the shock of being without a body, and I decided to try to do something fun to make me feel better—something I'd never in a million years have been able to do before.

I went to the zoo and swam with the seals.

It wasn't quite the same as being there in my body. The seals had no idea I was even around. But I was. At first it was awful because I wished so desperately that I could feel the water against my skin, and the cool smooth flanks of the seals, but I put that out of my head and concentrated on zipping my mind through the water with them and staring into their puppylike faces as they played together. It was strange . . . but magical. I loved it so much, I was dying to tell Mother all about it. I couldn't stop thinking about how incredible she'd think it was, and that she'd have to join me, and I wished like crazy I could tell her about it right now . . .

. . . and suddenly I was with her.

She hadn't been anywhere specific at the time, so I found her in that limbo space . . . but at the same time I was also with the seals.

I was equally in two places at once. There's no good way to describe how that feels. It's not bad, or painful . . . and it's not like I was less in one place because I was in the other at the same time. It was just . . . dizzying. At first I felt like I'd pass out, but I quickly got used to it, and the wild thing was I could function perfectly well in both places. I told Mother what I was doing, and she was amazed. I wanted her to join me, so she could experience it too . . . but she couldn't. If she thought herself to the seals, she left the limbo space, and vice versa. Even years later I was still the only one in the family who could be in two places at once.

Grandfather chalked it up to my brain being so young when we first took the Elixir. As the next youngest after me, Mother swore she'd be able to do it too one day. As far as I knew, she never had. Given everything that happened later, that was probably a very good thing. In fact, I sometimes wished I'd never told her being in two places at the same time was even a possibility for us.

For me, even after all this time, it was still a trick that amazed me. I'm very good at it now. All the weirdness is gone and it feels completely natural, like the way pianists and drummers train their hands to do two completely different things at the same time. It's exhilarating, but it takes a lot of energy. When I do it, I'm exhausted afterward and can't do much of anything. If I push too hard, it can leave me so tired that I disappear in that terrible dead-but-not-dead way, and I don't even realize it until I come back.

All told, life as pure consciousness wasn't ideal, but it wasn't without its surprises and pleasures. I knew we all wanted to get back to our bodies, and I knew Grandfather was *working hard to find a way to make it happen, but I never in a million years would have guessed how far he, Mother, and Father were willing to go.*

They were willing to kill someone innocent and turn monsters loose on the world, just to get our bodies back. When I tried to talk them out of it, I became the enemy. Mother in particular was so furious, she tried to hurt me . . . and she succeeded. That was a surprise — I didn't know we could hurt one another in this state.

I had to be careful. I knew my mind was stronger than any of theirs, but Mother's skills seemed to be growing, and she wouldn't let anything get between her and resuming her normal life. She had a plan in place that involved Lila and using her to drive a wedge between Clea and Sage. I'd have loved to tell Clea all about it, but Mother didn't trust me, and she was paying close attention to me.

How could I help Clea and Sage without Mother knowing?

I had an idea, but it was risky. I'd leave Clea a message. Soon, while Mother was hopefully weak from bringing Clea's dreaming mind to see Lila and Sage. The message would have to be vague, but it was my only chance. I had to hope Clea would be clever enough to figure it out.

Everything depended on it.

five

PETRA WAS GONE, but her words echoed in my head.

If you love someone, shouldn't *you try to stop their pain, even if it hurts you?*

I thought about Sage's ruined back. I knew the Elixir of Life that flowed in his veins would heal him from tortures even worse than that, but I also knew it didn't spare him from pain.

It didn't make sense. Sage had been captured by the Saviors of Eternal Life, a group descended from the Society, an ancient guild dedicated to protecting the Elixir. Sage had been a member of the Society hundreds of years ago, and the lone person intentionally spared when their meeting was attacked. "Spared" wasn't exactly the right word, since he was forced to drink the Elixir and endure horror after horror as his captors tested its ability to keep him alive.

Although almost all the other Society members were brutally murdered, their families and descendants took up the cause to find and protect the Elixir, which now existed in Sage's body alone. My dad had believed the Saviors of Eternal Life would treat Sage like a treasured museum piece under lock and key, but that wasn't what I'd seen. The kind of brutality I'd witnessed is what I expected of Cursed Vengeance, the descendants of those who attacked the Society and destroyed the Elixir beyond what remained in Sage. Their name came from the fact that their lives were cursed, and would be until the Elixir—meaning Sage—was destroyed forever.

So was Sage with the Saviors, or was he now being held by someone else? And if he was with the Saviors, why would they harm him? And why did Lila say they'd keep doing it until he gave up on me?

Petra said if I loved Sage, I'd stop what was

happening to him, but if that meant giving up on him, that was impossible. Sage and I were tied together for eternity. We couldn't change that; we just had to find a way to defy fate and make it better. Even if I *could* change it—if I could snap my fingers and change the past so Sage never existed—I wouldn't do it. A life without Sage would be easier, maybe, and it would surely be safer, but it would be life under novocaine, numb and empty.

I looked at my computer and tried to figure out what I could possibly put in a search engine to help me find that room where Sage was held. I couldn't think of anything specific enough. Maybe caffeine would help. I took the tray of tea my mom had made for me yesterday and carried it downstairs, relishing the early-morning quiet. While I brewed a new pot, I looked around for something to eat. I saw a cork-sealed glass jar of granola that looked and smelled amazing, but just as I was scooping myself a huge bowl, I remembered Piri's homemade horse snacks and dumped it back in the jar.

Instead of going back to my room, I went down to my father's studio and pored through more of my dad's books and computer files, hoping to find something connecting the Saviors to a frilly room decorated heavily in white wicker. It was a long shot, and after a couple fruitless hours I went back upstairs to shower.

I made it to the main floor.

"Clea!" Suzanne cried.

Oh, great. I shouldn't care, but running into Suzanne felt worse when I didn't look at least somewhat put together. I was wearing what I'd slept in—thrashed green sweatpants and an ancient T-shirt of my mom's that featured Grimace from McDonald's. Suzanne, on the other hand, was so buffed and polished, I could have sworn I saw the sun glint off her perfect skin.

Reflexively, I reached up to smooth back my hair, as if I could possibly conquer this rat's nest on my head with a single pat. "Hi, Suzanne."

"The senator was very sad she missed you last night. I was about to get her breakfast. Care to join us?" She looked me up and down. "Although I'm sure you'll want to put yourself together first."

Of course. Because who'd even dream about wearing nightclothes to have breakfast in her own house with her own mother at the wildly late hour of eight a.m.? But she had said "us," so . . .

"Yeah. I'm just going to run upstairs. Please

tell Mom I'll catch up with her later."

"I will."

She said it like she was finished with me, but she didn't turn on her heel and clip away. She just stood there, as if she wanted to say more but wasn't sure she should. This was so unlike her, I forgot how rumpled I looked.

"Suzanne?" I asked.

The uncertainty left her face and she somehow managed to pull herself up even taller. "You and Ben," she said. "Normally I wouldn't pry, but you're the senator's daughter, and I don't want to step on any toes."

She stared down at me, waiting for an answer, but I was having trouble believing the question. Was Suzanne asking my permission to date Ben? I couldn't figure out what surprised me the most: that she wanted Ben in the first place, that she was bothering to see what I thought about it . . . or that my stomach had started to twist in an uncomfortable knot that had nothing to do with wanting breakfast.

"No toe stepping," I assured her. "Ben and I are . . ."

I'd been about to say "just friends," but that sounded like an absurd thing to say about someone I didn't talk to anymore. It also didn't do justice to what we'd been to each other before.

If my hesitation sent mixed messages, they didn't bother Suzanne. She smoothed out her unrumpled skirt and smiled. "Good. That's settled then." She clicked down the hall with what looked like an added spring to her step . . . but I could have been mistaken.

I slipped up to my room but staggered back when I opened the door, overcome by a distinctly pungent odor. I recognized it immediately. When we were sixteen, Rayna had a mad crush on a guy who played in a Native American drum circle.

I know.

For six months she went to see him play several times a week, and she begged me to come along so her stalking wouldn't be so obvious. The circles started with a smudging ceremony. A leader would light a bundle of herbs, then douse the flame to smoldering embers, and wave the smoke around "to rid the space of evil spirits."

The herbs were sage, and their exact same odor coated the air of my room.

I shut the door and stalked downstairs. There was just one person in this house who actively battled evil spirits, and I'd thought we had an understanding that I'd rather her not battle them in my room. Apparently it was time to once again make that clear.

I found Piri in the laundry room, folding sheets. Piri is shaped like a fire hydrant, yet her whole body seems to elongate when she folds sheets. She never needs help, never needs to lay them on a flat surface, they never touch the ground, and they somehow end up in perfectly crisp rectangles.

Piri was humming happily to herself as I approached, but she groaned when she saw me enter out of the corner of her eye.

"Piri . . . ," I began.

She turned as if surprised to see me.

"Ah, Clea! I was just folding sheets. Hard on the old back, you know."

I did know. I knew she had no trouble with her back but thought she'd get more appreciation for her work if she did it through great hardship. It wasn't necessary—we knew the house couldn't function without her, but we went along with it since it made her feel good. Normally I'd play into it, but right now I just wanted answers.

"Piri, why were you burning sage in my room?"

"Burning what? Why would I burn sage in your room?"

Piri's not above lying, but she'd be a terrible poker player. She doesn't look you in the eye when she's avoiding the truth. Now she was looking right at me, and her face was genuinely confused. She was even letting the edge of the sheet in her arms touch the floor, which meant she was *seriously* thrown. She looked so befuddled that I felt crazy for what I was about to say.

"Because you wanted to . . . get rid of . . . evil spirits?"

"You have evil spirits in your room?"

"No! No, I don't. I just thought if you thought I did . . ."

"Why would I think you had evil spirits in your room? Did something happen?"

"No, I just—"

"Good." Piri snapped the sheet and went back to folding. "Holy water."

"What?"

"*That's* how you expel evil spirits. Holy water. Nothing else. You need some? I get it for you. I show you how to use it."

"No, that's okay. Thanks, Piri."

Piri nodded, then turned away from me, back in laundry mode. I watched her for a moment, then walked back up to my room. I moved slowly, breathing deeply, waiting to see when the scent would again hit my nose. It didn't. Not on the stairs, not in the hall, not two inches in front of my door. Not until I opened my door . . . then it slammed into me.

My nerve endings started to prickle.

This wasn't normal. An odor this strong wouldn't just sit in the room. It would seep out. And it would dissipate. Yet the scent was just as strong now as it had been when I'd first encountered it. Maybe stronger.

I walked in warily and went straight to the window, which I pulled open. There was a breeze outside, and my door was open, so the cross ventilation should have done the trick. I gave it a few minutes, leaning out the window and breathing in the fresh air. Hope made my pulse race and my heart pound, but I wouldn't give in to it yet. I had to be patient. I couldn't handle the disappointment if I was wrong. Part of me didn't want to pull my head back in, but finally I needed to know. I leaned in . . . and the scent was stronger than ever.

The scent of *sage*.

I was breathing heavier now, and excitement threatened to cloud my reactions.

Okay, Clea, calm down, I told myself. *Look for the logical answer first.*

I went methodically through my drawers and closet, looking for incense, a candle, potpourri . . . *something* that might have been placed here and would explain what I smelled. When I'd exhausted every hidden nook and corner, I closed my door, sat on my bed, and let the truth sink in.

There *was* no logical answer. The aroma of sage . . . was from *Sage.* He was reaching out to me. I didn't know how, but I knew it was true. He *had* seen me when I sat by his side in my dream, and he was trying to tell me he needed me to be strong. No matter what Petra and her otherworldly family said or did, no matter how lovingly Lila cared for him, no matter how weak and lost he seemed, the two of us were bound together for eternity. I would find him. We would be together again, and this time would be different. We would survive, and we would be happy.

But that was ridiculous. Sage didn't have that kind of power. He couldn't be in one place and make something happen in another.

But Petra could.

Was Sage reaching out to me through Petra?

Impossible. Petra made it very clear that for whatever reason, she wanted Sage and me apart.

Then I remembered Amelia, and the way her eyes belied her words. Could *she* be helping Sage reach out to me?

It was possible, and possible was enough.

Then my eyes lit on my computer screen . . . and I froze.

Since I'd come back from Japan, I'd changed my screensaver. It used to be one of the ones that came with the computer—a randomly changing design. Rayna had thought it was strange that I didn't use a slide show of my photojournalism assignments, but I was critical of my work, and seeing those photos frustrated me with thoughts of everything I should have done differently.

Now, however, I did have a slide show . . . of the pictures I knew held Sage deep in their backgrounds. I could barely see him in these uncropped, unenlarged shots, but I knew he was there, and it comforted me.

But Sage wasn't anywhere on my monitor now. None of my pictures was. The screen was dark . . . except for several words written in a bright blue, twelve-point font that scrolled along the top of the screen, too small for me to read from across the room.

I walked over, staring as the words became clear.

"Find Charlie Victor . . . beneath the flying pig . . . time is short. . . ."

Over and over again it scrolled by.

A message from Sage. A cryptic message, which made sense if Amelia was helping him, and wanted to keep her intentions from Petra.

I scrawled the message on a notepad, then tapped my keyboard. It hurt to do it—seeing the words blink away was like losing a bit of Sage. I Googled "Charlie Victor." I imagined he might be one of the Saviors, perhaps the leader. Or maybe he was peripherally connected to them. Maybe the place I'd seen Sage was owned by him, and I could track it down by his name. Maybe Sage wasn't with the Saviors at all, and Charlie Victor was the one behind the torture.

I used every form of the name I could imagine: Charlie, Charles, Chaz. I found countless versions of the man on endless social-networking sites, websites featuring businesses owned by him, homes he last bought. I wrote down every lead, but it was pretty clear that chasing down each one would be like trying to catch every bit of dandelion fluff once you've blown it off the flower.

I tried "beneath the flying pig," but those results

were even more random, although the reference started to feel more and more appropriate. The longer I scoured the Net, the more I thought Sage had been so clever with his clue that I would figure it out when pigs fly.

Time is short. . . .

I didn't need Google for that one. Whatever his captors were going to do with Sage, they were going to do it soon. If I wanted to find him, I needed to do it now, which meant I didn't have the luxury of stumbling through on my own. I needed help, and while he certainly came with issues, I could imagine just one person to give it to me.

After more than a month of near complete silence, it was time to go back to Ben.

six

I STOOD OUTSIDE my father's office, my hand on the knob.

Ben and I hadn't discussed it, but I knew he worked with the door closed for my benefit. I often rummaged through things in Dad's studio, moving them around and tossing them aside, but I did it in Dad's own spirit. The chaos I created came from following the same mystery he had loved. I was keeping his vision alive. I knew he'd approve.

What was happening in the office was different. Mom was having Ben disembowel it. Even though I'd made a kind of peace with Dad's death, Ben knew I wouldn't want to watch as he scrubbed Dad's memory out of our lives.

My stomach fluttered. I tried to convince myself it was because of the office, but I knew better. Turning to Ben might be smart, but it wouldn't be easy.

I remembered the last time we spoke. It had been a week after we got back from Japan, and I was quarantined to my bed. I claimed it was because of the gunshot wound I'd suffered in Japan, but that wasn't it. I was too heartbroken to function. I hadn't showered, my hair was a frizzy tangle, my face puffy from crying and screaming . . . and Ben would just stare at me with saucer-huge eyes, like I was the most beautiful thing he'd ever seen. I stared up at my ceiling. I couldn't even look at him.

"Clea, please . . . ," he'd begged. The tray of tea and cookies he'd brought in with him sat on my dresser . . . right next to the untouched one he'd brought the night before. "It's been a week. You have to talk to me."

"We talk."

"We talk about nothing. You tell me you're not hungry and you don't need anything. You tell me you're tired and you need time alone. That's it."

"There's nothing else to talk about."

"Are you kidding? How can you even say that? You were shot, Clea. You could have died."

"Who says I didn't?"

"I do. Sage would too. I know because he told me, before they took him away."

I squeezed my eyes shut. "I don't want to talk about this."

"You don't have to. Just listen. He said something to me, before they grabbed him."

The memories of that day flooded back to me. The Saviors standing in a clutch on the beach, guns drawn and pointed as Sage walked over the sand, away from me and toward them, his hands raised in surrender. Two men had been holding Ben, and they shoved him roughly toward Sage, who caught him and held him upright. Ben was nearly hysterical, but Sage gripped him by his arms and stared into his eyes. He'd said something to Ben . . . I couldn't hear what . . . and Ben nodded. He might have responded, or Sage might have said more, but before they could, two of the more powerful Saviors swooped in and seized Sage, their guns to his temples as they rushed him into their van and screeched away.

"He *thanked* me, Clea. He thanked me, and then

he said, 'This will end it, but Clea needs to go on. Make sure she goes on. Help her.'"

"Fine. You've done your part. You've helped me."

"You won't *let* me help you! But I want to, Clea. And I can. I know I can. I lo—"

"Don't say it, Ben."

"I have to. I'm not keeping secrets anymore. I love you, Clea. It's not like you don't know it. I love you, and I want to take care of you. I want us to be together. We'd be *good* together; I know you know that."

I wouldn't look, but I felt Ben lower himself onto the edge of my bed. He leaned closer, urging me to meet his eyes.

"This is how it ends. The chain of tragedy. That's why Sage made the sacrifice he did. It ends with you and me together, choosing life—real, mortal, human *life*."

"Don't you get it?" Fury threatened to burn me up inside. I whipped my head to finally look in Ben's eyes. "Sage didn't make a sacrifice; *you* sacrificed him! You ran onto the beach where the Saviors could grab you and hold you hostage. Sage didn't turn himself over as part of a grand plan; he turned himself over to save your ass."

Ben opened his mouth to respond, but I wouldn't let him.

"I know you didn't mean it that way, I know, and I swear to God that's what's stopping me from kicking and punching at you, but it's taking every bit of energy in my body not to do it."

"Clea . . ."

"You saw the same visions of the past I did. You never mean it, and you always regret it, but you do it every time. You destroy me."

"No! Not this time! Don't you see? That's why he thanked me! I *saved* you this time! Look, I'm not stupid. I don't expect you to just drop your feelings for Sage and be with me. I'm just saying we can move on from here. We can start over. We can—"

"Get out of my room, Ben."

"Listen to me!"

"I did listen! You need to get out of my room before I do something I'll regret."

"Clea, they have the dagger. Sage is gone."

"He's *not* gone. I don't believe that, and I won't believe it until I have proof."

Ben sat there a few moments, then sighed and got up. "Your tea's already cold. I'll bring you some more. We can talk about everything later."

"We can't. I can't do this, Ben. I can't act like nothing's changed and we're friends."

"What do you mean?"

"I need you out of my life. *That's* how I'm breaking the chain."

Ben's face wavered. He tugged at his front tuft of hair. "But . . . that's . . . wow. You can honestly just cut me out?"

"I can't see you anymore, Ben. Don't bring me tea, don't come check on me, don't e-mail me. . . ."

"You're just going to shut me out forever?"

"I don't know for how long."

Ben's upper lip twitched. I wasn't sure if he was going to scream or cry. His eyes were already red, but his jaw tensed, and I saw his hands clenching.

"You could do that?" he asked. "Let me out of your life without blinking? Like I'm nothing to you?"

It was the opposite. If he meant nothing to me, it would be easier, but telling him that would just muddle everything up and lead him on. I loved Ben, but I couldn't love him the way he wanted. He might have been willing to settle for that, but I couldn't. Not anymore.

"Please just go," I said.

I forced myself to keep my eyes on Ben as I

said it. I owed him that much. As he heard the words, I saw his face shatter.

He didn't say another word. He piled the contents of both tea trays together on a single one, then stacked the trays together and left, taking away not just himself but any evidence he'd ever been in the room.

Now after that, here I was, desperate for his help.

There was no reason on earth why he should say yes. I'd shut him out, and even if I hadn't, finding Sage wouldn't exactly be among his top priorities. But this was Ben. He and Rayna were the two people I knew I could count on no matter what.

My stomach did another flip-flop as I knocked on the door of my dad's office.

No answer.

I knocked again, harder.

"Ben?"

Nothing.

I knocked and called a few more times—to the point of being ridiculous—when I could have just pulled open the door. I wasn't being polite. I'd been avoiding my dad's office for a long time now, and I was hoping Ben would just slip out. However, it was becoming painfully obvious that wasn't going to happen. He must have been listening to his iPod and hadn't heard me knocking.

I twisted the knob, pushed open the door . . . and gasped.

The last time I'd been inside my dad's office, it looked like a very small tornado had just spun through, leaving piles of strewn papers, reference books, and various anatomical models in its wake. No horizontal surface had been visible under the snowdrifts of clutter, and the one path across the floor required carefully tiptoeing around precarious towers of Dad's things.

Now everything was pristine. The only thing on Dad's desk was his computer. Nothing sat on his filing cabinet. His bookcase was decimated, with a few family pictures lined up on the top three shelves. Even the pile of fifteen moving boxes were stacked neatly in a single corner.

I'd once entered this room and been sure it had been ransacked. It felt horrible, like my father's memory had been violated. This felt worse. It was like he'd been erased. I walked to the desk and sat down in Dad's chair. It was something I'd done in the past when I wanted to feel close to him. I leaned the seat back, just like my dad had . . . but he wasn't here anymore.

Neither was Ben.

I'd been so stunned by the room that I hadn't even noticed at first, but he wasn't there. Had he finished the job? I tugged at one of Dad's desk drawers, and had to fight against the curl of papers to pull it open. It was wildly overstuffed, so Ben wasn't finished.

I checked my watch. Ten a.m.

Because Ben worked for my mom, I knew it wasn't like he had a time clock — she trusted him to make his own hours and work at his own pace. But Mom was paying him to do a job, and he took it seriously. He liked to come in by nine on weekdays and leave around three, so he had his late afternoons free to meet with the college students he advised. I used to ask him if he ever had trouble with the students, since at twenty he was younger than many of them, but he said it wasn't an issue. There was a reason Ben already had a doctorate, and apparently everyone who sat down to talk to him was so impressed by his knowledge that they quickly forgot his age.

He was probably sick, in which case I shouldn't bother him, but since I'd decided to reach out,

I wanted to do it immediately. *Time is short,* the message had said, and I couldn't waste a single second.

I went back to my room, grabbed my cell, and called his landline, figuring that's where he'd be if he was sick. The machine picked up.

"Ben? Hey . . . are you there? It's me. When you get this, give me a call, okay?"

I hung up, then called back. That way he'd know it was serious and he'd grab it.

The machine answered again.

"Hey, Ben . . . sorry, I know you're probably sick, but I just need to talk to you, and —"

I heard a click as he picked up the line. "Hello?"

"Hey."

"Who is this?"

Was he kidding?

"It's me, Clea."

"Oh."

That was it.

"Can you meet me at Dalt's?"

"Now?"

I got it. He was making me pay. I understood, but it still tried my patience.

"Not *now,* but when you can get there. An hour?"

"An *hour*?"

"Ben, I know you're sick. I wouldn't have called if it wasn't important. I—"

"I'm not sick. Why would you think I was sick?"

"I don't know; I just . . . you weren't here, so . . ."

"So you assumed I have no life outside of work?"

This was going far worse than I'd imagined. I was tempted to say "forget it" and hang up, but I didn't have that luxury if I wanted to find Sage.

"Ben . . . please. If you won't come, just tell me."

"No, I'll come. Give me a couple hours though. I'm recovering."

"Recovering?"

"I had a long night last night."

There was something coy in his voice, and it turned my stomach. He was with Suzanne last night. I didn't take the bait.

"Noon then. See you there."

I clicked off. Ben could try to annoy me if he wanted. It didn't matter, as long as it got me to Sage. The scent he'd left was gone now. With the message delivered, it was like it hadn't even existed. I treated myself to a long, hot shower, during which I forced myself to specifically *not* think about Ben and Suzanne.

I spent extra time shaving and giving my hair a deep conditioning. When I got out, I slathered my body with my favorite grapefruit lotion, put some makeup on, and blew my hair dry so it draped over my shoulders. I put on my best beat-up jeans and T-shirt, and threw on my favorite earrings. I told myself I was putting in the effort because I had time to kill, so why not use it to look my best. Never mind the fact that I preferred to look completely inconspicuous in public, and rarely ventured out without a baseball cap and sunglasses. My parents' celebrity—and my own recent tabloid splashes—made me eager to stay incognito, and yet here I was, practically making sure anyone interested would recognize me.

I pulled my ancient mint-green Bronco into the Dalt's parking lot at exactly noon and scanned the windows for Ben. The place was built like a long train car, with the booths pressed against the windows, so I'd have seen him if he was there. Dalt's had been our favorite meeting place for years—the greasiest of greasy spoons, twenty-four-hour diners—and there hadn't been a single time I'd arrived before Ben.

Until now.

I considered waiting in my car, but I could see there was one free booth, and I didn't want to get stuck talking to Ben at the counter.

I walked in and immediately regretted trying to look good. Several tables of people looked up and stared, nudging the friends opposite them so they could turn and get a not-so-subtle gaze in too. I gave a half smile to the people who met my eyes, then slipped into a booth of my own. I turned my concentration to the menu, despite the fact that I knew it by heart, but I could hear the squeak of stools as people at the counter turned to peek at me as well.

This is the problem with living in a sleepy part of the Connecticut coast. Other places in the world I might be recognized, but I was hardly the biggest story around. Here, the Weston family was like royalty. Even more so now that Mom was spending more time here than in D.C.

I checked my watch. Twelve fifteen. No sign of Ben in the diner, or of his car in the lot outside. Was he going to stand me up? I pulled out my phone to text him for his ETA, when a throat cleared behind me, and I turned to see a gangly guy about my age. He wore thick glasses, jeans, and a T-shirt so worn he must have had it since he was twelve. I pegged him as one of the people obsessed with my dad's quest for the Elixir of Life and the meaning behind it. I used to call them "alien lovers" and write them off. Now I knew better. If Ben didn't show up soon, I'd be tempted to have this kid join me and pump him for any information he might have on one Charles Victor and his connection to airborne swine.

"Clea Raymond?" the kid asked.

I nodded—a gesture he took as an invitation to join me in the booth. He slipped into the seat facing me and leaned his forearms on the table. "I know you're not officially part of Senator Weston's team," he said, "but you have her ear. There is a bill coming up for vote on the Senate floor that could ruin the economy of this great state of ours, and I'm afraid from everything I've read your mother is on the wrong side of the issue."

I'd misjudged the guy—he was a follower of my mom, not my dad. He kept talking, but I wasn't listening anymore. It's not that I didn't care about the state's political issues, but I had long ago decided that I'd form my opinions by reading and talking to sources I trusted, not from random strangers trying to use me as their mouthpiece.

This guy was at least polite, and he was clearly passionate about his argument. I did my best to give him a studied expression while he spoke.

That's why I didn't notice when Ben walked in.

"Sorry . . . am I interrupting something?"

He stood at the end of the booth, smirking down at us. Like my new political friend, Ben wore a T-shirt and jeans, but there was no comparison. The same outfit that made my booth mate seem more nondescript enhanced Ben's sudden air of easy confidence.

Was it sudden? Or had this been building in him the whole time he was off my radar?

"Yes, you are," the guy with the glasses said. "I was trying to impress on Miss Raymond the necessity of—"

Okay, that pushed it over the line. Now the guy wasn't being polite; he was intruding.

"Actually, we're done," I told him. "Thanks for your thoughts."

He opened his mouth to say more, but I smiled in a way that thankfully conveyed what I felt.

"You're welcome. And thank you."

The guy slipped out, and I saw him walk over to his booth of friends. They slapped him on the back and celebrated his bravery. Had I seen his crowd, I wouldn't have misjudged him as an alien lover. Every one of them wore the pressed khakis and oxfords I'd come to expect of the poli-sci majors who followed my mom's every move.

"Did he get you to sign his petition?" Ben asked, sliding into the space the guy had just vacated.

"Hadn't pulled it out yet. It was just a matter of time."

"You asked for it. You're out of uniform."

I felt myself blush.

"I see you got dressed up too," I said. "No wonder it took you so long to get here."

Ben's hair was rumpled, the slightly overgrown front tuft hanging a bit in his face. His clothes looked like he'd slept in them, and he hadn't shaved, though the growth was so minimal you'd have to know him well to realize it.

"Yeah, well . . . I kind of fell back asleep after you called. . . ."

"Right," I said. "Late night last night."

Ben didn't answer. He just let that sit between us a bit. The waitress came to take our orders. I got a toasted bagel, knowing full well that at Dalt's "toasted" meant "buttered and fried on the greasy grill to within an inch of its life."

"I'll have a veggie omelet with egg whites,

well-done and dry. No toast or potatoes—sliced tomatoes instead. And a side of fruit," Ben said.

Now I wanted to change my order, but the waitress was already gone.

"When did you get so healthy?" I said.

Ben shrugged. "You should try it."

Asshole.

"So," he said before I could respond, "I was kind of surprised you called me."

"I know. I just—"

"Then I realized you probably need something. And you couldn't ask anyone else, which means whatever you need has to do with Sage."

"Wow. Cutting to the chase."

Ben shrugged. "Am I wrong?"

"No."

"And you think I'll be willing to help you because of our years of close, meaningful friendship?"

"Something like that."

"I see. So when you said you needed me out of your life, you meant you needed me out of your life . . . until you needed to use me *in* your life."

"You could have just said no." I pulled out my wallet to throw down money for our food. It hadn't arrived yet, but there was no way I was staying. "Forget it. I'm sorry I dragged you out of bed."

"I'm not saying no. I'm just noting the circumstances."

So he was willing to help, but he wanted to torture me first. Fine. I guess I deserved it.

"Are you denying you cut me out of your life?" he asked.

"No, Ben, I'm not denying it. I'm not. I was shitty to you, is that what you want to hear? I was. But if you think I'm going to scrape around and beg for your help, it's not going to happen. I'm sorry you were hurt, but I'm not sorry I said what I did. I couldn't be around you then, and I couldn't give you what you wanted."

"Then we're in luck. Because I don't want that anymore."

There was no reason his words should have hurt, but they stung. Could I do this without him? I was sure I could ask Rayna for help. She knew Sage's whole story, and she'd love the drama of searching for him, and Sage and I reuniting.

But Rayna's memory was short. She wouldn't remember the kind of details I'd need to help me locate Sage. She also had no background whatsoever in the mythology of the Elixir, whereas Ben had spent countless hours talking it over with my dad. Sure, with Rayna as a sounding board I could figure things out somewhat faster than on my own, but I had the distinct feeling that time was running out on Sage's life. I couldn't let pride get in my way.

I put my wallet back in my bag and settled back into the booth, just as our food arrived. I spread a thick layer of cream cheese on my grilled bagel and let Ben tuck into his breakfast before I started.

"Can the Elixir of Life create ghosts?" I asked.

"Ghosts? There's no such thing as ghosts."

I just looked at him.

"What?" he said. "There's not. Demons, guardian angels, displaced spirits, phantasms, poltergeists . . . those things, sure. But 'ghosts,' that's just a watered-down term for anything with an otherworldly presence. It doesn't mean anything."

"Fine. Then give me another word for people who blink in and out of existence, speak inside my head, and take me places in my dreams."

Ben froze, his egg-white-laden fork halfway to his mouth. He set it down and looked at me, and for the first time since we started talking, I saw my old friend, the guy whose eyes had gleamed when he and Dad dug into the finer points of all things paranormal. This time when he smiled there was nothing cold about it. He was excited, and there was no way he could hide behind hurt feelings.

"Tell me more," he said.

seven

"SO WHEN YOU THINK ABOUT IT, the woman — Petra — manifested in three different ways," Ben said. He had devoured everything on his plate while I told him the story, then spent hours grilling me for every possible detail. He was even more excited now that he was dissecting the story, his eyes glimmering as he worked to ferret out its meaning.

"The first time," he said, "she appeared with the three others, at which point she spoke, but she couldn't move. Correct?"

He knew this already; I must have told him four times.

"I don't know if she *couldn't,* but she didn't," I said. "She was like a statue. The other adults were too."

"Exactly. But when you saw her with Sage, she wasn't a statue."

"Yes . . . but I'm not sure she was *with* Sage. . . ."

"It sounds like she was . . . not physically in the room, but she was there somehow. That's how she could bring you the vision of what was happening in real time."

"Right."

"And she could move normally then."

"Totally. Like you or me."

"So those two manifestations are different, and then you said she also spoke in your head. What exactly did she say?"

I glanced down at my watch. We'd spent most of the afternoon here, and I felt no closer to finding Sage than when we'd started.

"I think you're missing the point, Ben."

"You came to me for help; I'm trying to help. What did she say?"

"I can't remember the words, exactly. It was more stuff about telling me to give up on Sage, that I shouldn't trust him."

It wasn't the entire truth, but I wanted to stay vague about the precise moment Petra had spoken to me, and what she said. While I was sure Ben would love to hear a paranormal apparition was admiring him, I couldn't tell him Petra had been trying to play matchmaker for us. I could already imagine him puffing out his newly buffed chest and telling me in great detail that he didn't need anyone's help in the romance department. Besides, he was already way off track from where I needed him to be.

"Got it, okay. . . ." He ran his hand through his hair and looked around, searching. "Do you have a pen? A pad of paper?"

"That's your thing," I said. Ben was usually Boy Scout prepared, his ever present canvas satchel stocked with pens, notepads, and the leather organizer he insisted he preferred to any computer app. But today he'd come to Dalt's empty-handed, and he blushed when I called him on it.

"Yeah, well . . . I didn't think I'd be here long enough to need much. It's okay. I'll punch it in."

"So four people," he muttered as he worked the keypad on his phone, "an older man, a younger man, Petra, and Amelia, the girl . . ." Ben dropped the phone on the table and thrust both hands into his hair. He was like my dad—his mind worked faster than he could type; he needed the freedom of a longhand scrawl.

"Let's go to your dad's studio," he said. "You can go through the details again, and I can cross-reference with some of his books, figure out what we're dealing with."

"Ben, stop. I don't *care* what we're dealing with. I want to figure out the message Sage left on my computer. That's it. Then I can go find him."

"You mean *we* can go find him."

I clenched my teeth. Did he really need me to go into what happened when he joined me on adventures involving Sage? They did not turn out well.

"No," I said. "I don't mean that. I need to find Sage myself."

"Why?" Ben asked. The thrill of the mystery had drained from his face, and he sat back in the booth, scrutinizing me. "You're afraid I'm going to mess up your happy ending with your five-hundred-year-old boyfriend?"

"You know what I think. And you know why."

"Let it go, Clea. It may have taken me lifetimes to get the hint, but I did get it. I have no desire to get in the way of you and Sage. If he's out there and we bring him back, I'm cool with it. I'll dance at your wedding. I'll dance at your fiftieth anniversary, assuming Sage can handle being with someone who looks like his grandmother. It's one of those pesky issues when you fall for someone immortal."

For a second I saw it: a dance floor full of applauding friends and family, a giant anniversary cake . . . and Sage, young and vital as ever, pushing the wheelchair that carried my stooped and withered body.

I pushed the image out of my head.

"Then why do you want to come? Are you trying to protect me?"

"I want to come because I'm interested. I'd be interested even if it had nothing to do with you or Sage. This is what I do, remember? I study mythologies. I have an advanced degree in it. I research paranormal activities for fun. You come to me with an eyewitness account of humans popping in and out of existence, speaking telepathically, manipulating the world around them . . . hell yes, I'm going to come."

Ben had a point. If Sage's life weren't hanging in the balance, I'd give in, but as it was, I couldn't.

"So?" Ben asked. "Are we going together to the CV?"

"The CV? But the clue is to help us find Sage. He's not with the Saviors?"

A smirk played on Ben's face. "That's not what Charlie Victor says."

"You know who that is?"

"It's not a who, it's a what," Ben said. "The NATO phonetic alphabet. It's used mainly in aviation. 'Alfa, Bravo, *Charlie*, Delta . . .'"

"So 'Charlie Victor' . . ."

"They're initials. 'CV.' Sage's clue—the clue we think Amelia helped him place—is telling us to find Cursed Vengeance."

"So Cursed Vengeance took Sage from the Saviors. That's why he's being tortured."

"Seems that way," Ben agreed. "They must not have gotten the dagger, or Sage wouldn't be alive right now."

"That makes sense. So 'Find Charlie Victor' is 'Find Cursed Vengeance.' But 'Beneath the flying pig'?"

"I know that, too. At least I think I do."

"Great—where?"

"Not telling you. I know you too well, Clea. You think I'm going to mess this up for you and Sage. I have to keep some things to myself if I want to stay involved. Plus I want to do a little more research to make sure I'm right." Ben was already sliding out of the booth. "Meet you at your place."

He was out the door before it even sank in that he'd stiffed me for the check. I tossed some bills on the table and followed.

"You're welcome for lunch, by the way!"

He got in his car and didn't answer.

I was right behind him as we pulled in the gated driveway. It ended in a large parking area—widened recently, to accommodate Mom's added staff—but it was nearly empty. I checked my watch. It was five o'clock, but that meant nothing. Mom's staff didn't exactly keep nine-to-five hours.

Ben and I walked to the front door . . . and were practically knocked over by a fashion spread straight out of *Vogue*.

"Oh!" Suzanne cried, surprised to find people in her way as she zipped out the door. The red in her cheeks matched the shade of her scoop-neck sleeveless gown. She wore it with a delicate crystal necklace, and her long blond hair curled in loose waves over her shoulders. The outfit was simple but somehow made her look both professionally conservative and jaw-droppingly hot at the same time. I know this for a fact because Ben's jaw had dropped between his feet. He was knocked back for a second before he pulled it together and gave Suzanne a knowing smile that made her blush even deeper.

"Running out for a carton of milk?" Ben asked.

"No," she smiled. "Dinner at the Governor's Mansion. With the *president*. I'm sure you heard he's in town. It's a very small event. Very high level. Most staff members weren't invited."

"You're not most staff members," I said.

Her snark detector must have been off. She beamed. "No, I'm not. In fact, the senator says she trusts me more than anyone else up here."

She purred as she said it. I knew for a fact that my mother wasn't including me in that group of people, but something in Suzanne's gaze implied she was.

I guess her snark detector was working just fine after all.

"You look stunning," Ben said.

"Thank you." Suzanne dropped her gaze as if the compliment was too much for her to take. When she looked back at him, I could see the space between them struggle to keep them apart.

"I was going to call you from the car. I know we wanted to try to get together tonight. . . ."

"Just call me when you get back," Ben said, gently pushing a stray wisp of curl out of her face. "Have a great time."

"Thanks."

That was her exit line, but she didn't move. She just gazed at Ben expectantly, waiting for him to lean in and—

"Say hi to my mom!" I chirped.

Suzanne jumped, just enough to prove she'd blocked out that I was even there. "I will do that," she said, "but now I have to go."

Ben said nothing, but his eyes stayed on her as she clicked her way to her car and folded herself inside. He exhaled deeply and pulled on his front tuft of hair.

If he thought he was being subtle, he wasn't.

Of course, neither was Suzanne. She pretended she didn't notice Ben staring, but then the car lurched forward.

"Oops!" she called out the window. "Guess I should have put it in reverse!"

I rolled my eyes as she made a goofy "silly me" face, then finally pulled away.

"Can we go now?" I asked. Ben's eyes were

rooted to the spot where Suzanne's car had disappeared.

"Sure," he said with a shrug. I followed him into the house and toward the stairs.

"Clea! Ben!" Rayna's voice rang out from the family room. "Come join us!"

I didn't want to lose any more time, but I couldn't just blow off Rayna. I peeked inside and saw her sprawled out on one of the room's three overstuffed gray couches. Her back was propped up with one of the large, muted-red throw pillows, and her denim-clad legs and bare feet stretched across the couch seats and onto Nico's lap. The better for him to gently knead her right calf, of course. He bent over the task with furrowed concentration, barely looking up when Ben and I came in.

Rayna, however, went wide-eyed. She raised her eyebrows, and I shook my head subtly. Rayna let it go and smiled, brilliantly changing the subject we hadn't even spoken aloud.

"Can you believe it?" Rayna said. "I'd just climbed on Kennedy when I got this horrible cramp!"

"Amazing," I said. Referring, of course, to the fact that Rayna had found yet another way to get Nico's hands on her.

"So it's a true charley horse!" Ben said. I had to smile. Ben's dorky sense of humor hadn't changed.

Nico shook his head. "Rayna was on *Kennedy*. There is no horse named Charlie."

"Right," Ben said.

Rayna scruffed Nico's hair like he was a well-trained golden retriever. "Isn't he sweet?"

Nico turned to me. "I hope you don't mind that I'm in here. Rayna said it would be okay, but I don't want to overstep or anything."

Rayna caught my eye and mouthed over Nico's head, "Too cute!"

"Of course it's okay," I said. "Ben and I just have to run and check something on the computer."

"Mind if I come along and check my e-mail?" Nico asked. "I've been expecting something from my mom, but my machine's down."

"That's a great idea!" Rayna said. "You go with Ben; Clea can stay here with me."

"Rayna, I really need to—"

"No, it's cool," Ben said with a smirk. "I'll take Nico, and you hang here with Rayna."

Nico cradled Rayna's legs, lifting them until he could put the other giant throw pillow beneath them. "Keep that elevated, okay? I'll be right back."

"You're so bossy," she chided, blowing him a kiss. "Get out of here."

Nico nodded and trotted at Ben's heels, heading upstairs.

"Since when do you elevate a leg cramp?" I asked, plopping on the couch next to her.

"What leg cramp?" Rayna asked.

I frowned.

"What? Little white lies don't count." She flung the throw pillow to the floor and curled her legs under her so she could lean in close. "So tell me . . . is the Ice Age ending?"

"For some people it is."

Rayna scrunched her brows and blew a curl of red hair out of her face. She had no idea what I meant.

"Ben and Suzanne," I said.

"Oh, that."

"You knew?"

Rayna nodded. "They hang out on the porch every time 'the senator' gives her a break. It started a couple weeks ago. He smelled some hazelnut-chicory monstrosity in her coffee cup, and the next day he brought her a giant tin of the stuff. He's been reeling her in ever since."

So Suzanne was a coffee drinker. I hated coffee.

I was a tea person, and Ben had been trying to convert me for most of our friendship.

"How do you know this?" I asked Rayna. "You're at school all day." Unlike homeschooled me, Rayna was finishing up her senior year at Vallera Academy.

"I have my sources." She twirled a curl around her finger and pulled it in front of her to study it. "And he might have told me some things . . . maybe asked for some advice. . . ."

"Advice? You were helping him with this?"

"He *needed* help! This is Ben! But I did *not* tell him to start playing cribbage with her. I thought that was kind of sacrilege."

"Why didn't you tell me?"

"About the cribbage?"

"About any of it!"

"Does it bother you? You should be happy! If Ben's in love with Suzanne, doesn't it kill the whole love-triangle-through-the-ages issue with the two of you and Sage?"

I was all set to keep at it, but she was right. I should be thrilled Ben was crazy about someone else. Why wasn't I?

"Psych 101?" Rayna asked. "'I Don't Want Him But I Don't Want Anyone Else to Have Him'?"

"Ugh, I hope not. That's awful."

"But normal."

I thought about it. Was I jealous that Ben liked Suzanne more than me?

"Okay, if there is some of that—and I'm not saying there is—it's just the littlest, littlest bit," I admitted.

"Then what else?"

"I think it's just . . . he's playing it up. A lot. If he's really into her, that's great. It just feels like he's doing it for show, which is creepy. And wrong."

"If he was doing it for show, he wouldn't have started with her when you weren't talking," Rayna said. "He's a guy. You rejected him. She didn't. Of course he'd play it up around you."

"You're right." I gave it a moment, then said, "So he's actually into *Suzanne*."

Rayna rolled her eyes. "I don't get it either. But, hey, whatever makes him happy. So what brought on the sort-of thaw with you guys?"

I smiled, feeling a warm glow spread through me.

"Sage. I saw Sage."

"WHAT?" Rayna cried. "When? And by the way, *completely* unacceptable that you didn't start the conversation with that. What the hell?"

I took a deep breath and filled her in on the highlights. Her expression went from excited to concerned, until her brow was furrowed.

"So you're just going to run off and chase the CV? Aren't they the big scary guys who attacked you and Ben in Brazil?"

"Japan, too," I agreed.

"With guns, right?"

I nodded.

"So even if you find them, what makes you think you and Ben can just walk in together and find Sage? If Sage is even there."

"Sage has to be there," I said. "He left me the message."

"What if he didn't? What if it's a trap?"

"By the CV? Why? If they don't have Sage, taking me won't help them get him. And if they do have him, why bother trapping me?"

"So this is it. And you think Ben will help?"

"He's making me bring him. Maybe you're right. If he's all about Suzanne, it might not be a problem."

"Let me go with you," Rayna said. "Maybe I can help stop him if . . . you know . . . he makes a mistake again."

I shook my head. "Dangerous guys with guns,

remember?" I saw Nico and Ben approaching the door, so I gasped theatrically. "Rayna! Didn't I say you shouldn't try to walk yet?"

Rayna got the hint and winced as Nico raced in. "Are you okay?" he asked, settling her gently back onto the couch.

"I think so. . . . Too much too soon, I guess. Ooh, that feels much better." Nico resumed his post massaging her left calf. "Thanks, Nico."

Nico was no brain trust, but even he had to realize no leg cramp could last this long . . . or magically migrate to Rayna's other calf. He clearly liked her.

I turned to Ben, standing in the doorway. "Did you figure it out?"

"Yep. I know exactly where we're going."

"Where?"

"Nope, not telling. Ready to go?"

I gave a silent prayer to the universe that Rayna was right and things were different now.

"I'm ready."

eight

Good. Ben and Clea were on their way. I had been peeking in on Clea periodically since she found the message I left, and I saw what Ben was looking at on the computer. They were going to the right place. I took my mind away from them. It had been dangerous to even peek, but I'd reached out with my mind and felt that Mother was with Father and Grandfather. Tied to them, she couldn't follow me and see what I was doing. Not unless she'd developed the same skill I had, of being in two places at once.

I didn't think she had, but I made my peeks very fast, just to be sure.

Sending Clea to Cursed Vengeance was a gamble, but

an educated one. My family had been spending a lot of time around the Saviors of Eternal Life. It was part of the Grand Plan — the Saviors were very impressed when we showed our skills, whether we were astrally projecting ourselves into their midst, speaking inside their heads, or playing poltergeist and moving things around the room. The more they saw, the more eager they were to do exactly what we — what my family — needed them to do.

Since I was playing the good daughter and granddaughter, I hung out around the Saviors as much as anyone. More, even, since I needed to prove I was on my family's side. The benefit was that I heard all kinds of conversations between members of the Saviors. Most of them made me sick, but some were useful. Like the things I heard about Cursed Vengeance, the CV. The Saviors were apparently on constant alert, because the CV would do anything to find Sage, take him, and destroy both him and the Elixir. If that happened before the Plan was complete, it would ruin everything. Some of the Saviors were worried, but most of them felt confident in their remote location and — if the worst happened — their large arsenal of weapons.

The Saviors had an enemy! This was incredible news. I'd been searching for a way to free Sage before the Plan happened, but Mother was making it difficult.

She didn't trust me, and paid such close attention that more than half of the time if I uttered Sage's name, or

Clea's, or any such word that might raise an alarm, Mother would appear. It happened if I was speaking with Father or Grandfather, if I was speaking in one of the Saviors' dreams or minds. It was as if these words set off alarms in Mother, and brought her to me immediately. It was a new skill, and it made things much trickier. I couldn't save Sage myself because my family was on alert for that. I couldn't tell Clea where to find Sage—even hinting at his location would send a red flare to Mother's consciousness. Even if it didn't, the Saviors were armed and dangerous. I doubted Clea could handle them on her own. If I sent her to them and she tried to save Sage, she'd probably be killed.

But maybe I could send Clea to the CV.

I listened in to more conversations about Cursed Vengeance. They were a common topic among the Saviors. The CV wanted Sage destroyed, so they weren't exactly the good guys, but at least they wouldn't unleash hell on earth with their plans.

From stories I overheard, I knew the CV had used Clea to find Sage before. Now she and they had something in common: They both wanted Sage away from the Saviors as much as I did. The CV scared the Saviors. They were strong. If they helped Clea, she'd stand a better chance. I'd just need to bring Clea and the CV together, then give them more information without Mother knowing . . .

I could try.

devoted

It wasn't hard to find out where the CV were located. Several of the Saviors had ideas, so I waited until Mother was distracted, then briefly checked out each location until I found the right one. I didn't tell Clea; I left a vague clue to be safer. The scent of sage was risky, but so far Mother had been tuned into sights and sounds, not smells.

I'd worried that Clea wouldn't understand the message, but I felt better now that she was on her way. Things were so complicated now, and it was all my fault. If I hadn't drunk the Elixir . . .

If I hadn't drunk the Elixir, we'd be long dead. Would that be better?

Sometimes I thought it would.

More often I wished Grandfather had never discovered the "cure" that would get us back into our bodies. Maybe if there was no other way, we all could have been satisfied with this new way of life. But no, even though it took him years, Grandfather finally found a way. He gathered us to share the news.

"I know how to end this," he said. "I know how to get our lives back."

The trail to success started on the computer, he told us, when he found a report about scientists having limited success in rats with a synthetic Elixir of Life. It worked, Grandfather told us, by multiplying mitochondria, organelles that create energy.

"What's interesting about mitochondria," he said, "is that millions of years ago they were independent creatures."

"My, that is interesting," said Mother, rolling her eyes.

Grandfather wasn't dissuaded. "Who knows anything about vibration theory?"

"Dad . . . seriously?"

"Quiet, Petra. Vibration theory dictates that every living thing in the universe functions on vibrations. Every creature has its own unique vibration. Disharmonious vibrations lead to everything from fatigue to cancer."

Mother opened her mouth to speak, but Father raised a hand. "I'll do it." He turned to Grandfather. "What does any of this have to do with us?"

"Petra, when you said you wanted to marry this young man, what was my only caution?"

Mother stifled a smile. "He didn't listen."

"He didn't listen," Grandfather agreed. "Now, vibration therapy is a medicine that brings disharmonious vibrations back into harmony. It's very effective, but its most miraculous results have been in treating otherwise fatal diseases of the mitochondria."

"Mitochondria?" I asked. "The stuff the synthetic Elixir affects?"

"Amazing," Grandfather said with a smile. "Two non-listeners like you give birth to the only one who pays attention. Yes, Amelia. That's right. Since mitochondria were once independent creatures, each has its own vibration, so they're particularly sensitive to therapy. In fact, many believe the vibrations of mitochondria are the key to human vitality."

Grandfather had me now. A Wind in the Door by Madeleine L'Engle was one of my favorite novels, so mitochondria holding the key to humanity was perfectly reasonable to me. "How?"

"Think about singing," Grandfather said. "If one person sings, there's a certain level of sound, but if five people sing, it seems like there's more than five times the sound of one. Why?"

"Vibrations?" I asked.

"Vibrations!" he agreed. "Sound waves vibrating together, complementing one another, and enhancing one another. Same with the mitochondria. Their vibrations complement and enhance one another too. As new people are born, those vibrations are constantly refreshed, strengthened, and reenergized. That doesn't happen with us."

"Why not?" Mother asked.

"What, you're interested now?" Grandfather teased. "It doesn't happen, because our mitochondria are fundamentally different from that of mortal humans. The Elixir mutated them."

We didn't ask how he knew. He could go anywhere and move things with his mind. He could have taken a cell sample from his own dormant body, looked at it under a microscope, and compared what he saw to normal mortal cells.

"With different mitochondria, we vibrate at a different frequency than mortals. Their vibrations don't refresh and strengthen ours. Without that constant refueling mortals have, our vibrational energy has petered out. We survive, but we no longer thrive."

"So . . . what would we need to do?" Father asked. "Have more kids, so they'd have the same mutation? I don't even know if that's possible."

"No new children," Grandfather said, "but we do need more mitochondria like ours in the world. We need many more people to drink the Elixir of Life."

"Great!" Mother said. "I'll pop over to the store and grab a gallon of Elixir we can share with the neighbors and—oh right, there is no more Elixir."

"That's not quite true," Grandfather said, "as I learned on a most enlightening trip to Greece. . . ."

He said "trip to Greece" as if he'd hopped a plane or cruise ship, rather than bounced his consciousness across the globe. He'd gone to the National Historical Museum in Athens, where the archives are filled with ancient books and writings not open to the public. He hoped to find some Elixir lore he didn't already know—something that might tell him if more of the liquid existed somewhere in the world. He found nothing, but instead of coming home right away, he let his mind wander through the museum, gazing at the antiquities from our mortal lifetimes. It was nothing but nostalgia, but it led him to Albert.

Albert was an American tourist, in the middle of a heated conversation . . . about the Elixir of Life. Grandfather listened in, and was impressed by the man's knowledge—so impressed that he let his mind follow Albert to his hotel room that night, and visited the man in his dreams to chat. It turned out Albert was one of the senior members of a group called the Saviors of Eternal Life, and they had recently scored the ultimate coup: They captured the vessel of the Elixir of Life.

"What vessel?" Father asked.

"A man," Grandfather said. "Albert told me the whole story. The man's name is Sage, and he apparently drank the Elixir some five hundred years ago."

"You mean . . . there's somebody else out there like us?" I asked.

"Well, not like us the way we are now," Grandfather clarified, "though he will be in a thousand years or so if things don't change. But, yes, there is another immortal. Truth be told, we're lucky he exists. His mitochondrial vibrations helped our bodies stay active as long as they did."

"So you believe he's real?" Father asked.

Grandfather nodded. "When we went to the pool of Elixir, it was smaller than I had first seen it, remember? I didn't think much of it, given our circumstances, but someone else must have drained it, probably bottled it up. There were vials excavated a few years back—ancient vials said to have held the Elixir. I didn't believe it then, but now it fits. Some of that Elixir must have ended up in Sage."

"That's all fine," Mother said, "but what does it mean for us? Whatever vibrations Sage gives us clearly aren't enough."

"True," Grandfather said. "But there's a way to get the Elixir out of Sage and share it with many others. They will then have the same mutation we do, and together they'll create a vibrational force strong enough to bring our bodies back to life."

"How?" Mother asked.

Grandfather told us. It was Albert who believed it was possible. In their dreamtime conversation, he admitted he was in Greece to research ancient texts. He knew there was a ceremony that would drain the Elixir from someone who'd taken it, return the Elixir to the earth, and destroy it and the person forever.

"Wait—," I said. "You mean . . . we can be . . . killed? Even though we've had the Elixir?"

"Yes and no," Grandfather replied. "We can, technically, but it's a very involved ceremony. We're not in any danger. That's not the point though. You were so good at listening before, Amelia. Please."

I nodded, and he went on. Albert had found references to a variation of the ceremony—one that would drain the Elixir but maintain its power. He'd hoped to find the text detailing the ceremony in the museum, but after talking to several researchers, it seemed like the ancient book he wanted was in the home vault of an Italian man with a vast private collection of antiquities. Albert had contacted the man, but he wasn't interested in letting anyone see his books.

For Albert, the whole conversation was only a dream. He was shocked to wake up and find Grandfather standing at the foot of his bed, still as a statue. Grandfather knew the astral projection would have more impact than anything else he could say or do. He offered Albert a deal: Grandfather would transport his consciousness to the Italian man's private collection and read the text Albert could not; in return, Albert would bring together a group of people who believed in the Elixir and were ready to enjoy the gift of eternal life.

Albert was only too happy to agree.

Grandfather left immediately, and read about the details of the ceremony. It was very similar to the ritual Albert had told him about—the one that would destroy the Elixir—but with a variation. This ceremony had to be done during the full moon—the time of renewal. The first part untethered the victim from all earthly delights, while the more gruesome second part happened at the stroke of midnight, when the blood of the victim was collected in a bowl of unadulterated silver, the metal of purity. That bowl would transform the blood back—for a short time—into pure Elixir, which could be shared immediately with others and render them immortal.

"Which will bring us back to ourselves." Mother sighed.

It sounded heavenly, and yet . . .

"But, Grandfather . . . what about the man? Sage. Won't the ceremony kill him? Or can he drink from the bowl and come back to life?"

"What kind of a question is that?" Mother asked.

"I just wondered. . . . I mean, if he can't . . . aren't we murdering him?"

"We're sacrificing him," Grandfather said. "To save our lives, and the new lives of many, many others — our new brethren, the Saviors of Eternal Life. At least, the group of Saviors handpicked by Albert to join us. They took Sage from the larger group and relocated to a safe place, where we can do the ceremony tomorrow, with the full moon."

Tomorrow? Mother and Father leaped up, cheering and hugging each other. I wanted to share their excitement . . . but Sage . . .

"Amelia, come on!" Mother said. "Celebrate with us!"

"I would . . . it's just . . . I mean, he's a person. How is it okay to kill him?"

"Amelia," she said, "would you rather see him alive and us dead?"

"We're not dead. We're just —"

"You need to think of the bigger picture, Amelia," Grandfather said. "The salvation of many is worth the sacrifice of one."

"But there's no salvation. We're not trying to survive; we're just trying to make things a little better for us."

"A little better?" Father gaped.

"I'd think you of all people would be more considerate, Amelia," Mother said. "We only drank the Elixir in the first place to make things better for you. Is it so horrible now to try to make things better for us?"

My face flushed. She wasn't wrong, but killing someone . . .

"Let me talk to the child," Grandfather said.

Mother and Father nodded, and I felt their minds slip away. I was alone with Grandfather. He put an arm around me.

"You've had an extraordinary life, Amelia, haven't you?" he asked.

"Yes."

"And you've been happy?"

"Very happy, Grandfather."

"Would you have rather grown up? Grown old? Gotten sick?"

"No."

"Would you have wanted to watch the rest of us get sick, and old, and die, leaving you one by one?"

Tears sprang to my eyes and my voice trembled. "No, Grandfather."

He gave my shoulders a gentle squeeze, pulling me closer. "It's okay. Don't cry. You've never had to face any of that, and you never will. It was a mistake when you drank the Elixir, but look at all the happiness it's brought us. Now we can share that gift with others. Albert and his friends are good people. Wouldn't it be kind to give them centuries of joy like we've had?"

I nodded. It would be an amazing gift to share. But still . . .

"Sacrifice me," I whispered. "Not Sage. Take me instead."

Grandfather shook his head. "The Elixir is already too weak in our family. Even in you. It has to be Sage."

After a long time I looked up at Grandfather. "Will he hurt?"

"The ceremony will be swift and painless. And when it's over, after thousands of years on our own, we'll have a community. One with enough members that we'll stay strong and vibrant for ages to come."

A community. I imagined what it might be like . . . a whole group of us, grateful for our expanded life spans, devouring each day, constantly learning and growing and exploring the world. I adored my family, but it would be exhilarating to spend time with new people who really understood my world. I supposed eternal life with the Saviors would be like living on a traveling commune, or a college campus.

By the next day—the day of the ceremony—I was so excited by the idea of our new life that I stopped thinking of Sage as anything but the Sacrifice—a hurdle to jump so the rest of us could reach utopia.

devoted

When I realized how wrong I was, it was too late. Only Sage's love for Clea saved him then, but soon the Saviors would try to do the ceremony again . . . and if Mother had her way, by that time Sage and Clea's bond would be destroyed.

Sending Clea to the CV was good, but it wasn't enough. I had to do more. I had to strengthen her faith in Sage, so much that Mother couldn't drive the two of them apart.

I had to bring Clea and Sage together.

If Mother found out, she'd destroy me. I couldn't even try unless I found the perfect moment, when I could do it without her knowing.

It wouldn't be easy, but I couldn't live with myself if I didn't at least try.

nine

BEN AND I DIDN'T TALK on the drive to . . . wherever we were going. He turned up the radio the second we were in the car and tapped out the beat with his fingers on the wheel. He was ignoring me on purpose—his way of telling me he wasn't going to tell me more than he had to. It was his signal that he was still keeping our destination a secret.

I didn't press it. I'd know soon enough.

I considered trying to fall asleep. Maybe Petra would appear with another vision of Sage. But with no idea how much time I had, it seemed like a bad idea.

After an hour I saw the signs for Bradley International Airport. Wherever we were headed, it wasn't close.

We parked, and I followed Ben to the kiosk to check us in.

"You might as well tell me where we're going now," I asked. "I'll find out at the gate anyway. You're just stressing me out."

"Cincinnati, Ohio."

"Cincinnati?"

"Also known as 'Porkopolis,' thanks to its history as the hog-packing capital of the country."

"You found this online?" I asked.

"I did." Ben started pressing buttons on the check-in machine, which soon delivered our boarding passes. I followed as he strode off toward the gates.

"Isn't it a bit of a leap from 'Porkopolis' to 'beneath the flying pig'?"

"In 1988 Cincinnati celebrated its bicentennial with a new park. The park's entrance was marked by four smokestacks, topped by four flying-pig statues, to honor all the little swine who gave their lives so the city could thrive."

"How did you find that? I didn't find any of that."

"I knew the Cincinnati part right away. One of my students ran a marathon there last year—the Cincinnati Flying Pig Marathon."

"So why didn't we come here right from Dalt's?"

"I had to be sure. I had to find out what was *beneath*."

I was done with Ben talking in cryptic circles. I waited until we got through security and made it to our gate. We had two hours before our flight—more than enough time to do research. I found a seat by myself, pulled out my phone, and Googled "beneath Cincinnati Ohio."

"Pretty amazing, huh?"

I turned to see Ben in the seat behind me, on his knees and twisted around so he could look over my shoulder. He was grinning like someone who knew he'd just delivered the greatest surprise Christmas present ever.

"It's incredible, but . . . you think the CV's there?"

I was staring at images from the 1920s, massive tunnels of cement and steel. A subway system, unfinished and unused. Buried under the streets of Cincinnati since 1925, sealed off for decades.

devoted

"I do," Ben said. "It has two miles of tunnels, plus three full station platforms, and it's hidden from the public. There's even electricity down there, from when they tried to use it as a bomb shelter in the sixties. I don't know. . . . If I were running a covert paramilitary operation, it's where I'd want to be."

"But it's not where I saw Sage. The room I saw was frilly and airy and open. It looked like an inn, not an abandoned subway."

"I thought about that. I see three options. One is that Petra lied to you. She didn't show the real Sage, just an image of him."

I shook my head. "She specifically said it *wasn't* an image. He was there."

"And you believe her?"

I imagined being there with Sage in the room, how real it all felt. I nodded.

"I do. Not because I trust her . . . it just felt right. He was there. I know he was."

"And you think he was there at that moment? She wasn't showing something from the past?"

"No. He was there. I'm sure of it."

"Okay," Ben said. "Two more possibilities then. Either they're moving Sage down there and he found out about it; or he's not there at all, but

144

that's where we'll find out how to get him."

"Find out how? Ask someone?"

It wasn't a real question. The CV weren't exactly friendly. It was highly unlikely one of them would offer up the information we needed. I had to have faith that if Sage was sending us there, it was because he knew we could find it on our own . . . somehow.

To prepare for what lay ahead, we spent the rest of the time before the plane took off poring over the web, scouring it for every scrap of information we could find about the abandoned subway. The images were eerily post apocalyptic: massive vaulted caverns, abandoned tunnels, and wide staircases leading no longer to the world above but to cemented dead ends.

Decades after it was abandoned for good, the ghostly subway welcomed small groups of the wealthy and the curious, who ponied up thousands of dollars for the privilege of wandering its secret passageways. But the last of those tours had been thirty years ago, and the entrances were then sealed shut. Since then, the few people who somehow found their way down to explore reported new barricades, stopping them from going more than twenty feet. Conspiracy theorists claimed the tunnels had been blocked for a reason: alien dissections, perhaps; or secret research on chemical weapons.

"Think the Elixir counts as a chemical weapon?" Ben asked.

He said it playfully, but to me it wasn't funny.

"It did for Sage," I said.

It was true. Even as the Elixir saved Sage's life, it poisoned him, and poisoned the lives of everyone who came into contact with him. Not even my dad had been spared.

"Ben . . . do you believe in reincarnation?"

It was an odd question from someone who knew for a fact she was on her fifth life, but I had a feeling Ben would know what I meant.

"You mean normally?"

I nodded.

"Yes and no," he said. "I think souls are meant to move on. To heaven or hell, depending on how they lived. I don't know if either of those places is like it is in stories, but I do think they exist: eternal reward or condemnation . . . maybe with a chance to redeem yourself, maybe not. Reincarnation happens, but it happens when something goes wrong, like if your iPod was stuck on repeat, and the same song kept playing over and over."

"So if Sage hadn't been forced to drink the Elixir . . ."

"After the attack on the Society? If Sage had been killed like the others? Can't say for sure, but my guess is your soul and his would have gone to heaven. Mine . . . not so much."

Ben's eyes had darkened, and he stared down at his hands. With one finger, he traced the lines of his jeans.

"Ben . . . you don't think . . . if the cycle did end at some point and our souls moved on . . . do you honestly believe? . . ."

"My soul doesn't exactly have the greatest track record, does it? Even then, that first time. I was the one who blabbed about the Society. All those people killed . . . it was my fault. And it's not like I learned. I've always had blood on my hands." He pursed his lips a moment, and when he spoke again, his voice was soft and raspy. "I can't imagine there's any kind of huge reward waiting for me. Maybe that's why I keep the cycle going, even when I think I'm not. Maybe on some level I know what's coming, and I'm afraid of it."

"Ben . . ."

I reached out for him, but the PA system announced our boarding call, and he leaped to his feet. He wouldn't look at me as we stood in line — just kept his eyes focused on a single spot ahead, blinking quickly, as if trying to hold back tears.

By the time we slid into our seats, he was clear-eyed. The flight to Cincinnati would take two hours, but since there was Wi-Fi and seat-back computers on the plane, we'd be able to keep researching possible entrances to the hidden subway system. I figured we'd spend the entire flight doing that, but I didn't count on how oddly comfortable and cushy the seats felt . . . or how lulling the white noise of the engine would be . . . or how heavy my eyelids would get. . . .

I wasn't in the airplane anymore. I was standing, but I was in blackness. Not *just* blackness, exactly . . . I wasn't floating. It was like I was standing in a room painted in black: black floor, black walls, black ceiling. No windows, no lights, no door . . . and yet it wasn't dark. I could see perfectly — my hands in front of my face, my body. . . . I could see as clearly as if I were standing outside on a summer day.

"Clea? Oh my God, *Clea?!*"

"Sage!"

He was right behind me. Tears welled in my eyes as I felt his arms wrap around me. I felt his heartbeat, his lips against my hair, the warmth of his body. He pulled me so tightly I could finally breathe. His touch was my air. I wanted him to pull me even closer, to pull me into him so I could disappear in his arms, safe and happy and protected.

"Clea . . ." His voice broke on the word. "You feel so real. I've dreamed you so many times, but you feel so real. . . ."

He started to loosen his grip, but I squeezed my arms tighter around him.

"Don't. Don't let go. Promise me. If you do, I'm afraid I'll wake up."

"You won't," a voice said. "At least not right away."

I knew that voice. It was a child's voice. . . .

She was there. Amelia. The last time I'd seen her, she'd been the one animated person among human statues, but now she sat very still, legs crossed in front of her. She looked like she was meditating, taking deep breaths through her nose and pushing them out through her mouth.

"Hi, Clea," she said. She smiled, but it looked strained. Like she was hurting.

"Hi," I said.

"Clea?" Sage sounded confused. I looked up to

try to explain but immediately got lost in his face. The hollows of his cheeks, the dark brows over his endlessly deep brown eyes, the tiny bulge at the top of his nose from a childhood fight . . .

. . . but the scar lines on his face were fainter. And the scruff was gone.

I reached up and ran my hand over the smooth contours of his face.

"You're healing," I said. "The scars are fading."

"Yeah," he said, raising his own hand to his face. "But . . . how did you know?"

"I'm so sorry," said Amelia. "There's not much time. They're busy now, and they think I'm with them, but if they realize I'm not . . . if they find out I got you together . . . they'll punish me. . . ."

"We're not dreaming, are we?" I said. The words were for Amelia, but my eyes wouldn't leave Sage. My fingers traced over the faded remnants of his scars. He stared at me with a mix of joy, hope, and disbelief. He placed one hand over mine, pressing it to his skin.

"Not *entirely*," Amelia answered. "You're both asleep . . . but this is real. Like what you saw when you were with my mother."

"But I couldn't touch you then," I told Sage. "I could see you, but I couldn't touch you. I—"

Sage interrupted me with a kiss, and everything else went away.

"*Listen!*" Amelia hissed.

I didn't want to listen. I wanted Sage. I wrapped my arms around his neck, pulling him even closer. His mouth on mine, his hands on my back, then entwined in my hair . . . it was everything I wanted, right here, for all eternity.

"If you want more than this moment, you have to listen!" Amelia snapped. Her voice had a frantic edge I couldn't ignore. It hurt to do it, but I turned away from Sage to look at her . . . though I clung to him even more tightly to make up for it.

The outburst seemed to hurt Amelia. She was coated in a sheen of sweat and winced against an unseen pain. When she spoke again, it was in gasping spurts she struggled to get out.

"I can help. . . . Don't let Mother know. . . . She'll destroy Sage . . . and others. . . ."

She yelped now, and red spots rose high in her cheeks as she fixed her unearthly bright blue eyes on mine. *"Don't give up, Clea."*

I felt a tug at the center of my body. Sage must have felt the same—he placed his hand on his stomach. "Clea?"

There wasn't time to explain. I turned away from Amelia to face him.

"I love you," I said.

"I love you."

I tried to kiss him again, but even as our lips touched I felt my body start to pull away . . .

. . . and suddenly I jolted awake.

ten

Everything lined up perfectly when Clea was on the plane. She and Sage were both asleep, and my whole family was occupied with the Saviors. We were almost always with them now, but every week Albert brought the group together to meet with "The Elders," as they called us. We would appear in our astrally projected bodies and answer all their questions about eternal life. We'd impress them with tricks like speaking inside their minds or moving objects. Father and Grandfather always had to vanish before they could do things like that, but Mother and I didn't.

The whole thing was goofy to me, but the weekly meetings kept the Saviors mesmerized by us and focused on their goal of performing the ceremony so they could be just as astounding.

For me, the best part of the meetings was the way they distracted my family. All of them—even Mother—were so focused on performing that I was willing to take the huge risk of bringing Clea and Sage together. I had to. I couldn't let Mother break their bond. I couldn't let the ceremony succeed.

I still remembered every second of the last time. It happened at the Saviors' compound, a long-vacant bed-and-breakfast in Vermont. It was a beautiful white colonial mansion set on fifty acres of rolling fields and pastures. A river flowed through the grounds. An ancient but beautifully restored barn sat on the property, and goats, llamas, sheep, and pigs roamed freely.

It was heavenly.

I imagined we'd live there once we had our bodies back. We'd travel, of course, but this place could be home, one we'd share with our new extended family.

I couldn't wait.

Yes, there was a sacrifice to make, and that was sad, but we would honor it with the solemnity it deserved, knowing it was for a greater good.

As we moved behind the mansion, I saw there was a party going on. Twinkle lights glistened like fairy dust in the trees, and tiki torches blazed in welcome. I saw around twenty guests, but a buffet table groaned with champagne and delicacies for ten times that number. The revelers ranged in age. The youngest seemed in their twenties; the oldest in their sixties. Music played, and several of the tuxedoed and gowned guests twirled wildly on the parquet floor covering the grass. At the side of the dance floor stood a huge digital readout mounted on a pole. It displayed the time: 11:15:29, with the seconds constantly flipping forward.

It felt like New Year's Eve.

"What's going on?" I asked Mother.

"Just stay with us, and follow what we do."

Following what they'd do was fine, but staying with them wasn't. The party felt wrong—disturbing, even, considering what I knew was going to happen.

Mother had asked me to stay with them, and part of me did . . . but I peeled off a splinter of myself and let it float around the party, listening to snippets of conversation:

"The others will wish they had listened to us. . . ."

"I can't wait for my fiftieth high school reunion. They'll look like shit, but me . . ."

"We can have anything. We can walk in and rob a bank. What are they gonna do, shoot us? We'll be rich. . . ."

"Any woman. Any time. Can't fight us off, dude. . . ."

"Don't think small. We'll be indestructible. You know what people would pay for that? You know what countries would pay for that? . . ."

"My God, we could ask for anything. . . ."

"We'll be like what those freaks talk about. Shadow government. We can make all kinds of shit happen."

". . . someone pisses us off, wouldn't even have to do it ourselves . . ."

". . . whole world afraid of us . . ."

". . . everything we want . . ."

". . . unstoppable . . ."

". . . forever . . ."

"Amelia!"

It was Mother. She was looking at me funny, even though I'd kept the bulk of my consciousness right at her side. I snapped myself together and pretended everything was fine.

But it wasn't.

The party guests — the Saviors of Eternal Life — weren't what Grandfather had described at all. They wanted immortality for power . . . for revenge . . . for everything my family and I were against. And yet, we were going to help them. We were going to kill someone innocent for them. And when we did . . . when the Saviors were indeed immortal . . . they truly would be unstoppable.

"Come, Amelia," Mother said. "It's time."

The large clock had stopped at 11:30:00, and the Saviors were on the move. We followed, still invisible. Champagne glasses in hand, they trooped to an area off in the trees: a clearing marked by an array of large boulders. A New

England Stonehenge. Tiki torches lit the perimeter, but what sat in the middle was horrifying.

A flat rock altar . . . with a man chained to it.

He was shirtless, his muscles standing taut in the torchlight.

The chains pulled his arms wide above his head, and his feet were shackled together and bound tightly to the altar. A gag blocked all but the most guttural sounds as he struggled against his bonds. Sweat poured down his face.

Sage.

Two men flanked him, each holding a Taser. They'd let him struggle to the point of ultimate strain, then zap him unconscious.

Both men wore tuxedos. They drank champagne between shocks, clinking glasses with their newly arrived friends. No one else glanced at the tortured man on the rock.

A digital clock stood among the boulders, just like the one on the field. This one was running. When it hit 11:45:00, Grandfather nodded to Mother, who nudged me.

"Do what we do," she said, "but keep still, like us. Your grandfather says they like that; it impresses them."

She, Father, and Grandfather manifested into physical form. I did the same and stood as rigid as the rest of them.

"Welcome to your destiny!" Grandfather boomed. The Saviors turned and gasped, then cheered like wild.

"A toast to immortality!" one man called.

"A toast to the Elders!" another cried.

"The first with champagne, the next with the Elixir of Life!" a woman yelled.

Another roaring cheer. They raised their glasses and drank.

"Are you prepared?" Grandfather asked.

An older man stepped forward. He looked like someone who had once been an athlete, but whose body had seen better days.

"Albert," Grandfather acknowledged him.

"We have fire," Albert said, gesturing to a blaze at the foot of Sage's rock. "We have arranged tokens of earthly pleasures the Sacrifice must relinquish."

He pointed out one of the other rocks around the perimeter of the ceremony. I had been too transfixed by Sage to notice before, but it was laden with things a person might miss if leaving the world forever: flowers, pictures of beautiful places . . . and framed in the middle, a large photograph of a young woman. She had blond hair, blue eyes, and fair skin. She was smiling confidently in the image, but there was something sardonic in her eyes, like it was secretly a big joke that she was posing for the picture.

Albert held up a silver bowl.

"We have the bowl," he said, "a vessel of purest silver, in which we'll catch the blood of the Sacrifice at exactly midnight, under the full moon of renewal."

"And the dagger?" Grandfather asked.

Albert turned to one of the Taser wielders, who reached behind a boulder and took out a large velvet box. He opened it to reveal a golden hilt and scabbard. With great ceremony, Albert took the hilt in one hand, the scabbard in the other, then separated the two, brandishing a glistening-sharp dagger.

Everyone gasped appreciatively.

"A plunge into his heart will sever his soul," Albert said.

There was silence . . . then applause.

Behind his gag, Sage screamed.

I felt ill.

The clock read 11:59:05.

How could my family be okay with this? They must be having second thoughts. I looked at their faces. No. No second thoughts. They looked . . . ecstatic.

If they weren't going to stop this, I had to . . . but I was terrified. Not because I thought they'd do anything to me — back then I didn't know that was possible — but because I knew that if I ripped this opportunity from Mother, Father, and Grandfather, they'd never forgive me. Never. That meant an eternity on my own. Could I really handle that?

I waited until the last possible second. I told myself that was because I didn't want to give my family a chance to stop me, but I actually just wanted to put off the choice as long as possible.

11:59:50.

In the blink of an eye, I saw my whole long, wonderful lifetime flash in front of my eyes. One way or another, the next ten seconds would change everything forever.

Albert raised the dagger high above his head.

I prepared to lunge.

Albert started his downward arc . . .

"STOP! ABORT THE CEREMONY!"

The desperate ferocity in Grandfather's voice froze everyone . . . everyone but me. I staggered forward, unable to stop my momentum.

Mother noticed. She eyed me suspiciously.

The clock clicked to 12:01:00.

It was no longer midnight.

"Why did you stop us?" a woman demanded.

"Look at the dagger," Grandfather rasped.

The dagger glowed bright red. Albert screamed and let it thump to the ground.

"It's hot!" he cried, then glared at Grandfather. "What happened? You promised us! You promised us immortality!"

"And you will have it," Grandfather said. "But only if you prepare properly. You've read the texts, Albert. The red-hot blade means he's still tied to the mortal world. Had you stabbed him, the ceremony would have failed."

"That's impossible!" Albert sputtered. "We did everything right!"

"Apparently not," Mother snapped. "Maybe next time we'll offer this gift to someone more competent!"

The crowd roared with such terrible fury, I had to remind myself they couldn't actually hurt us.

"My daughter speaks out of turn," Grandfather said. "All is not lost. We will find out and fix what went wrong. By the next full moon, I assure you, the ceremony will succeed. I ask you to be patient, and hold the Sacrifice until then. Do not falter, for immortality still awaits."

Grandfather nodded imperceptibly to us, then disappeared, taking his mind elsewhere. We all followed, drawn to Grandfather in the familiar limbo space.

"How did that happen?" Mother raged. "I should be in my body right now!"

"It's just as I said, Petra. The red glow means his earthly ties weren't properly broken. It won't happen again."

"How can you be sure?"

"I know how," I said. "We could decide not to make the Saviors immortal at all."

Three pairs of eyes glared at me.

"Is this about the Sacrifice?" Mother asked.

"No!" I said. "It's about the Saviors and what they'll do with eternal life."

"They'll bring us back to our bodies," Mother said.

"Okay . . . and then what?"

"Then they're no longer our concern," Grandfather said.

"They are! Didn't you hear them talking? If they drink the Elixir, they'll hurt people. They're planning it!"

"People say all kinds of things," Father said. "Doesn't mean they'll do it."

"Even if they do," Mother added, "that's their choice, not ours."

"But if we give them eternal life, aren't their choices our responsibility?"

"We're not giving them anything," Grandfather said. "They'll do the ceremony all by themselves."

"Because you taught them how!"

"So what are you suggesting?" Grandfather asked. "We find a more acceptable group of people, then bring the Sacrifice to them? How do you propose we find them, a Facebook post? 'Click here to apply for eternal life'?"

I took a deep breath, my insides fluttering, already imagining their reactions. "Maybe we don't need to make more immortals. We'll find another way to get our bodies back. Or we won't, and maybe that'll be . . . you know . . . okay."

"Amelia." Mother's voice was calm, but her fists clenched at her sides and the muscles in her neck bulged. "Tell me you're not suggesting we stay like this for eternity."

"Would it be that horrible?" I asked meekly.

"Listen to me, Amelia. I need to know you will not get in the way of this ceremony. You have to promise me." Mother's voice worked to push through her tightly clenched jaw.

"I want my body back too," I said. "It's just, if we have to kill someone, and give eternal life to bad people—"

"Amelia . . . ," Mother warned.

"I'm just saying, it might not really be worth it—"

"SHUT UP!" Mother howled.

I didn't have time to say another word. My mother lunged at me, eyes flashing and talon-arms straining for me.

Had we been in our bodies, she'd have knocked me to the ground. Instead her hands clawed right through me.

The pain was immediate and blinding, but tempered by shock. My mother had never hurt me before, not even in our mortal lives. Now she had . . . and in a way I hadn't known was possible. Before, these visions of our bodies had obeyed the laws of physics. We hugged, we touched, we held hands . . . But now Mother tore inside me, inside my consciousness to claw me apart until . . .

I blacked out before I could fully comprehend it.

I was gone.

I didn't know for how long. Eventually I started to exist again, to be aware . . . but I had no sense of place or being. I had no clear thoughts, just half-formed nightmare images . . . and pain.

When my thoughts returned, it was almost worse.

My own mother had tried to destroy me, and my father and grandfather did nothing to stop her.

There was no question now. I was completely on my own . . . and even though I'd been alive for so many years, I was only seven years old.

I wanted my blanket — not the pink threadbare one tucked in with my body, but the one I'd had when I was just another mortal. My mother had woven it when she was pregnant with me. It had disintegrated centuries ago.

I wanted my mommy . . . but the person I wanted didn't exist anymore. She had changed, and it was all my fault. Everything was my fault. I wanted to die.

I thought about the dagger. Couldn't I do the ceremony on myself? Steal the dagger, find a way to get it to my sleeping body in Switzerland, prepare the ritual, and at the stroke of midnight drive the blade into my heart?

But if I was gone, who would stop my family from making the Saviors immortal? No one.

Did Mother realize that too? If she did, would she send someone to Switzerland to get rid of me once and for all?

It was possible, but I couldn't let it happen. I had to be strong. I had to pull myself together and convince my family I was on their side. I had to believe they wouldn't destroy me unless they thought they had to. If I was very good and obedient, if I had a true change of heart, I could bide my time until I could stop them.

I waited until I'd regained some strength, then reached out and called to them.

In no time I was back in that limbo space with Mother, Father, and Grandfather. They stood far from me, their lips pursed in disapproval.

I put on my best little-girl smile. "Hi, Mommy," I said. "I missed you."

She looked away, her eyes to the ceiling.

"Daddy?"

He didn't look at me either.

"I know . . . I was very bad. I'm so sorry."

"You were gone a long time, Amelia," Grandfather said. "It was not unpleasant."

Ouch.

"I . . . I don't know what to say. . . . I messed up."

"Yes, you did," Grandfather said. "I worked very hard to bring us back to ourselves. I'm still working hard at it. We all are. It's most frustrating to have my own granddaughter getting in the way."

"I know. You're right. I'm sorry."

"Are you really?" Father asked. "Or are you just saying that so you won't be in trouble?"

In trouble. Like they were thinking of grounding me, not getting rid of me.

"I'm really sorry. I want the ceremony to happen. I want to go back to the way things were."

"Even if it means the Sacrifice dies and the Saviors get eternal life?" Grandfather asked.

"If that's what it takes," I said. "I won't stand in the way. I'll help. I promise."

Grandfather's and Father's eyes were softening. They wanted to believe me. Mother still looked suspicious. I took her hand.

"Mommy?"

She thought a moment, then knelt down smiling. She brushed my hair out of my face, then took both my hands.

"Amelia," she said. "I believe you want our bodies back. I do. I believe you want to stretch to the sky, run through the grass as fast as you can, feel the sun on your skin, smell chocolate chip cookies baking in the oven. . . ."

Her words painted beautiful images in my head . . . but I saw them through the wrong end of a pair of binoculars. They were tiny and far away. What did chocolate chip cookies really smell like? I couldn't remember. What did it feel like to have the warm sun on my face? How did newly mown grass crumple under my feet and tickle my nose?

I couldn't remember any of it, and the rush of longing brought tears to my eyes.

"You do want those things, don't you, Amelia?"

I nodded. I didn't just want them, I needed them, and if I tried to speak, I might break.

"But do you want them enough? Enough to look the other way from the Saviors' shortcomings?"

Shortcomings. I guess that was one way to describe a murderous streak.

I nodded again. "Daddy was right. They were probably just talking. None of our business anyway."

"And the Sacrifice?" Mother asked.

"It's sad . . . but it's the only way."

Mother considered. "I'm proud of you, Amelia," she finally said. "You've grown up a lot."

She hugged me, and for just a minute I let my guard down. I was a kid, she was my mom, and everything was okay. She pulled back and held me at arm's length, a kind smile on her face.

"It's funny," she said. "I've never been a disciplinarian, but you respond so well to punishment. I'll have to remember that."

There it was. The threat. She gave me a last squeeze — a little too hard — then blew me a kiss as she stepped away.

I was on notice, but I was back in the family fold.

"So," I began nonchalantly, "did you ever find out what went wrong with the ceremony?"

Grandfather had. The problem, he realized, was Sage's connection with Clea Raymond, the woman from the picture. It was no secret to us that Clea and Sage were in love, or even that their love had spanned lifetimes and reincarnations. This was all information Albert had known and shared with Grandfather.

devoted

What we hadn't known, and what Grandfather had learned from a wealth of "alternative" practitioners, was that letting go of a soulmate is not a simple process.

"Soulmate" is an overused term, but a true soul connection is very rare, and very real. Two people who meet and share such a connection do more than fall in love; they change each other both deeply and irreversibly. Real soulmates will always weather difficult times; they have to. They're eternally bound together, drawn back to each other no matter what.

This was the bond Sage had formed with his first love, Olivia, and that biological "soul tag" was passed down to every reincarnated version of her.

Breaking a soul bond apparently took more than a framed picture on an altar of earthly sacrifices. A soul bond is so rare and wondrous that it's sacrilege to sever it. It can only be done with the darkest black magic. Moreover, the bond breaking can't be forced on a couple. It's a choice that must be made by one of them. His or her verbal acceptance primes the body. Without it, no magic is strong enough to sever a soul bond.

It took Grandfather many dreamtime visits to self-proclaimed witches, voodoo priestesses, and sorcerers, and many run-ins with frauds and charlatans, but eventually he found one ceremony on which the most reliable dark practitioners agreed.

Now the mission was simple: Get either Sage or Clea to agree to break their bond.

At first, Grandfather told me, they tried to torture Sage's acceptance out of him. When that didn't work, Mother had come up with a better idea. The torture would continue — at least as long as it was helpful — but she also had Albert hire an actress, Lila. Lila's role was "junior member" of the Saviors, someone who could believably be critical of them. Lila was put in charge of Sage's care, and followed her script to a T. She was loving and gentle, and slowly but surely let Sage know she was falling hard for him. Mother wanted Lila to win him over with her kindness and understanding, until eventually Sage would fall for her as well, and agree to break his bond with Clea.

That was the idea, but there was no way Mother would rely on anything as fickle as human emotions. To make sure Sage responded the way she required, she had the Saviors drug the water and salves Lila used to take care of Sage. It was a smart move — Sage might worry about poisoned food or drink, but when he was weak and in pain, he wouldn't worry about Lila's balms. The drugs in question were made to help put people into hypnotic states. In Sage's case, they left him more open to suggestion, and apparently his feelings for Lila were growing every day.

Mother, however, was still impatient. She was moving to the next step: working on Clea. Mother thought Clea was unlikely to willingly break her bond to Sage, but she thought she could use Lila and Sage to drive Clea to someone else, even for a little while. If Mother could show that to Sage, she thought it would push him to agree to sever their bond—ideally before the next full moon.

At the time, that brought me up to speed. I said I'd do anything I could to help them, which is when they started bringing me to hang around the Saviors and join in the weekly meetings. They kept a close eye on me at first, especially Mother, but the more I behaved, the more they relaxed.

Then I messed up. The first time the whole family appeared to Clea, I tried to signal that I was on her side and different from the others. I thought I was being subtle, but I wasn't—not subtle enough. That's when Mother locked in on my words and started her surprise visits. Her suspicions and paranoia only grew as the next full moon loomed closer and closer. It was a miracle I found that perfect moment when Clea was on the plane to bring her and Sage together.

I only hoped I'd given Clea enough to cling to.

As for myself, I was spent from the effort. I needed to rest. I wouldn't have the strength to split myself and check in on Clea for quite a while. I hoped she'd stay strong. I hoped she'd hold tightly to Sage, no matter what.

Everything was riding on it.

eleven

"NIGHTMARE?"

I wheeled to face Ben, hazy from my dream, or visit, or whatever had just happened, and in that second it was like he wasn't asking a question but announcing the truth: He *was* my nightmare, mine and Sage's, and even if he tried to change things, that wouldn't change.

"No! I mean . . . I don't know. . . . I don't remember what I dreamed. . . ."

The cabin lights were dimmed, and as Ben leaned closer, eerie shadows sank his eyes into blackness and arched his brows. "Are you sure?" he asked.

My breath caught in my throat.

"Ladies and gentlemen, we welcome you to Cincinnati, Ohio," the flight attendant said over the intercom. The lights flicked back on and the shadows flew from Ben's face.

"I'm sure," I said. "I'm fine."

"Okay, good."

We stayed quiet as the plane taxied to the gate, and prepared to get off. The silence gave me time to think about what I'd seen. It was real—as real as what I'd seen with Petra—and I was sure Sage had seen the exact same thing. He'd *been* there . . . wherever we were . . . just as I'd been. And yet . . . he didn't seem familiar with Amelia the way I was. So it was definite—Amelia, Petra, and the two men weren't related to Sage in any way, nor were they anyone he knew.

So who were they? And why had they come to me? And why did Amelia bring Sage and me together, when the rest of her family wanted me to forget about him? I felt like she'd tried to explain it, but what she'd said didn't make any sense to me. Maybe Ben could help me figure it out, but I worried about him. I didn't think he'd do anything on purpose to get between Sage and me, but that didn't mean it wouldn't happen. I decided to keep my mouth shut.

I gasped out loud when I realized I'd missed an opportunity. I had just seen Sage. I could have *asked* him where he was and the best way to get to him. I told myself I would have if I'd had more time; I was just so overwhelmed to finally be with him, to touch him and feel his arms around me, there was no way I could think strategically. It was a lost opportunity, though, and I was furious. I couldn't let that happen again.

Ben and I had made it off the plane and were walking through the terminal. It was late. The place felt half-abandoned.

"So," I began, "you said there're two miles of abandoned subway."

"Right."

"Then how do we know the right place to try to get in? What if we burst into the middle of one of their training exercises? We could get killed before they even know who we are."

"Ghost stories," Ben said.

"'Ghost stories'?"

"That's today's mythology: ghost stories."

"I thought you believed in ghost stories. Now you're saying they're myths?"

"I believe in the inexplicable, things beyond what most of us know and understand."

"Aren't ghost stories about the inexplicable?" I asked.

"Usually it's the opposite," Ben said. "Ghost stories are about something *easily* explicable . . . but the person telling the story doesn't realize it. Ghost stories start because people experience something they don't understand, and come up with a story to explain it. It's just like ancient Greeks who watched the sun move across the sky and decided it was being pulled by a giant chariot."

"Okay . . . but what does that have to do with finding the CV?"

"I did some research while you were sleeping. The Cincinnati Symphony Orchestra Music Hall has been around for more than a hundred years, so it has a history of ghost stories. Most of them are what you'd expect: phantom music everyone says was played by a star violinist who committed suicide on the symphony's opening day; ghostly sightings of their most famous conductor, dead but hoping to lead his orchestra one last time."

"Sounds like your kind of place."

Ben flashed a smile. "I'll admit I'm intrigued. But what's *more* interesting is that for the past ten years, the ghost stories have changed. They're about noises coming from *underground*. There're whole websites now about how the Music Hall was built over an ancient cemetery, and the ghosts of displaced bodies are out for revenge."

We were in baggage claim now, and Ben beelined for a small kiosk with a picture of a taxi above it.

"So tell me," I said, smiling because I was sure I knew the answer, "is the Music Hall actually built on top of an ancient cemetery . . . or on top of an ancient subway?"

"The largest of the underground stations is Race Street, a few blocks away from the Music Hall. All the ghost stories I found were centered around that area; none of the stories had anything to do with the other end of the subway."

"Because the CV is operating underneath the Music Hall."

"Around there, yeah," Ben agreed.

We had made it to the front of the taxi line. "Twenty-three twenty-two Ferguson Road in Cincinnati, please."

"Out these doors, cab three-oh-nine."

I followed Ben outside and into the cab.

"So here's what I think we should do," I whispered. The cabdriver blared music in a language I didn't know, but that didn't mean he wouldn't be intrigued by our conversation. "We find a way to sneak into the subway as far from Race Street as possible."

"I agree," Ben said. "Based on the noises, that's where we're least likely to be caught."

I didn't ask what would happen if we *were* caught. The CV weren't exactly reasonable people. If we were caught, we'd just have to scramble to make sure we stayed alive, found Sage if he was there—and if not, found whatever Sage needed us to find—and got back out again.

"So where is the cab taking us?" I asked. "Did you find an entrance?"

"I did, but that's not where we're going. We need to make one more stop to prepare."

Several minutes later, the cab came to a stop in front of a giant box with a blue-and-white sign. We'd pulled into Walmart.

Ben leaned forward and handed the driver some cash. "We'll be back as soon as we can. Please wait here."

We passed through the automatic glass doors and into fluorescent light so harsh I wished I'd worn my sunglasses.

"Good evening," said a white-haired woman

in a blue vest covered with smiley-face pins. "Welcome to Walmart!"

Ben sped past her and I walked quickly to keep up, but the woman was undaunted. "Please be aware we're closing in just ten minutes," she shouted after us, "so if there's anything I can do to help speedy-up your shopping trip, you just let me know, okay?"

"Thank you!" I called back.

Ben wound his way through the store, picking up flashlights, trowels, batteries, backpacks, wire cutters, rope, heavy gloves, thick sweatshirts, surgical face masks, a compass, energy bars, serrated folding utility knives . . . and a parade of middle-aged to ancient blue-vested people who I at first thought might be alarmed that our shopping cart looked like it belonged to John Dillinger but were apparently far more worried about rousting us from the store before closing time.

"Four minutes!" a heavyset man chirped, his smile straining his face even more than the "How May I Help You" vest strained his ample stomach.

Ben ignored him.

"Do you think we have enough knives?" Ben asked.

"How many knives do you think we need?"

"I don't know. . . . What do you think of this one?"

"Ben, that's a machete."

He just looked at me.

"Put it back," I said.

He did but kept scanning the blades. "This one has a gut hook," he said.

"Two minutes left!" a new blue-vester cried as she joined us. "May I help you to the checkout?"

"Yes!" I said, dragging Ben by the arm.

"What can you tell me about your gun selection?" he asked the woman.

She frowned a bit, her eyes darting nervously. "We don't carry firearms here."

"That's fine," I said. "We'll just check out, please."

The woman nodded and walked quickly toward the registers.

"What do you think you'd do with a gun?" I hissed to Ben.

"It's the CV. I just want to be prepared."

"What happened the last time you shot a gun?"

He'd done it once, and I'd been there. He'd been with me on a photojournalism assignment where I'd sat in with a female police officer for a week, and she'd taken us to a shooting range.

"That was different," Ben said.

"You broke your collarbone!"

The heavyset blue-vester chuckled. When I turned to him, he covered it up by coughing into his fist. Ben's face reddened and his mouth became a line.

"Very nice, Clea."

He went ahead to the checkout counter and wouldn't look at me as our purchases were rung up and bagged.

"So long!" called the heavyset man as we left. He pointed his finger and thumb at us and "shot" a farewell, then cried "Ow!" as he recoiled his own hand into his shoulder.

He was not helping.

We climbed back into the cab, and Ben gave him another address.

"Is that near the entrance we want?" I asked as we pulled away.

Ben didn't answer.

"Oh come on, Ben. They didn't even sell guns anyway. Let it go."

"You always underestimate me, Clea. You're the one who came to me, remember? So if you want me to help, how about you trust me to help?"

"I do trust you, Ben."

He glared at me. I had to be honest.

"I trust your *intentions*."

Ben didn't answer. He spent the rest of the cab ride unpacking our purchases and tucking them into our new backpacks. He put on one sweatshirt and handed the other to me. The knife he folded into its protective sheath, which he hung from his belt. Then he handed me mine so I could do the same. He filled the flashlights with batteries and clicked them on to make sure they worked, then stashed a couple in each pack, leaving one out for each of us.

"About a mile farther, please," he told the driver as he slowed. "You can let us out on the side of the road."

If that raised any kind of red flag for the driver, he didn't show it. He pulled over exactly where Ben asked, then zipped off into the night once he'd been paid and we were out.

Right away I realized something about Cincinnati: It is not a twenty-four-hour town. It was ten thirty, and around us were nothing but darkened buildings and the occasional passing car.

"This way," Ben said.

There was a stone fence next to the road, and Ben walked over to it then leaned over it to peer down below. I joined him. Maybe twenty feet below sprawled a sea of gravel and scrub, separated by a guardrail from what looked like a major road, with a regular stream of cars whizzing by. The web surfing I'd done made me think this was I-75, the major thoroughfare through the city.

"We're on top of it right now, aren't we?" I said. "The far end of the subway."

Ben nodded. "We just have to jump down there, and we should be able to find a way in."

"It doesn't look that far," I said.

Although it did. Especially in the dark, it looked very far. And the road rash from a fall on that gravel would hurt. A lot. We both just stood there, looking down.

Then Ben vaulted over the wall.

twelve

I DID NOT LIKE THE SOUND of the thud as Ben hit the ground. I strained my eyes to see where he'd landed.

"Ben? Are you okay?"

"I'm fine. Make sure you wear your gloves."

I pulled the gloves out of my backpack and pulled them on, then climbed over the stone fence, throwing my legs over the top and hanging down so the actual drop would be as short as possible.

I let go and fell for a very long second before the ground smacked into me. I did land on my feet, but I couldn't stay on them, and toppled backward onto the gravelly pavement.

"Here," Ben said, holding out his arm. "You'll want to grab my wrist."

"Your wrist?"

Then I noticed the heel and palm of his hand were covered in scratches.

"Ow! Ben, are you okay?"

"I'm fine. I just should have thought of the glove thing *before* I jumped. Come on."

I grabbed his wrist and he helped pull me to my feet, then I checked out his other hand, which was just as scraped up. "This needs to be cleaned out. That's what we should have been looking for—not a gun, a first-aid kit."

Ben whipped back his hands and walked away from me. I sighed and followed him.

Up ahead, the stone wall over which we had vaulted protruded into our path, and on the wall facing us rose a massive archway.

The entrance to the subway.

It was maybe fifteen feet tall and ten feet wide, the top four feet filling the curve of the arch with a rusted lattice of steel. In the long-ago subway planners' eyes, the area below the lattice would be wide open, the right side crammed with commuters climbing down to the train cars, the left spilling people out at their destination. Looking around now, I couldn't imagine this area as the same kind of urban hub as New York's subway stations, but it had been about a hundred years since it was built, so things must have been much different then. In a way, it was like I was looking at a portal into that past world.

A closed portal. The entire area beneath the steel lattice was welded shut with a thick metal wall, covered by a layer of steel jail-cell-like bars. To top it off, the brush grew thick and deep around the bottom third of the wall, reaching up as high as my waist. It was as if Nature herself wanted this entrance to remain permanently sealed.

"There's no way we can get inside," I said.

"You think?" Ben asked.

He tromped into the brush, but made it just a few feet before he was hopelessly tangled. He swung the backpack off and pulled out his gloves, then unsheathed his knife and started sawing through the more difficult thorny branches.

Ben was right. We had to try.

I unsheathed my knife and started hacking and sawing as well. The brambles were thick, and within minutes the muscles in my arms were screaming. I heard Ben's grunts of breath and knew he was feeling the same thing, but neither of us let up for an instant.

"You know what would really be helpful right now?" Ben huffed between slices of his knife. "A machete."

"You don't say." I gave another knife hack, and made a mental note that when this was over, I'd have to call him on the double standard of him giving me a hard time when I couldn't do it to him.

Or I could just ignore the double standard entirely.

"You're the one who knew where we were going," I said. "If you knew we'd need a machete, you should have said something."

"I didn't know. The pictures of this place were ten years old. The plants weren't like this then."

We carved paths at opposite sides of the portal, but we reached the door at the same time. By then I was drenched with sweat. I'd have taken off my sweatshirt, but its long sleeves were keeping my arms from getting scratched to shreds.

I reached out and grabbed one of the bars. It was thin but solid. The wire cutters we had wouldn't come close to doing the job. We needed the Jaws of Life. And even then there was the small matter of the metal wall.

"Ben?"

I didn't see him anywhere.

Something latched around my ankle.

I screamed.

"Shhh," Ben's voice hissed. "Come down here."

I ducked down and saw him. He had reached through a tangle of branches to grab me. He was about two feet away, but the wall of brambles made the distance seem much farther.

"This way," he said.

"Move your arm, then."

He pulled it back and I started hacking at the branches. Ben did the same on his side, and it wasn't long before I was crouched next to him, in the low, fortlike clearing we'd carved into the brush.

"Look," he said. Just in front of him, the ground was raised in a low dirt mound, as if something was buried there. Ben grinned, then pulled out his trowel and dug at the mound, kicking back the dirt until he'd revealed a large slab of mold-softened wood.

"Help me."

The wood slab was buried deep in the dirt, which was far more dense and hard packed than the mound, and it took both of us digging with our trowels for what seemed like forever before it was loose enough for us to wiggle out.

When we did, we were rewarded by a gaping hole in both the wooden bars and the metal sheet behind it.

A rush of musty air rose up from the subway below. It was like the grave exhaling on us.

The hole wasn't large. It would be a close fit for me, and a tight squeeze for Ben. With his broader chest and shoulders, Sage wouldn't be able to make it through. If we did find him inside, we'd have to get him out another way. The edges of the hole were slightly jagged in places. One particularly nasty shard reminded me of the gut hook Ben had been eyeing at Walmart.

I tried to remember if I'd had a tetanus booster in the past ten years.

Ben shone his flashlight into the darkness. "Nothing nefarious. At least not at this end." He smiled up at me. "Ladies first?"

"How chivalrous." I grimaced.

I knelt down and shone my own flashlight into the darkness. There was no need to do it — Ben had just told me there was nothing dangerous inside — but I had to see for myself.

The hole sat at the top of a long flight of cement stairs, leading down farther than my light could reach.

Ben and I used our knives to clear away more of the brush, so I'd have room to lie on the ground, stomach down, and ease myself back into the hole, feetfirst. Despite the fact that I'd just seen with my own eyes that the subway was empty, panic surged through me. As I sidled along, keeping the sharp metal edges from catching my clothes and tearing through my skin, every childhood nightmare flashed through my mind. I felt the fur of giant, terrible-clawed monsters swiping at my legs, the hot breath of sewer alligators ready to close their teeth on me and drag me deeper and deeper into the bowels of the earth.

I was grateful when I made it inside and my mind could stop playing tricks on me. I crawled backward down several steps so I'd have room to turn around.

When I did, I was amazed.

I was alone, dwarfed inside an enormous cavern.

I sat on the lowest riser of the top tier of the

staircase. Another step and I'd be on a five-foot-long, flat piece of concrete that led to the second tier of stairs. At the bottom, my light gave dim shape to concrete columns stretching floor to ceiling, spaced along a massive platform. I could barely make out the edges of deep trenches on either side of the platform, carved out for train cars that would never arrive.

Thanks to my parents' international lifestyle, I'd traveled the world. I'd spent countless hours in the New York subways, the Metros of D.C., Tokyo, and Paris, and the London Tube. Every one was an underground city, teeming with commuters, buskers, and vendors; roaring with the sound of trains, conversation, and countless clicking and stomping footsteps; bright with lights and the colors of posters, newsstand magazines, and the strewn detritus of wrappers, pocket change, and other trash.

Here there was *nothing.* The bones were there—the shapes that were so familiar to me from riding in those other undergrounds—but it was deathly silent and empty. I felt like an archaeologist visiting the site of an ancient community, wiped out by some horrible disaster.

I felt that, but I knew it wasn't accurate. From

my reading, I knew this place hadn't been finished, much less used. Yet here it was, a subterranean world lurking just beneath the city's surface. And most of the population walking above had no idea.

"Makes you want to believe in ghosts, doesn't it?"

I jumped at the sound of Ben's voice. It echoed over and over through the cavern as he settled next to me on the step, his own flashlight adding its glow to mine.

"We should keep our voices down," I whispered. Even my whisper echoed, an indistinct susurration like a million hissing snakes. "We don't know how far into the tunnels we'll find them. We don't want to warn them we're coming. We want to slip in, find Sage or what he wanted us to find, and slip back out."

Ben nodded. He rose but waited for me to do the same and lead the way. The message was clear: He was happy to help, but this was my rescue mission.

I got up and walked down the second flight of stairs. Once again I was glad Ben had thought to bring the sweatshirts. Even though mine was oversize and thick, I felt the chill of the catacombs.

If the urban legends centered around a spot

two miles away, we could have a long walk before we saw any sign of the CV's lair. The platform on which we stood extended for another thirty feet. To go farther, we'd need to climb down into one of the tunnels that would have held the subway tracks. I walked to one of them, and found it filled with large plastic tubing.

"The water main," Ben said. "It runs through the subway on this track."

"So it could give us some cover if we need it," I said.

I shone my flashlight along the side of the water main to find a layer of watery muck. The main *might* give us cover, but wading through the muck would take much longer. And much as the main could help hide us, it also took up so much of the tunnel that we could be trapped if we hit a narrower section.

"We'll use the other tunnel," I decided.

Ben followed me across the platform to the other track, and I shone the light down to the floor, about five feet below—nowhere near the kind of leap we had to make earlier from the road.

"Hop down. I'll light your way. You're wearing your gloves, right?"

I couldn't help it, but this time he didn't act

offended. He held up his gloved hands, waggling them in front of his face, then crouched and leaped down. He shone his flashlight at my feet so I could see as well. I hopped down, and this time I stayed on my feet.

"Thanks," I said, shining my flashlight so it glowed on Ben's face. He had a huge, loopy grin that made it hard not to laugh out loud.

"What?" I asked.

"It's pretty cool. We're down on the tracks. Haven't you ever wondered what it would be like to be down on the tracks?"

I totally had—I knew exactly what he meant. I kind of think it's impossible to stand on a subway platform and *not* wonder what it would be like to end up down on the tracks. Usually it's a sick thrill of a feeling, like looking out over the rail of a high balcony and wondering what it would feel like to fall. You don't want to experience it, but you can't help thinking about it. Now here we were. And we were perfectly safe . . . at least perfectly safe in terms of speeding trains. Safe from evil groups out to destroy us and the man I loved? Probably not so much.

Without thinking, I pulled out my phone to check GPS and get a sense of our position, but of course I had no service in the catacombs.

"That way," Ben said. He had pulled out the compass and was checking its glowing dial. "If we follow the tunnel that way, it'll take us to Race Street."

I nodded and started to walk.

"Clea," Ben said. "Watch out for the third rail."

I rolled my eyes and continued walking. The tunnel floor was at least twenty feet wide, and very flat, so walking was easy. While there *was* no electrified third rail, parallel wood beams that would have held the two main rails for the subway cars ran the entire length of the tunnels. Ben and I fell into step on either side of one of these.

The path felt eerier once we left the "station" and moved into the tunnel. While the station had felt familiar but vacant, this was an area where people were never meant to stand. The concrete walls arched all around us now. It was like a massive tomb, and I had the unsettling and completely irrational feeling that we'd reach a dead end, and the way back would somehow seal itself up, trapping us forever.

"Here," Ben said, handing me an energy bar from his backpack.

I hadn't even realized I was hungry, but the

second I saw the bar, I was ravenous. My stomach growled to prove it, and the sound purred through the tunnel. Ben smiled.

"Thanks," I said, opening the bar. It was a Clif Bar, Blueberry Crisp flavor, my favorite choice whenever I go rock climbing. I adjusted my flashlight so Ben's face was illuminated by the edge of its glow, but he was moving forward again, munching on his own bar.

He knew me so well. Even better than Sage, in some ways. He knew details—like my favorite brand of energy bar, my favorite tea, my favorite place to sit on an airplane, and a million other favorites. They were the kinds of things anyone who spent enough time around me would know, if they cared enough to pay attention, and Ben had. Sage wouldn't know any of those details, but he knew *me*. He knew my darkest places and deepest flaws, and he loved me not despite them but *for* them.

It drew me in deeper than Ben's most detailed list of Clea Raymond trivia ever could.

I trained my flashlight back on the tunnel ahead. The darkness was so thick, it had weight and body. Ben and I were twin lighthouses, slicing through the inky blackness. With no landmarks, no change in the scenery, and no sound but the soft echo of our own feet and the dull white noise of the world just above, time slowed to a crawl. It was difficult to believe we were moving. We hadn't gone far—the entire length of the tunnel was two miles, and we hadn't even covered a quarter of that yet—but the near complete lack of sensory input left me quickly exhausted.

I turned my mind's eye to Sage. I let myself feel his arms around me as they had been in the dream-that-wasn't-a-dream. I breathed deeply, remembering his scent. He had left a sign for me to come here, and I needed to stay strong and alert for him.

Then I heard a low, gravelly laugh, and my blood ran cold.

I spun to Ben, nearly blinding him with my light, but I had to see his face—had he heard what I'd heard?

He had. I could see it in his eyes, wild now and darting around the darkened shaft.

Then his eyes met mine. He gave a pointed stare and nod, then turned off his flashlight.

I understood. I did the same.

Without even realizing I was doing it, I took sideways steps toward Ben. He must have been doing the same, because I quickly felt him next to me.

The laughter came again, female, but harsh and raspy. Its echo raced up and down the tunnel so we couldn't tell where it was coming from.

Everything was suddenly very real. A chill ran up my spine and I squeezed Ben's hand, hard. I hadn't even realized I was holding it, and now it was the only thing keeping me from screaming out loud.

Ben pulled me toward the wall. We were too exposed in the middle of the tunnel. With the wall as our guide we could keep moving forward, and before long we'd be out of this section of tunnel and in another open platform area.

I pressed my back against the wall . . . and felt something cold and wet seep into my hair. I jumped away and reached up to feel it, letting go of Ben's hand as I did. The goop was thick and sticky, and I had a horrible certainty that if I turned on my flashlight, I'd find my hand full of blood.

Then the laughter came back . . . along with scratching, like a wild animal clawing at the cement walls. But the scratching was too loud— the animal would have to be a dragon, a giant beast raking its talons from ceiling to floor.

I had to turn on my flashlight and see, but before I could, I felt a whoosh of air as *something* shot by me, slapping the flashlight out of my hand as it went.

"Ben!" I screamed.

I heard a clatter and knew the flashlight had been knocked out of his hands as well.

I reached for my backpack—we had more flashlights inside—but I was yanked backward as the pack itself was ripped from my back. I fought against the disorienting darkness and remembered my Krav Maga, throwing an elbow strike behind me, but I hit nothing. Whoever had been there was already gone. I kicked and punched into the darkness, trying to aim for anything I heard, but the echoing catacombs threw me off. I grew more and more frantic as each blow found nothingness.

Finally one of my kicks made contact.

"UGH!"

Shit. I'd hit Ben.

"Ben! Are you okay?"

I staggered blindly forward until I found him. He was hunched over, gasping for breath.

"Ben, I'm so sorry. . . ."

Then I screamed as something landed on my face.

And started crawling around.

Several somethings.

They were on my hands, too. Crawling up my sleeves.

My hands flew to my face and I clawed at it, pulling away . . . spiders. They were spiders, crawling on my *face*, crawling toward my *mouth*. . . .

I was losing it. I was going to be sick. I brushed frantically at my face, my hands, my body. I yanked off my sweatshirt and shook it out, then wiped it over myself, trying to brush the spiders away.

Then the laughter started again. More of it than before, bouncing around from every direction. High-pitched, insane giggles mixed with the deep rumbling sound we'd heard before.

It was too much. The darkness, the goo, the invisible attackers, the spiders . . . my nerves were on overload, and my body was exhausted from punching and kicking into the nothingness. I could feel myself shutting down. I could imagine myself curling up on the ground and falling asleep, hoping to wake up in my own bed, with this just being a terrible nightmare.

My knees started giving way . . . until I heard the pitter-patter of tiny clawed feet and felt a large lump clamber over my foot, a thick rope tail slipping under the cuff of my jeans to tickle my ankle.

A rat.

I kicked it away and heard the sick thud as it smacked against the wall . . . just seconds before I heard a much more horrible sound coming from Ben.

He was screaming, as if he were in agonizing pain.

"Ben? *Ben?*"

A gunshot.

Then silence.

"BEN!"

I staggered blindly around the tunnel, reaching out for him. Where was he? What happened? Was he alive?

Rough arms grabbed me from behind, and before I could kick back at them, someone else pulled a rope around my legs, tying them tightly together. I struggled, but within moments my wrists were tied as well, my arms held behind my back.

"Hello, Clea Raymond. Remember me?"

I did, and I didn't need to see him to know it. His thick European accent and the hideous stench of his breath gave him away. He was the man who had attacked Ben and me in Brazil. The man who'd have kidnapped us had Sage not gotten in his way.

The man clicked on his flashlight—*my* flashlight—and shone it up at his face. I could see his black, rotten teeth, his sunken cheeks, his pustule-covered skin, and the tattoo across his throat: a skull with fire in its eye sockets, branded "CV" for Cursed Vengeance.

"What did you do with Ben?" I asked through gritted teeth.

He smiled his putrid smile.

But before he could say anything, twin beams of brightness snapped to life several feet in front of us.

Headlights. From what looked like a Hummer. After so much darkness, my eyes had trouble adjusting to the blinding lights pointed straight at us. What I could see was a silhouette standing just in front of the car, legs spread wide, hands on its hips. Several large men with guns stood in a V formation, flanking the vehicle and spreading out from its nexus. I could see at least ten, but I could tell there were more, just out of reach of the light.

"You shouldn't be asking questions right now,"

the silhouette in front of the Hummer said. She had a woman's voice, but there was nothing feminine in its tone. "What you want to do is give me one reason I shouldn't kill you right now."

thirteen

"CLEA," BEN CROAKED.

I spun around. It was dark where I stood, but there was enough headlight glow for me to see Ben, three feet away. He was tied up like I was, and it looked like he'd just managed to work a cloth gag out of his mouth so he could speak. He didn't look good, but he didn't look like someone who'd just been shot.

"Are you okay?" I asked.

"Of course he's okay," the woman in silhouette said. "What did you think we'd do, shoot him?"

"I'd shoot him," Rot-Mouth said, leaning close

to my face. "I'll shoot him right now." He pulled a pistol from his belt and pointed it at Ben.

"Give it a rest, Damian," the woman said. "We're on the same side."

"We're *not* on the same side," I said.

"'Course we are. We both want to find your boyfriend, right? Same side. So it's time we had a little chat."

She left her position in front of the headlights to hop in the passenger seat of the Humvee. Someone else started it up and pulled it next to us. With the headlights no longer blinding us, I could see the car was a convertible, and I had a fairly clear view of the woman. She was tiny, and her ragged jeans and drab-white tank top clung to a body ripped with muscles. Her long hair grew black at the roots but was bleach blond beyond that, and was pulled into a greasy-slick ponytail. Her arms bore full sleeves of vivid tattoos—what looked like scenes of death and dismemberment. The one I could best make out was on her right bicep: a voracious wolf with bloodstained teeth disemboweling an agonized boy. The wolf's eyes peered up from its work and glared out of the picture, as if warning anyone who looked that they'd be its next victims.

"What are you waiting for?" she asked me. "Get in."

I looked down at my bound ankles.

The woman laughed.

"Damian, toss her in," she said.

Rot-Mouth treated me to a putrefying smile. "Love to."

I tried not to breathe as he pulled me close, crushing me into his body.

"Jesus Christ, Damian, pick her up and dump her in the car. You're not dancing at the fucking prom," the woman said.

Damian pressed me tighter into him, and I tried not to puke at the bulge in his pants that grew rock hard, then subsided.

"Was it good for you, too?" he breathed into my ear. "'Cause it was real good for me."

He swept his hand under my knees, pulling me into a fireman's hold, then climbed up and tossed me into the backseat of the car just as Ben was dropped down in the seat next to me.

"You sure you're okay?" I asked him again.

The woman spun around in her seat. "Get over it. He's fine."

"Where is Sage?" I shot back. "Did you bring him here?"

"If he were here, he'd be dead, princess. We don't have him, and we weren't expecting you, but once we got the heads-up you were coming, we rolled out the welcome wagon. Did you like it?"

"Heads-up?" I looked at Ben—did she mean she saw us coming into the subway, or something else?

The woman ignored me. "Now I'll tell you why we're going to work together. You'll even get the grand tour." She turned to the shirtless, ink-covered mountain of a driver next to her. "Go."

The man kicked the Hummer to life. As the car sped faster and faster, she clambered into the backseat and leaned back between Ben and me. "I'm Sloane." She nodded to the road in front of us and grinned. "Check this out. It's like Six Fuckin' Flags."

Her grin grew wider and wider as the Hummer kept speeding up. The exhaust fumes in the closed space stung my eyes and choked me, but I wouldn't flinch.

"Um . . . Sloane?" Ben choked out. "We're heading straight for . . ."

He couldn't even finish, but what we were heading straight for was a thick concrete wall that filled the entire tunnel.

Sloane pulled the stub of a much-mouthed cigar from her sports bra and lit it up, sucking it in until it smoldered.

I was calm at first. There was no way Sloane was seriously going to smash us into a wall of concrete. She'd said we were on the same side. Even if she was lying about that, would she kill herself and her driver just to get Ben and me? It made no sense.

But the CV was filled with zealots. Making sense wasn't a priority for them. Accomplishing what they wanted; that was their priority. And if killing Ben and me was what they wanted, they wouldn't have a problem incurring a couple casualties. They might even enjoy it.

"Scared yet?" Sloane asked.

My heart *was* pounding now. I understood everything—luring us here had been the CV's idea. *They'd* left the message on my computer, not Sage. Of course—they were the ones who could physically *get* to my computer; Sage was held captive. I'd been so ready to believe Sage and Amelia were working together in some supernatural way that I'd let it destroy my common sense. I should have known right away this was a trap. Sloane was lying—the CV *did* have Sage, and killing Ben and me was their way of breaking him before they finally destroyed him.

I stole a glance at Ben, expecting to see him cowering in the farthest corner of the seat. He wasn't. His jaw was clenched, and the sweat was beading on his face as he breathed hard, his nostrils flaring with the effort . . . but he was sitting straight up, eyes wide open and waiting for what came next.

If he could be that strong, so could I. I stared at the oncoming wall.

A memory flashed in my head — me at six years old, looking up at my father.

"Daddy, what happens when you die?" I asked.

He sighed, then lifted me into his lap. "Physiologically? You just . . . stop."

"But what about heaven?"

We weren't religious, but Rayna's parents were, and they'd been talking a lot about heaven since Rayna's grandmother had died.

Dad pursed his lips together, as if wondering whether to tell me the truth or what he thought I needed to hear. "I don't know. I want to think there's an actual heaven, a place where our souls go after we die. Sometimes I *do* think that. Sometimes I think our souls come back to earth to learn something new. But sometimes . . . sometimes I think we just stop, and what we think of as an eternal afterlife is simply the last thought we have before we die."

I furrowed my tiny brow. "So if I think about you right before I die, I can be with you forever?"

Dad smoothed my hair. "Something like that."

I nodded. "Then that's what I'll do. But maybe I'll think about puppies, too. And candy."

The whole scene flashed through my mind with vivid detail in less than a blink. Now was my chance to make good on my promise, but I wasn't going to think about Dad, or puppies, or candy. I concentrated on Sage. On the two of us together, living in peace for eternity.

The Hummer screeched to the side at the last possible second. We fishtailed wildly, the squeal of the tires echoing back to us a million times over. My stomach somersaulted as I was thrown back and forth against the door and then Sloane, and for an instant I bounced off the seat entirely. I was sure I'd be thrown from the car, or it would roll over, crushing us.

Instead, the driver regained control and drove back into the darkened tunnel from which we'd come. About halfway back, he pressed a button on the car visor—it looked like a garage-door opener—and a steel panel I hadn't seen on our suicidal drive the other way lifted so we could drive through.

"Hope you didn't wet yourself," Sloane said. She grabbed a folding knife out of her jeans pocket and whipped it open. The blade was dangerously sharp.

"Nice gut hook," I said.

Sloane grinned. "You like it? Thanks. Don't move."

It was easier said than done. We'd slowed down, but the car was bouncing and swerving. Not moving wasn't exactly an option.

"Just keep in mind, I've got hundreds of soldiers down here who'd kill you if you tried anything. There."

I felt the rope around my hands loosen and fall away.

"Turning my back on you now. You can either be good, or dead. Your choice."

As she turned to cut the ropes on Ben, I looked around for the first time since we'd gone through the steel door.

No, not the steel door. We'd gone down the rabbit hole. This place was nothing like the hundred-year-old abandoned subway Ben and I had been exploring. We were in a tunnel, but this one was bright from the giant lights built into the ceiling. The place was crawling with people, most of them as buff and tattooed as Sloane and her driver, and in constant motion. From where I sat, I could see men and women rappelling in competitive heats down the walls. Others ran an obstacle course equipped with tires, rope swings over mud pits, climbing walls, hurdles, and football sleds. Still others did calisthenics to the screaming cadence of a drill sergeant.

"This is . . . incredible," Ben said, rubbing his wrists where the rope had dug in. Sloane had pulled away the remnants of his gag and sliced the rope from his legs, and now bent to do the same for mine.

"'Course it is. We work our asses off down here. Have for years. I'll show you the place, but you need to move. The Hummer's for the outer tunnels; here it takes up too much space."

Sloane's driver pulled the Hummer into a parking spot. He got out of the car and opened Ben's door so we could pile out, then Sloane led us to a golf cart. Her driver followed, but she waved her hand dismissively.

"I've got it," she said. She climbed into the cart, then nodded for us to join her. I sat next to her in the front seat while Ben slid onto the bench behind us. "Should go without saying," she said as she turned the keys and started driving us along the tunnel, next to the soldiers-in-training, "but you try anything and you're dead. If I don't get you, my team will."

"Your team?" I asked.

"I run this place," she said. "Elder statesman. Have been for three years now. If I'm lucky, it stays mine for another four months."

"What happens in four months?" Ben asked.

"I fucking croak," she said, then winked at me. "Unless I kill your boyfriend first. That's the plan."

"So you can get rid of the curse," Ben said.

"Oh, that's what you bring to the party," Sloane said. "You're the smart one. Yeah, so I can get rid of the curse."

"You believe the curse is real?" I asked.

Sloane gave a single barking laugh. "Ask that again and you'll see how fast my gut hook can take out your jugular."

My heart pounded against my chest, but I kept my voice calm. "I'm sorry. That was rude. What I mean is that we don't know very much about the curse, beyond that one exists."

"Damn straight it exists," she muttered.

We kept driving through the retrofitted subway tunnel, surrounded constantly by the beehive of people going through what seemed like Navy SEAL training. Everyone was focused; if anyone ever rested down here, there was no evidence of it. Nor was there anyplace to do it—there wasn't a spot of open space that wasn't designed as part of a workout area. Even the tall wooden crates that *could* double as stools were occupied by people grunting as they did two-footed leaps on and off them while another of the drill sergeants screamed at them.

Eventually we moved out of the tunnel and into what must have been created as another station, though it was impossible to tell from its current condition. It had become a giant barracks: rows and rows of beds and footlockers. The CV were masters of using their small space to its best advantage: They'd built multiple platforms up the sides of the station, each with identical rows of the beds and lockers. Ladders extended up the open ends of the platforms, giving access to the beds on the higher levels. The lights were dimmer in this part of this station, and I noticed that several sections of the barracks were occupied by sleeping people.

"We operate twenty-four/seven," Sloane explained. "We sleep in shifts."

"Are those . . . kids?" Ben whispered.

I followed his gaze. He was looking at one of the higher platforms, which was hard to make out in the dim light, and from so many feet below. But a couple of the sleepers had their heads close to the edge of the bed . . . and I could see the puffy roundness of baby-faced cheeks and lips.

"Speak up," Sloane barked. "I can't hear you when you whisper."

"Sorry, I just . . . People are sleeping. . . ."

"They need to grab sleep when they can, even if bombs are going off around them, so don't whisper. And yeah, they're kids. We stick them up top so they get over any fear-of-heights bullshit right away. Not on the very top—that's reserved for people getting their party on. Gotta keep the new soldiers coming, right?"

"I don't understand," Ben said. "You act like you're training for war, but as I understand it, and forgive me if I'm wrong . . ." He didn't sound frightened, but I could tell he was choosing his words carefully. ". . . the entire mission of Cursed Vengeance is to find and destroy one man: Sage. Your ancestors were cursed because they stole the Elixir and forced him to drink it. Now you need to undo that crime by returning the Elixir to the earth. That's how to break the curse, and to do that, you have to empty the Elixir from Sage, killing him in the process."

I didn't care if he was just placating Sloane — it turned my stomach that Ben could talk about killing Sage as calmly as if he were leading one of his college advisees through a tricky mythological passage.

"You know your shit," Sloane said. "But you're clueless about what the hell that means. We're after one guy — one guy who is fucking *immortal,* and has gotten very good at disappearing and protecting himself. He's also got the Saviors on him, so we know if we want him, there's a good shot we'll have to fight them for him. And we can't kill him unless we have the dagger, so we'll probably have to fight for that, too. All that's *part* of why we're so organized, but it's not the most important part."

"What is?" I asked.

Sloane drove the golf cart out of the station

and into another stretch of tunnel. This one was apparently an ammunitions training ground. The wood beams on the floor had been pulled up so the ground was soft earth, and CV members commando-crawled over it with rifles, then rose up to shoot at targets before ducking down again. Sloane smiled at the sight of one soldier who was particularly adept with the rifle — a girl who couldn't be any more than twelve. She was slight, but she looked tough.

"Nice shooting, Jaymes!" she called. "Proud of you."

The girl looked up and gave a rock-on sign, then went back to obliterating her target.

"Look around at my soldiers," Sloane said to us. "Notice anything about them?"

I noticed they were well-oiled fighting and killing machines, but that seemed like it would be stating the obvious.

"They're under thirty," Sloane answered. "That's the curse. We die before our thirtieth birthday, which is usually the capper to a life of pure shit."

I took a closer look at the soldiers swarming around us. It wasn't easy to make out most of their faces while they were crawling and shooting, but

I did see what looked like a whole group of very young kids—some as small as the local kindergarteners whose classrooms Mom would visit every year to tell them about how the government works.

"What about Damian?" That was what Sloane had called Rot-Face. I could smell the reek of his breath, and see his black teeth and scarred and abused body. There was no way he was under thirty.

"Twenty-one," Sloane said. "We didn't find him and bring him in until he was nineteen. If we hadn't, he'd be long gone."

"Bring him in?" I said. "But aren't people born into the CV? You're descendants of the same group of three people."

"Three people who scattered, stayed on the run, and had piss-poor lives where everything went wrong. They did sleep around though, and left kids who had no idea who their fathers were, or what they had done. Those kids grew up with the curse over them and died before they were thirty too, but not before they had another generation of kids with even less idea of what the fuck their grandfathers had done. It was a couple hundred years before anyone had their shit together enough to figure it out. Those people started the CV, but it took even longer to get seriously organized. That's a lot of years and a lot of short generations. So yeah, you're born into the CV, but there's a shitload of kids out there who have no clue they're part of the club."

As she spoke, Sloane drove the cart out of the long ammunitions-training tunnel and into another station area, this one bigger than the other two had been. Much of it was dedicated to a mess area, with large group tables and a cafeteria-style kitchen line. This was the part of the underground network that seemed to offer a chance for relaxation. There were open areas where men, women, and children wrestled like lions struggling for dominance within a pride. Groups of sinewy soldiers sat against the wall and smoked cigarettes and cigars, their crass jokes and gritty laughter echoing through the room. A jungle gym, rope course, and zip line doubled as both further training grounds and a playground on which knots of people shoved for position.

Like the last station area, this one had been maximized with several vertical levels. These were walled off by what looked like Plexiglas, so anyone inside could see what was happening outside and below. Inside, they resembled the kind of offices you'd find anywhere, outfitted with desks, chairs, and computers.

"Those offices?" Sloane said. "About half of them are for our computer jockeys. They research the genealogy. When we find family, we bring 'em in. It's their one shot at a life with purpose and hope. Out there they're lucky if they die young. If not, they get caught in the kind of shitstorm that spits 'em out like Damian."

Sloane stopped the golf cart and got out, beelining for one of the ladders that stretched to the upper levels. She didn't ask Ben and me to follow her, nor did she look back to see if we would, but of course we did. Without breaking a sweat or even breathing heavily, Sloane scaled four ladders, climbing up to the very top of the station. Even with his newly developed muscles, Ben couldn't keep up with her. I was impressed, though—before, a climb like this would have been impossible for him. Even if he'd had the strength to do it, he couldn't deal with heights. As it was, I had to work hard to remain just behind him as we rose higher and higher toward the ceiling.

"What do you think?" I asked, huffing as I tried to take advantage of our time out of earshot of Sloane. "Is she telling the truth?"

"Doesn't contradict the mythology," Ben said. He tried to cover it up, but I could tell he was huffing too. "And it explains why getting Sage is so important to them. It's life and death."

Ben clambered up to the top platform, and I climbed out after him. We'd entered a kind of command center. One wall was covered in monitors showing portions of the two-mile underground subway system, both the renovated ones and the older areas Ben and I had struggled through at first. These were dark, but were scanned with heat sensors that showed any motion in fiery colors.

Sloane was already seated, feet up on a utilitarian metal desk, a beer cracked open in her hand. Looking at her, I imagined what it would be like to have a time stamp on your life. I suppose I had one too—none of my lives had lasted very long—but there was something merciful about not knowing when it would happen.

Since I'd found out about them, I'd been certain the CV were the bad guys—cold, heartless, and evil. But there was more to it than that. Knowing the full story, I felt sorry for them. I wondered if there were other things I'd misunderstood when it came to the Elixir.

devoted

"So what do you say?" she asked. "We have a deal?"

I looked at Ben, but he shook his head. He was just as confused as I was. As far as I knew, Sloane hadn't offered us a deal.

"A deal for what?" I asked.

"Your boyfriend," she replied. "You find out where the Saviors of Eternal Life have him; we'll help you get to him, and we'll help you fight them off. If you can get away with him, you go on the run and live happily ever after . . . for as long as you possibly can."

"What do you mean if I can get away with him?"

"If you can get him away from us," Sloane said, taking a big swig of her beer, "before we kill him."

---

fourteen

I LAUGHED OUT LOUD.

"That's it? *That's* why you broke into my room and left the message on my computer? You thought I'd help you get Sage?"

Sloane looked at me like I'd sprouted another head. "What message?"

"The message," I said. "'Charlie Victor . . . beneath the flying pig . . .'"

"What are you talking about?"

I looked at Ben, but he wasn't even paying attention to the conversation. He was scanning the monitors, no doubt taking mental notes for the book he would one day write about the fascinating mythology of the Saviors, the CV, and the Elixir of Life.

"Here's what I know," Sloane continued. "The Saviors of Eternal Life grabbed your boyfriend in Japan. Because *you* set them up. Hell of a girlfriend."

"She saved his life," Ben said. Apparently he *was* paying attention.

"Whatever," Sloane said. "When the Saviors got him, they got the dagger, too. We intercepted them crowing about it before they cut off known communication lines. We've been trying to find them, but we can't."

"And you thought I could help you. That's why you left the message on my computer."

"Stop with the message. I did *not* leave a message on your computer. If I wanted to bring your ass here, I'd have had my soldiers grab you, tie a cute burlap sack over your head, and *bring your ass here.* My plan was to watch you and tail you if you got intel and went after your boyfriend. When I found out you were coming to visit, I changed it up. You got our whole sob story, you know why we do what we do, and now I'm offering you a damn good deal—your best shot at getting your guy out alive."

"For the two seconds before you grab him and kill him."

Sloane shrugged. "I didn't say it was a good shot, just that it was your best. Hell, we might find him before you—then all this is b.s. But I know the history—you have a way of meeting up with this guy. Thing is, you go after the Saviors by yourself, you're screwed. They're not as organized as we are, but there's a bunch of 'em, and they won't give up Sage without a fight. They'll trap you, they'll kill you, but they sure as hell won't be stopped by you. You work with us, we got your back. We'll take on the Saviors, and believe me, we'll win. So tell me . . . we got a deal?"

I stared at Sloane, kicked back in her chair. She guzzled her beer and grinned around her stub of a cigar.

"What if I say no?" I asked. "Won't you just watch me and follow me anyway?"

"Oh hell yeah. But you've slipped us before, so why not just play nice together from the start?"

"Because you're trying to kill the man I love," I said.

"We are not the bad guys!" she roared. "Don't

you get it? I am a walking corpse. Living to twenty-nine in the CV? It's like knocking around at a hundred and five in the real world. We live in fucking dog years. And the curse isn't kind. We don't go to sleep and not wake up. We're nailed with the most god-awful plagues to ever hit humanity. Five-year-olds with flesh-eating viruses, rare diseases that rot you from the inside out and make you drown in your own blood. That shit happens even in here, every day. All we can do is save them from the crap out in the big world: car crashes, shootings, overdoses . . . the ones you hear about that seem so random? It's not random; it's the curse. The three guys who stole the Elixir may have been assholes who deserved what they got, but they've been dead five hundred years. That's *five hundred years* of innocent people born without a shot in hell at any kind of life, with parents who die young after drowning for years in their own crap. You honestly think your boyfriend's life is worth more than *every single one* of ours?"

Her eyes were wild, but I couldn't look away. She was right. No one life—especially one that had already gone on for centuries—was worth sacrificing so many others. Sage himself would say the same thing. I knew that, but tears filled my eyes because I also knew no matter how wrong it was, no matter how many other people had to suffer, I couldn't help her.

"I don't want Sage to die," I whispered.

Sloane took a deep breath and blew it out toward her blond-black greasy hair. She even smiled.

"I know," she said. "The soulmate thing. But I'm counting on that, remember? That's what'll lead you to him. I'm just asking you don't run off after him without letting us know. We'll help you get to the Saviors. We'll help you beat them back. You will get your hands on Sage. You have my word as a dying woman. If you can get him the hell out of there before we do, have at it. We'll be on your ass until we find him, but you'll have your shot. It's more than the Saviors will offer you, and further than you'll get on your own."

"Why should I trust you?"

"It's not about trusting me. It's about trusting yourself. And your friend here, right? I'm guessing he'll be coming along for the ride?"

"Yes. Yes, I will be there," Ben said. "Absolutely."

"So there you go," Sloane said. "My soldiers and I will give you a fighting chance. It's slim, but it's there."

devoted

I thought about it. What Sloane said was true. Especially now that I'd seen their operation, I knew working with the CV would give me a huge advantage against the Saviors, whom I might not be able to handle on my own. And it wasn't like I was a stranger to using my enemy to help me. That had been my whole plan in Japan: contacting the Saviors so they'd interrupt Sage doing the ceremony that would destroy him. I knew we'd have just a slight chance to escape from them when they attacked, but I had enough faith in Sage and myself that a slight chance was enough.

Ben had destroyed that slight chance. Would he destroy it again?

I glanced over at him. He was looking around the room as if memorizing it. I got it, I guess. Seeing the CV in operation and learning their secrets was probably an Elixir-lore fanboy's dream come true. Of course he'd want to be involved when we somehow found the Saviors, but I wasn't sure it was a good idea.

I didn't have to deal with that now, though. I turned back to Sloane.

"We have a deal."

"Good. When you know where your boy is and you're ready to make a move, you tell our guy."

I cringed, thinking about Damian. "You're sending someone with us?"

"Don't need to. I told you, we've got you covered."

So there was someone watching me at the house. At this point I wasn't even surprised. I'd have to figure out who it was when we got back.

"Here — I'll show you to the door." Sloane leaped off the desk and moved to a far corner behind her. There was a ladder leading up to the ceiling, and she practically sprinted up it. I stayed right on her heels. Ben lagged, taking a last look down at the inner workings of the CV before he followed.

At the top of the ladder was a round porthole, maybe three feet in diameter, right in the ceiling. Sloane pushed it open to reveal a dark, earthen tube with another ladder built into its side. I couldn't see how high it climbed; the inside was pitch-black. She turned back to me and grinned. "You're not afraid of the dark, are you? Small spaces?"

She didn't wait for an answer. She pulled herself into the tube and kept climbing. I followed, and was soon swallowed by the darkness, though if I looked down I could see the faint glow from her office below.

"Shut the door behind you," she said when Ben had made it inside.

When he did, the darkness was complete. I heard Sloane's footsteps above my head and followed, but the blackness was disorienting. The smell of dank earth, which hadn't seemed so powerful with the glow of light, now filled my nose. It made my head swimmy, and I had to force myself to concentrate on each rung, hand by hand, foot by foot.

"Shit!"

The shout came from below me, and was followed by a frantic scuffling of hands and feet, then a loud thud.

Ben had lost his grip.

"You'll want to watch your step," Sloane said, her voice snakelike as it floated down. "Complete darkness messes some people up."

She waited until we heard Ben breathing directly below me. "Okay," he said. "I'm good."

"Hadn't asked," Sloane said, then scrambled a few more feet. I heard sounds I couldn't place, then a loud cracking. A fluorescent green line appeared. A glow stick. In its light, I could see we were at the top of the earthen tunnel. A round metal door sat just above Sloane's head, and a tiny monitor was built into the wall next to it. In the green glow, she turned on the monitor, which showed a vacant street.

"Four a.m. and all's clear," she said.

She let the glow stick drop to the bottom of the tunnel, then pushed and slid the metal door. A cold gust of air blew down on us. It reeked of garbage and decay. I felt like I'd been underground for an eternity. As my eyes adjusted to the moonlit glow, I saw Sloane had shifted to the side of the ladder so Ben and I could climb out. We did, and with a final, "You'll be in touch," Sloane pulled the door back in and disappeared.

We were in an unlit alley, several feet from an overflowing Dumpster. The circle of asphalt that hid the door from which we'd emerged blended in perfectly — it was completely invisible.

The Dumpster stench was overwhelming. I started walking to get away from it.

"Wait up." Ben bounded a couple steps to catch up with me. His eyes were dancing. "Pretty amazing down there, right? I mean, look around — you'd have no clue it was right below us. Even people who've lived here their whole lives — people who know about the old subway — even *they* don't know what's going on. It's like — "

"Stop! This isn't fun for me, Ben. I'm not

researching a dissertation. I'm trying to find Sage. *He's* the reason I'm here."

"I've been thinking about that . . . and I don't think it's true."

"What do you mean? Of course it's true."

"Well, yeah, I mean, he's the reason you're here. You're here because you want to save him. But he's not the *reason* you're *here*."

"Ben . . . English . . ."

"I don't think Sage left you the message. You said it yourself—he doesn't have the kind of power where he can be in one place and simultaneously go to another."

"Right. He'd need help. Petra or Amelia or someone else in the family."

"But Petra and the men want you away from Sage. So it would have to be Amelia."

"Fine, yes. Amelia." It was what I'd assumed before, but even as I said it, I realized a flaw in the idea. When I was on the plane and had the vision of Sage—a vision I knew was real—Sage hadn't recognized Amelia at all. Had she appeared to him as a voice in his head? Is that how she helped him deliver the message?

"When we came here," Ben said, "we thought the message was from Sage—an SOS telling us the CV had taken him from the Saviors, and he needed us to rescue him."

I wasn't going to bother correcting him on the "us" thing. I let him continue.

"But it turns out he's not here. He's still with the Saviors."

"Right . . ."

"So how would he know about this place? And even if he did, the last time he was around the CV, they were shooting at him. I think whoever sent us here did it because they thought we could use Sloane's help. I don't buy that Sage would ever think help from the CV was even a possibility."

"You're right," I realized. "He wouldn't. So then was it . . . just Amelia?"

"I can't think of anyone else. You said she seemed like she wanted to help you . . . and that she wanted to keep that from her family. . . ."

Ben was right, and he didn't even know about the last time I saw her. She'd made it clear that she wanted Sage and me to hold on to each other, and that her family would hurt her if they knew.

Amelia must have sent the message. She used the scent of sage because she knew it would get my attention. She wanted me to join forces with the CV.

She thought I needed backup.

It felt right . . . but there was so much that didn't make sense. If Amelia wanted to leave a cryptic message, couldn't she have left one telling me where I could find Sage? It was fine to get me help if she thought I needed it, but a cavalry was useless without anyplace to go. And I still couldn't wrap my head around why it mattered to her. Why would Amelia or her family care whether Sage and I were together?

For the moment there was nothing to do about it but head back home. The good part of having Ben in the loop was he could help me sift through the few facts I had about Sage's location, so maybe we could find it faster.

Ben pulled out his phone and checked flight times. We had a few hours to kill, but not enough to check into a hotel for a nap. So we walked. The sun rose as we did, tingeing everything the light pink of early morning. I didn't say much; I was mentally planning my next meeting with Amelia, putting in order everything I wanted to ask her.

That is, if there *would* be a next meeting. I remembered how frightened she sounded when she talked about hiding what she was doing from her family. I hoped she was okay.

Ben and I had no destination in particular

but ended up on the Purple People Bridge, a pedestrian overpass connecting Cincinnati and Kentucky, where we'd catch our flight. The bridge was scarcely populated at this hour. I looked up at Ben, but the sun was rising out from behind his head and I had to squint and look away.

The silence between us was light and companionable. Ben didn't so much break it as skate seamlessly on top of it.

"So . . . Rayna and Nico," he said.

"From the second she saw him," I agreed.

"They seem good together," Ben said. Then he smiled, adding, "And here I didn't think Rayna was a stable person."

"Oooooh." I winced at the bad joke.

"What? I'm just horsing around."

"Ugh, Ben!"

"You're saying I should *rein* in the humor?"

"Oh my God, you're killing me."

"I hope not. I really, really hope not."

His voice had grown serious. I turned to him, but his eyes were downcast. I knew what he was thinking, but I had no idea what to say.

We walked for a while more.

"I want to make up for everything," he finally said. "I need to."

We were still walking, and his eyes were on his feet. He spoke softly, barely loud enough for me to hear.

"It's my last chance," Ben continued. "If he dies, and I haven't done everything I can to try to make things better . . ."

"He won't die."

"But he *could*. I'm not saying it to get you upset, Clea. I hope he doesn't. But he could . . . and then I'm done. I can't make it up. Ever."

"I don't believe that. You're not a bad person, Ben."

Ben choked out a laugh. "A good person with a bad soul."

"No . . ."

"I know you have good reasons not to want my help on this. I know you wouldn't have even brought me here if I hadn't kept everything from you until the last minute. But please . . . I need to do this. I need the chance to get it right, before . . ."

He didn't have to say it.

I had no idea how to respond. I wanted to tell him I'd trust him . . . but I didn't know if I could, and I couldn't play with Sage's life because Ben wanted one more chance to make things right.

"You don't have to answer," he said. "Just . . . you know . . . think about it."

I nodded. I could promise him that much.

We walked in an awkward silence awhile longer.

"So . . . you and Suzanne?" I asked. I figured that would be safer ground.

"Kind of . . . yeah."

"I'm glad. I'm happy for you."

"Yeah?"

"Yeah, I am."

"Thanks."

We kept walking, staying silent the rest of the way across the bridge, but it was an easier silence. When we made it to Kentucky, we were both too exhausted to do much of anything. We wound up sitting in a diner with a TV, zoning out in front of bad morning shows while we nursed cup after cup of coffee (him) and tea (me). When we finally left for the airport, got checked in, and boarded, I collapsed into my seat as if it were a feather bed. The second before I drifted off, I thought about Sage. If I could be with him in my dream again, I knew I could handle anything.

After no more than a blink, I opened my eyes. I sat in a white, wooden reclining chair in the middle of a massive open lawn. In the distance the sun glowed over lush mountains puffy with treetops.

"Beautiful, isn't it?"

I turned to my right. Petra sat there, in a chair matching my own. She lounged back, soaking in the sun. Her curls were pulled back in a loose ponytail, and she wore a pair of oversize sunglasses. She leaned toward me, lowering them on her nose. "You look surprised to see me, Clea. Why? There's no one else hanging out in your dreams, is there?"

She said it playfully, but there was a flame of something violent in her eyes.

"I don't know if I could handle anyone else," I said. "I'm still trying to figure out if *you're* real."

"Oh, I'm real," she said, relaxing back into her seat. "If you just trust it, you'll find I'm the best friend you've ever had. I'm going to save you a lot of heartache. Oh look, baby goats!"

I followed her glance to a flat meadow in the distance. Sure enough, there were several baby goats grazing as they galloped, leaped, and head-butted.

Standing among them were Sage and Lila.

Instantly I was by their side. "Sage!" I cried,

and reached for him . . . but I couldn't touch him.

"Honestly, you're a very slow learner," Petra said, pulling me back. "He can't see-you-feel-you-hear-you, so please don't waste our time."

Her words stung. She seemed to know it.

"Now, a bit of Best Friend You've Ever Had advice," Petra said. "You find out much more when you sit back and observe."

It wasn't her advice that made me do it. It was Sage.

Last time I saw him with Lila, he was in a lot of pain.

This time he was smiling.

He ambled along, perfectly in step with Lila. His hands swung loose at his side, and he seemed to bask in the breeze that blew his hair back from his face.

He looked content. More than content. He looked . . . happy.

"Are you ready for this?" Lila asked. She reached into a small tote bag slung over one arm and pulled out a handful of baby carrots. She waved them toward the grazing goats. "Hey, guys! Look what I've got!"

It was a baby-goat stampede. Ten of them. Their snouts were everywhere, nosing their way into her hand, the bag, the hem of her sundress. She gave a playful scream.

"One at a time, okay? There's enough for everyone!"

She tried to mete out the carrots, but the baby goats had no time for patience. They were everywhere, and she was screaming and laughing so hard she couldn't breathe. "Sage!" she cried. "Help me!"

"I don't know. . . . I think you've got this pretty much under control."

"SAGE!" A goat surprised her by rearing up on its back legs, pushing its front hooves on her stomach, and knocking her to the grass. Baby carrots spilled everywhere, most of them onto Lila, and the goats went nuts, nosing and bleating and batting at one another as they fought for the bonanza. Lila squealed and laughed, petting the goats as they nosed into her face, rolling away a bit when they clambered too hard with their hooves. She couldn't go far, though; she was completely penned in by the feeding frenzy.

I entertained a quick fantasy of the baby goats suddenly turning into rabid wolves. Technically I was dreaming, so I thought I had a shot . . . but it didn't happen.

"Sage!" she cried again between gasps of laughter, and this time he didn't refuse. He waded into the sea of goats, and when they bleated at him, he bleated right back at them. He reached Lila and scooped her into his arms, sending her into another flurry of squeals. The goats stayed behind with the abandoned carrots as Sage carried Lila several feet away, bride-over-the-threshold style. When they were safely away, Lila finally stopped squealing and instead looked into his eyes.

"You saved me!" she said.

Gross.

"My pleasure," Sage said.

"Put her down," I said out loud, despite the fact that he couldn't hear me. "Put her down now. Put her down."

He did . . . but he let her soft body slide down his before her feet hit the ground. Then he kept his arms around her a moment, like he was afraid she would topple.

She was in no danger of toppling.

Their eyes stayed locked, and for a horrible second I was sure they were going to kiss.

"Thank you," Lila said, inching closer.

Sage stepped away, breaking the spell.

"You're welcome," he said, but he wasn't

looking at Lila anymore. His eyes were far away.

"I saw her again, Lila."

"What?!"

The exclamation was from Petra. She had appeared right next to me, and her face contorted with fury. Of course. She had no idea Amelia had brought Sage and me together.

My heart was pounding and I felt Petra's angry stare before I heard her hiss, "He did?"

I shrugged and shook my head. If Sage had seen me, I knew nothing about it.

Petra moved closer to Sage, standing unseen immediately in front of his face.

"We were . . . I don't know where we were, but I could see her, and touch her, and there was this . . ."

He was going to say it. He was going to say something about Amelia. I willed him not to. If there was such a thing as psychic energy, I begged it to work right now. I didn't know who or what Amelia truly was, but I had a terrible feeling that if Petra found out what she'd done, it wouldn't just be Amelia who was destroyed . . . it would be Sage and me as well.

A shadow crossed Sage's face, then he shook it off.

"It was a dream, that's all. It just felt . . . it felt so real. . . ."

Petra had gone back to looking at me, those eyes hunting for the truth, but I concentrated on staring at Sage as if my life depended on it.

It wasn't hard.

Then his eyes were on mine in return.

I moved closer. I couldn't help it. He was looking right at me, the longing in his eyes so beautiful but so much more painful because it was for me, but I was *there*, I was right there in front of him, he just couldn't see. I didn't know why he couldn't see when he could before, but he couldn't.

I reached up and placed my hand on his cheek, knowing I'd feel nothing. Tears welled in my eyes.

"She's life to me," he said, his eyes going through and past me, even as I leaned up to try to kiss him, hoping he would finally feel and know. . . .

But he turned away as Lila sniffled. Her head was down and she was crying a bit, though she tried to cover. Sage rested a hand under her chin and tipped it up.

"I'm so sorry," he said. "I know this isn't fair to you."

"You can't help how you feel."

"No . . . but I don't have to tell you about it.

That's not right. Not after what you said."

What she said?

She gave Sage a hurt, puppy-dog smile.

Fury roiled inside me, and I jumped in between them, which didn't interrupt their moment in the slightest.

What did she say, Sage? That she loves you? And you believed her?! She's one of them! One of the Saviors! Why would you ever believe what they say? They took you! They're holding you captive! They're hurting you! These are the people who swore they wanted to protect you, and they're hurting you! And you believe one of them?!

I screamed the words inside my head, knowing he couldn't hear me.

Sage and Lila started walking again. Watching them hurt so bad.

Petra grinned.

"Have you noticed," she asked, "the last time we saw them, Sage was being held prisoner. Now he seems to be wandering around quite free. Free to run away . . . or to take long, romantic walks with a woman who clearly adores him. How interesting to see which one is his choice."

I scanned the horizon. Sure, it *looked* like he was free, but the tree line was probably riddled with barbed wire. Or snipers. Or an invisible fence—like for dogs, but for people.

I thought this, but at the same time I knew it wasn't true. If Sage wanted to escape, he could. He just . . . didn't.

Impossible.

There had to be something else. I'd thought before that he was betraying me, or that he was dangerous, and I'd been wrong. I couldn't jump to conclusions. Questionable behavior from Sage usually came from him trying to protect me. Is that what this was? Had the Saviors threatened my life if Sage tried to escape?

Had they threatened *Lila's* life?

Were they willing to sacrifice their own people like that? I wouldn't have thought so, but then again, I'd thought the CV were ruthless and bloodthirsty; I'd thought the Saviors wanted to keep Sage protected. I didn't know half as much as I thought I did.

But what if Lila's life was at risk? Did Sage care enough about her that he'd stay to save her?

I had to know more. I raced after Sage and Lila, running as fast as I could . . .

. . . but that tug in the center of my being pulled my feet out from under me.

The world was spiraling wildly now. I was the

center of a whirlpool, getting sucked farther and farther away from the swirling mouth. . . .

"Clea, are you okay?"

It was Ben, and he was one of twenty people whose eyes were fixed on me.

I'd woken up on the plane screaming.

fifteen

I still hadn't recovered from bringing Sage and Clea together. It had taken more out of me than I thought. I was only barely keeping myself from slipping into that state of nonexistence. Doing nothing, focusing on nothing . . . that helped, and it was exactly what I was doing when a viselike grip crushed my mind.

Mother.

"What do you think you're doing?" she snapped.

"Ow! Nothing!"

"You haven't been visiting Sage?"

"No! Ow! Stop!"

"Are you sure? Because I heard Sage say he dreamed about Clea."

"If he did, it was a dream! A regular dream!"

"Really? Because he shouldn't be dreaming about her anymore. We want him falling out of love with her, remember? That won't happen if someone's bringing them together in their dreams, Amelia."

"I'm not! I swear, I'm not! Please, you're hurting me. . . ."

"I want to believe you, I do. But if I find out you're lying . . . if you're getting in the way of our plans, it won't just be me hurting you. It will be all of us."

"Okay, but I didn't do anything! Ow!"

"Good. Then don't. Because if you do, I'll know." She released my mind from her grip. "You'll be happy to know that the dream didn't affect Sage. He's all about Lila. We'll be ready by the next full moon."

She gave my mind a final squeeze before she left. I didn't have the energy to fight against the nothingness. The last thing I thought before I disappeared was, "Another way . . . I need to find another way. . . ."

sixteen

"IT'S OKAY!" Ben said. He was standing in front of his seat in the airplane, turning to address everyone. "Just a panic attack. She gets them sometimes. Nothing to worry about." He lowered his voice into a dramatic whisper and added, "She's on medication." He sat back in his seat and looked at the doctor who was hunched over my chair, listening yet again to my heart through a stethoscope.

"Sounds good, doc?"

"Sounds great."

"Terrific." He shook the doctor's hand. "Great

devoted

call having the stethoscope in your carry-on, by the way."

"Never know when you'll need it!" the doctor agreed.

Ben gave him a knowing finger point, and the doctor went back to his seat.

"Guarantee he's been waiting his whole life for someone to shout, 'Is there a doctor on board?'" I said.

"No doubt," Ben agreed. "So are you going to tell me what happened?"

I grimaced, unsure of how much to say.

Ben sighed. "How about this? I'll tell you what I think happened. I think one of them came to you in your dream again and showed you something you didn't want to see."

"Ben . . ."

"Was it Petra? Was it Amelia? One of the men? What did they say?"

I rummaged through the back-of-the-seat pocket. "I hate two-hour flights. Long enough to get bored, but not long enough for them to show a movie."

"I'm guessing they haven't done anything to Sage that can't be fixed. You recovered too quickly for that."

"Do you think they have any more peanuts?" I asked. "I could use more water."

"Who are they? What did they tell you? What do they want? Why do they even care if you and Sage are together or not?"

"Ben . . ."

"I told you, Clea. I want to be involved in this. I need it. You don't have to tell me, but if you don't, I'm going to keep looking into this thing on my own. Please don't cut me out. There's too much riding on it for me."

"I know, but . . ."

How could I explain it to him? He was worried about the safety of his eternal soul, which I understood, but it was intangible. I had no idea if there even *was* a heaven or hell. My dad didn't think so. He thought we just stopped, and if that was true, nothing Ben did now would change his ultimate outcome.

But Sage needed me in *this* world. I would do anything to keep him alive, and if that meant I had to hurt Ben's feelings, so be it.

"Fine," Ben said, reading the answer in my silence. "Tell you what — after we land, take a cab back home. I don't want to get in your way."

"Where are you going?"

He had gotten up and was already several rows down the aisle.

"The flight's not full. I'll see you." He stalked off to an empty seat in the back.

When we landed, I didn't wait for Ben. I didn't even turn my head to see if he was behind me. I did just what he suggested and caught a cab back home.

I didn't want to go to my house, though.

I called Rayna.

"Did you know you say 'ho' to make a horse stop?" she said without preface.

"I thought it was 'whoa.'"

"Apparently it's either/or, which I didn't know before Nico and I went out for a trail ride this morning. He had me lead, and when I heard him yelling 'ho'. . ."

"Oh my God, he called you a ho?"

"No! But I freaked out! I thought he'd read my diary or something."

I laughed. "You? Keeping a diary?"

"I know! Can you imagine?"

"Where are you right now?"

"Just finished the postride shower and am about to collapse in front of the worst reality show I can find."

"That sounds awesome."

"My brain rot is your brain rot."

The whole time we'd been talking, I'd been making my way toward the guesthouse Rayna shared with her parents, Wanda and George. I walked in and went straight for the kitchen, remaining on the phone despite the fact that I could now see Rayna, already sprawled on the couch in the living room. She waved. I waved back.

"Are these seriously blackberries?" I asked from deep in the fridge.

"Grab 'em. And a couple Diet Cokes. And if you nuke up a popcorn, I'll be your best friend for life."

"You're already my best friend for life."

"So you can bring me along to the next one. I'd be way cooler than Ben."

"You have no idea," I said.

I hung up the phone, and five minutes later I had a tray loaded up with the popcorn, blackberries, sodas, and several slices of cold mushroom pizza that had been close enough to the front of the fridge that I guessed they were reasonably fresh.

"Ooh, good call," Rayna said, grabbing a slice.

"Protein," I agreed.

Rayna found a makeover show on TV—one

of those where they sneak up on unsuspecting people going about their business, accost them with cameras, and tell them they look like crap in front of a zillion people, make them cry, then build them back up with a new makeup job they won't be able to replicate and outfits so intricate they'll never remember how to fit them together.

It was perfect.

We sat for a while, just munching and watching. It was one of the things about Rayna I loved. She could tell when I had something on my mind, but she also knew when I was okay talking it out or when I needed time to keep it to myself. Maybe it was because she knew sooner or later, whatever it was, I'd tell her anyway.

"What do you think Sage did between Olivia and Catherine?" I finally asked.

"What do you mean?"

"Or between Catherine and Anneline. Or Anneline and Delia."

"Or Delia and you?"

"You're sensing a pattern?"

"I thought he told you," Rayna said. "He pined for you miserably."

"Right. But when he *wasn't* pining for me miserably. I mean, he's a guy."

"Okay . . . let me make sure I have this right. You're upset because you're worried Sage cheated on you . . . before you were born? You're losing it."

"It sounds lame when you say it that way."

Rayna arched an eyebrow.

"Fine," I said. "But it's not about me being jealous. I was just thinking about it, and it makes sense that he's probably fallen in love with other girls and had relationships before."

I was making the case like a lawyer, but I was pleading with my eyes for her to tell me I was both wrong and absolutely crazy for even considering such a thing.

"I know you want me to say he hasn't . . . and maybe he *hasn't* . . . but yeah, he's a guy. And a hundred years between dates is a freakishly long time. No matter how close he is with his hand, that's a lot of years for the two of them to be exclusive."

I knew it was true, but it wasn't what I wanted to hear.

"But, Clea, even if he did have other relationships—and I'm not saying he for sure did—it's not like he was cheating! You weren't even alive! He didn't know if you'd ever come back! Not for sure. And now that you *are* back . . ."

She saw it in my face.

"Oh please," she said. "Is this about the wound-washing slut at the girly hotel? Not a chance. Sage is *not* cheating on you. The boy is *obsessed* with you! Remember, I was hanging on him when we played boyfriend and girlfriend for your mom, and I got *nothing* back. Nothing. That doesn't happen. He's yours."

"There's more."

"Of course there's more!" Rayna wailed. "You and Ben ran off to chase down big guys with guns and bring back Sage; now you're here, Ben and Sage aren't, and I've been shockingly patient about not shaking you to get the dirt!" She took a handful of popcorn then froze.

"What?"

"The popcorn. It totally needs parmesan cheese."

She bounced up and ran to the kitchen, then shook the cheese generously over the bowl.

"Okay, I'm ready. Tell me."

I filled her in on everything that had happened. I didn't go into the CV stuff, except to say Sage wasn't with them and they'd give me backup against the Saviors. The other stuff would bore her. But I told her the dream with Sage and Amelia, my dream on the plane ride back, and

Ben's freak-out over his immortal soul. Rayna took it in.

"Whatever. Ben will get over it."

"I don't know. This is deep with him."

She waved it off. "So you think Sage and Goat Girl? . . ."

"She said she loves him."

"You didn't hear her say that."

I just stared at her. I'd told her their conversation verbatim. Was there any other conclusion?

"Okay, yes, she probably said that."

I raised an eyebrow.

"Fine! She said it! She loves him! So what? You think every time I tell a guy I love him, he automatically falls for me and loves me back?" She thought a second. "Okay, maybe that's a bad example. . . ."

"He was sympathetic about it. He apologized for talking about his feelings for me. Like being in love with me was something he felt awful about because it hurt her. Your 'soulmate' isn't supposed to do that."

"Maybe he's acting," Rayna said. "You said yourself you thought they might be threatening you and using that to keep him there. And how do you know there *isn't* some kind of human electric fence, or hidden people with guns pointed at him? You don't."

"I don't know. . . . It's not like he's never been with anyone else but me. . . ."

"Seriously? You don't see the difference between Sage *maybe possibly* having a quickie with someone when you didn't even exist, and him acting any way he has to act to protect the woman he loves, or just to stop from getting tortured?"

I stared at her, open mouthed. For long enough that Rayna threw a piece of popcorn into my mouth.

"I'm an idiot," I finally said after I finished choking and laughing.

"You're a jealous girlfriend," Rayna said. "Very similar, but different. Now *I*, on the other hand, have no reason to be jealous. I'm fairly certain Nico was a nun before he met me."

"You do know nuns are women, right?"

"A boy nun. What is that, a stag?"

"A monk. A boy deer is a stag."

"Bummer. I'd rather go with stag. It sounds kind of sexy."

"Agreed. He was a stag."

"Exactly," Rayna said. "He's twenty-one . . . and I'm his first girlfriend."

"Or so he says."

"Real deal, Clea. We're together all the time now. What do you think we do?"

She didn't even wait for me to answer.

"No! We don't! He's clean as driven snow! We *talk*. It's nice."

"Imagine."

"Shut up. I like it. It's just sad, mostly. I hear about his life and I want to have my parents adopt him . . . except then the incest thing would be a problem."

"I remember," I said. "Dead dad, poor family, four younger siblings . . ."

"*Two*," she amended.

"I thought you said he had four."

"He did have four. Did. Past tense. Two of them died."

"Oh my God. What happened?"

"Freaky shit. It's awful. One of his brothers was born with some super rare skin disease. The kid's skin was so hard when he was born, it was like a coat of armor. I looked it up online — it's for real, and there're some people who live until adulthood with it, but they're rare. The skin on these people is so hard that the eyelids flip inside out, and they have to drown themselves in Vaseline or else they can't move. . . . It's crazy."

"That's horrible. How old was Nico's brother when he died?"

"He made it to three. And his sister—totally random. She was sixteen and driving for the first time when this freak thunderstorm came out of nowhere. She didn't feel comfortable driving in the storm so she turned around to come home, and she's, like, two hundred feet from home when a tree branch gets struck by lightning and lands on her car. Crushed her. She decides to be *safe* and come home, and gets killed. Wild, right?"

"Yeah," I said, but it didn't sound wild to me. It sounded cursed.

"How old was his dad when he died?" I asked.

"Why?"

"Just curious—everything else is so awful, I'd like to think he at least had his dad for a while."

It was clumsy, but it was the best I could do. Luckily, Rayna was so into the drama of Nico's tragedy, she didn't seem to notice.

"Not even," she said. "His dad died right after the youngest brother was born. He was twenty-eight."

"Twenty-eight? How old was he when they had Nico?"

"Nineteen. His parents started *young*."

Of course they did, I thought. *That's what you do when*

you know you'll be dead by the time you're thirty.

"Nico gets depressed about it sometimes," Rayna said. "I mean, of course he does, but . . . he gets superstitious, too. He talks about his dad, and his brother and sister, and apparently his dad told him stories about other people in the family who died super young. . . ."

"His dad told him that when Nico was *nine*?"

"And younger. I know, right? It's amazing he's not completely messed up."

"Totally."

This was where I was supposed to say Rayna was good for him, but I couldn't bring myself to do it. Not when I knew what I knew.

"I bet it makes him feel good talking to you," I said. That at least was true. I doubted he would risk being so honest unless he felt like he needed to.

"Thanks," Rayna said. "I think it does. And if he won't let me jump him yet, at least I feel like I'm doing something good by making his life better. He's Maddox to my Angelina Jolie."

"That was so almost touching."

"Which is exactly my problem most of the time when I'm with Nico."

"Check it out," I said. "Makeover Woman's about to walk into her reunion."

"She looks hot," Rayna said.

"Totally."

We both focused on the screen, which was perfect because I could barely sit still and I didn't want Rayna to notice. I forced myself to make it through the rest of the show.

"Think Nico's at the stables?" I asked as casually as possible. "I kind of want to go for a ride."

"Let's find out."

No good. I needed to talk to Nico *without* Rayna.

"You know what, I think I just want to take a ride alone. I'll try to get some information before I go."

"Love it. Plus I get to finish the popcorn. I'll text him and tell him you want him."

"Cool. And I'll talk to him and tell him *you* want him."

"My God, if he doesn't know it yet, he *is* a stag."

She picked up the phone to text him, and I strolled out of the house, then practically sprinted to the stables. Nico was there, just slipping his phone back in his jeans.

"Oh hey, Clea," he said. "Rayna said you were coming to ride. Want me to saddle up Buchanan?"

"Nico, cut the crap," I said. "I know who you are, and I know what you're doing. I don't even give a shit that you're stalking me, but fucking with my friend is *not* okay."

Nico shifted uncomfortably from leg to leg. "I don't know what she told you," he said, "but we're not . . . I mean, we haven't . . ."

"I don't mean literally. You're with CV. Sloane had you get a job here when I came back from Japan, but it's bullshit. Your real job is spying on me. Messing with Rayna's head, *not* in the job description." My eyes grew wide as I realized. "Unless . . . Oh God, *is* it part of your job description? Did Sloane tell you to hook up with Rayna so you could get to me?"

"No! No, she didn't."

I expected that once I called Nico on his double life, he'd morph completely, but he didn't. His voice and mannerisms were the same as they'd always been. . . . Now he was just telling the truth. He plopped onto a stool and worked his hands.

"You're not gonna tell Rayna, are you?"

"She's my best friend."

That wasn't the same thing as saying I *was* going to tell her, but Nico didn't realize that.

"Aw, man . . . ," he said, "she's gonna think the same thing you did, and then . . ."

He hopped off the stool and walked around in anxious circles.

"You really like her?"

"Honestly, Clea . . . I love her. I hate lying to her, and I hate keeping her a little distant, but I had to stay focused. You've met them now. Sloane told me. All those people, cursed for something they didn't even do. That's the most important thing." Nico smiled. "But now, with you helping, we have a chance. We can get rid of this thing, and —

"Oh shit," he said, realizing he was talking to me about killing the love of my life. "Oh shit, I'm sorry, Clea. That was awful to say to you. I mean, Rayna told me some things about you and Sage — not that she's talking about you or anything, just stuff about how in love you are, not the stuff I know because of . . . you know . . . and I just . . . This has got to be so hard for you."

It was the most sympathy I'd ever gotten from someone who was as deeply involved with the Elixir as I was. I almost cried. It was twisted. I would do anything in the world to keep Sage alive. That hadn't changed. But at the same time I desperately wanted Nico to be rid of the curse he'd done nothing to deserve. He'd be good for Rayna, and she was already good for him.

I wanted Sage, and I wanted Nico, both with long lives ahead of them. The fact that I would never get both . . . I understood now why kids throw tantrums. I was about a second from falling on the floor in a kicking, screaming mess.

"It's got to be hard for you, too," I said.

"Yeah."

He didn't say anything else. I figured anything he tried would be the greatest understatement in the world.

"Did you really want to ride, or was that just to talk to me?"

"It was just to talk . . . but now I do want to ride."

"Want company?"

I smiled. Another time I might very much like Nico's company, but right now I wanted to be alone.

"No thanks. Not today."

He took Buchanan out of his stall and tacked him. I offered to do it, but Nico said it was his job—at least *part* of his job—and he wanted to do it himself.

I hoisted myself into the saddle and prepared to head out.

"Clea?"

"Yeah."

"If it comes down to it . . . you know, if we get the chance . . . to end the curse . . . I promise I won't be the one to do it."

Chills washed over me from head to toe.

"I can't ask you to promise that, Nico," I said. "It's your life."

"I know. And I can't say that I don't want it to happen, or that I won't do my part to help so someone else can do it . . . but it won't be me."

I felt tears threatening behind my eyes.

"Thank you."

I wanted to tell him I wouldn't hold him to it, but I saw in his eyes that he didn't want to hear that. He was telling the truth.

I clucked to Buchanan and started the long ride to the memorial I'd made for my father. I went at a slow trot, letting my mind clear so it could solve the puzzles rolling around it.

I thought of Nico being willing to sacrifice his shot at ending the curse, sacrificing it because he loved Rayna, and Rayna loved me, so he didn't want to hurt me. It was moving, but so absurd that I nearly laughed out loud. I imagined a new line of Hallmark cards: "Thank you for not killing my boyfriend, even if it risks killing you."

There probably wouldn't be a huge market for them.

The bigger problem was that even with everything I'd learned, I still had no idea where to find Sage. Goats. I knew there were goats. And huge pastures. Mountains in the background. Big wooden chairs. And what Rayna called the Girly Room.

It sounded like New England, a charming inn in New England.

Perfect. I'd narrowed it down to six states.

Time is short, the message had said.

How short?

Petra had made it clear that the visions she brought me were real, and happening in real time. That meant Sage had been alive and well not long ago for the goat feeding frenzy. The dagger would only work at midnight, so if he was alive earlier, he was alive now.

I dismounted once I could see the rock caduceus laid out on the ground.

"Hi, Dad," I said, walking to the memorial. "I'm sorry . . . I didn't bring you anything today. I kind of just needed to talk."

I noticed it from several feet away, but I couldn't believe what my eyes were seeing. I walked to the largest stone and knelt down right in front of it. I even ran my hand over its surface, as if it could have blended in, chameleon-like, and I just didn't realize it . . . but it wasn't there. Rage washed over me.

My necklace was gone.

seventeen

I CHECKED THE OTHER ROCKS OF the memorial, then scoured the dirt around them. Crawling on all fours, I ran my hands through the grass surrounding the site. I even looked up into the nearby tree branches, as if a small, targeted tornado might have come through this swath of land, then disappeared.

No luck. The necklace wasn't anywhere.

The logical part of me knew there were a million perfectly reasonable excuses. Birds like magpies collect shiny things. One could have grabbed the necklace and flown it up to a nest. It could have rained while I was in Cincinnati, and the necklace could have been washed off somewhere. A hiker could have come through and picked it up from the memorial. Any one of these and a million other options were possible . . . but I didn't believe any of them.

My necklace had been taken.

By Petra, maybe? Amelia?

I didn't know, but I felt a chill. Whoever took my necklace, I was certain it was a sign of bad things to come. I needed to do something, to lash out and take action. I wanted to see Amelia. She knew the answers. She wanted to help. If I could talk to her . . . if I could *call* to her . . .

But I couldn't. She'd said herself she'd get in trouble if the others knew she'd been with me. I didn't know what the rest of her family could see or not see, but if I screamed out for her, it seemed like there was a pretty good shot they'd take notice.

How could I reach her?

Could I reach her?

Maybe not . . . but I could try to reach someone who wouldn't get in trouble for speaking to me.

"Petra!"

Petra might not be on my side, but she definitely

knew more than she'd said. She would come if I called. I felt it. I screamed her name again and again, sounding as frantic and out of control as I felt.

"PETRA!"

I kept screaming, pleading to the sky, the trees, the ground. . . . I didn't even know if I was calling her as much as I was just screaming it out—Sage being gone but so close in my dreams, feeling helpless about how to save him, my fears about Lila and the cosmic unfairness of Rayna finally finding the perfect guy for her, who would die unless the love of my life was destroyed forever.

"PETRA!"

I felt so out of control. I fell to my knees by my father's memorial and started crying. I cried even after the tears stopped coming. I ended up curled on the ground, staring at the largest stone of the caduceus I'd laid out in the grass.

"Daddy," I whispered. "I wish you were here. I wish you could help me. I miss you so much."

As I reached out to touch the stone, a familiar lilting laugh sounded in my ear.

"Oh, sweetie, don't you know you can't count on family? They'll just disappoint you."

I bolted upright. "Petra?"

"You've seen it yourself, haven't you? Look at Sage. If you can't trust your soulmate to do right by you, you can't trust anyone, right?"

It was just her voice in my head this time, but I knew I could address it out loud. "Petra," I asked. "Where. Is. Sage?"

"That's the wrong question. The right question is this: Is Sage worth this? Look at you. Screaming, crying, losing control, rolling in the dirt . . . is that who you are? Is that the person you want to be? This man is taking your dignity, Clea."

"I love him."

Her laughter echoed inside my head. It sounded like church bells.

"That would be sweet . . . if he felt the same way about you."

"He does."

"'There are none so blind as those who will not see.' Poor, trusting Clea. You'll follow your heart, even if it leads you off a cliff."

"Why does it matter to you? How do you even know about Sage? How do you know about me? How am I supposed to trust you when I don't know what you are?"

"I'm someone who cares. And you don't need to trust me. Trust your eyes. You know the things

I've shown you are real. I'll show you more, too. We're not even close to done."

"Wait—don't leave! What about my necklace? Petra!"

But she was gone.

I climbed back on Buchanan and rode through the trails, then back to the stables.

Riding put me into a meditative zone. It stripped away my emotions, leaving me to see things more clearly. Once I did, I knew things weren't as tangled as they seemed. It didn't matter who Petra and her family were, I decided. They were part of the Mystery of the Elixir, and that wasn't my concern. That mystery was for my father, and for Ben. My goal was to find Sage. I had Nico to help me, and I had the rest of the CV, even though I knew they'd turn on me once I got Sage free. Petra and Amelia may have had their own agenda, but that only mattered if it helped me. And it did. By taking me to Sage, Petra had given me clues that pointed to a New England inn. It was vague, but it was something, and it was something I'd seen. I could do research online; I could look at pictures and maybe find the exact place I'd been in my dreams.

I brought Buchanan back to the stables and

handed him off to Nico. I didn't stay to talk. I liked him, and I loved him for Rayna, but if I spent too much time with him, I'd have to deal with the fact that if I got what I wanted—what I *needed*—I'd be signing his death warrant.

Not my fault. I couldn't take it on. He had nine years before his thirtieth birthday. There was a chance I'd have time to find another way to end the curse . . . *after* Sage was safe.

I spent the rest of the day on the computer, using everything I knew about the place I'd seen Sage in to try to find him. I was wired and knew I could stay up, but Petra had made it sound like she had more to show me, which meant I had to be asleep. I decided to go to sleep the minute the sun went down, hoping she'd bring me something that would help. I wanted to go downstairs and make myself a large pot of chamomile tea, but the idea of dealing with Piri, Suzanne, or even my mother was just too exhausting to bear. Instead I did some research and found a guided relaxation thing on the computer. It said it was a "calming, sleep meditation video." I tried it . . . but the guy telling me to "breathe in the white light of energy through your crown . . ." sounded too much like Anthony Hopkins in *Silence of the Lambs*. He also breathed heavily when he called me a "beautiful, shining being." It freaked me out.

Okay, so relaxation videos weren't the answer. I needed something that would exhaust me.

I walked down the hall to my father's office and opened the door. I was prepared for its barren landscape this time. I walked over to one of the moving boxes and opened it, pulling out the thickest medical journal I could find. I opened it to a random page. *Assessing the Feasibility of the American College of Surgeons' Benchmarks for the Triage of Trauma Patients.*

Perfect.

I hugged the book to my chest and brought it back to bed. I started reading it . . . and within minutes I was fast asleep.

Ten hours later I woke up.

That was it.

No visits from Petra. Nothing from Amelia. Nothing.

I didn't even dream.

It took me a while to realize it. I'd been so sure Petra was going to come get me that I expected to open my eyes at the inn. I was positive I'd be there, and kept looking around at my room, confused that it looked so different from the vision of white

devoted

wicker I'd expected. When I understood what had happened, I buried my head under my pillow and tried to force myself back to sleep, but there was a thin line of light blazing through the annoying crack in my curtains. Besides, I was more rested than I'd been in ages. There was no way.

Fine. If I didn't have more search fodder from Petra, I'd use what I already had.

First, a Sage check. Had he survived another midnight? I grabbed my camera, then pulled on a pair of jeans and a shirt, whipped my hair into a pony, and ran downstairs to grab tea and breakfast. Piri was already at work—I could smell pancakes and bacon, and my mouth was already watering. I called to her even before I walked in.

"Mmm, smells amazing! Did you make enough for me?"

But it wasn't Piri at the stove. It was Ben. He wore an old apron someone had given my mom as a gag gift that said POLITICIAN'S KITCHEN. He held the skillet high above the stove and looked like he was about to try to flip the absurdly large pancake inside it when he looked up and saw me. The joy in his eyes turned cold.

"No. There's just one for Suzanne."

I followed his gaze and saw Suzanne sitting

at the kitchen table, a huge grin on her face. "Morning, Clea," she chirped. Then she turned back to Ben. "Come on . . . you said you knew how to flip it!"

Ben slipped instantly back into his coat of charm, and carefully maneuvered the pancake on the skillet. "You ready for this?"

"Yes! Yes! Just do it already!" Suzanne cried.

Ben gave her an impish look and she blushed, darting her eyes to me. I pretended I hadn't noticed.

"One . . . two . . . three!" Ben cried, flicking the pancake into the air with a flourish. It flipped in midair, and he caught it expertly on the skillet. "YES!"

Suzanne laughed. "I thought you said you were a master at this!"

"Nope, first flipped flapjack."

"And you did it," Suzanne said.

"What can I say? You bring me luck."

Suzanne glowed.

"Are you done in there?" Piri's voice roared from the laundry room.

"Just about, Piri!" Ben assured her.

Piri harrumphed.

"Thank you!" Ben added.

"Piri wasn't very excited about Ben using the kitchen," Suzanne explained to me. "But he charmed her into it."

"I'm sure," I said. "He's quite the charmer."

I didn't want to stay in the kitchen anymore. It just felt toxic. I ducked into the pantry to see if there was anything I could grab and go.

I was impressed that Ben had convinced Piri to let him cook anything in her kitchen. She was clear about the fact that it was her realm, and swore the pots, stove, and oven responded to her specific touch and the tone of voice she used when she spoke to them, which she often did. Of course, I usually heard her cursing at them in Hungarian, so it's possible that cooking implements respond best to tough love. Either way, it was a very rare occurrence that Piri would cede her realm to anyone. I had a feeling it was more Suzanne's no-nonsense entitlement than Ben's charm that swayed her.

I found a Clif Bar and a bottled water, and headed out, waving a good-bye over my shoulder. As I went, I heard Ben presenting the finished meal to Suzanne. "A delicate balance of cakey, syrupy goodness, cut perfectly with the salted tang of the bacon . . ."

Suzanne's giggle was like nails on a blackboard.

I wondered if she'd eat either the pancake or the bacon. From what I'd seen, her diet was 90 percent protein shakes and Perrier.

Going out was a great choice. I felt refreshed and alive. Petra had said she'd come to me. When she did, I'd have more clues. In the meantime, I'd do what I could on my own.

I went for a hike in the woods behind my property, snapping photos. I took some time over a family of deer I found half hidden among the trees. The doe looked lovingly at her mate, and they both stuck closely to their fawn. It was beautiful, but it hurt to see.

It was early, but the weather was already hot and humid, and when I came back two hours later, I was ravenous and ready for a shower. Piri was back in her kitchen, grumbling in Hungarian to the cookware, and made me an omelet and a pot of tea, which I took up to my room on a tray.

I made myself shower before I checked my pictures. I'd decided that if I was truly going to handle things on my own, I had to keep my emotions in check and act logically. First shower, then pictures, then research.

I found Sage quickly this time. He was in the third picture I enlarged, lying in the grass far, far in the background of a shot I'd taken of a butterfly.

He was alive. That was enough to keep me going.

I printed the picture and taped it to the wall by my computer, then set to work.

I didn't know it then, but this would be my routine for the next several days.

Petra didn't come; Amelia didn't come.

I tried not to let it get to me. I started each day by finding Sage in a picture, so I knew he was okay . . . or at least alive. In the meantime, I got creative about my search for the New England inn. From my time as a freelance photojournalist, I had a ton of magazine contacts, many from travel-oriented publications. I approached them as myself this time, not Alyssa Grande, and sent them detailed descriptions of where I'd been. I used Photoshop to re-create a picture of both the room and the pasture I'd seen. I said it was a place I went on vacation with my parents several years ago, and while Mom and I wanted to go back, we couldn't remember the name. Involving my mother in the story was vital—people wanted to fulfill a request for Senator Weston, and they acted much faster than they would have if it had just come from me. Annoying, I know.

Within a day of sending out my pictures, I had a list of ten places that my group of travel editors thought I was showing them. Four were in Vermont, three in New Hampshire, and three in Maine. While I knew there was no guarantee any of them was the right one, I felt good about the possibility. I made phone calls to see if I could suss out anything unusual about any of them — I couldn't — and decided that if I didn't have any more dreams, I'd make use of the CV's military talents and have Sloane send out reconnaissance groups to each of the hotels. I felt uneasy about it, since it meant the CV might find Sage before me, and I had no guarantee that they'd give me a chance to escape with him, but Sloane had given me her word. I'd have to trust her.

The same night I decided that . . . I finally dreamed.

I'd cozied into bed with *Epidemiological Similarities Between Appendicitis and Diverticulitis Suggesting a Common Underlying Pathogenesis,* and made it about three pages in before my eyes slid closed.

I heard the music before I opened my eyes, and at first I thought I was having a flashback to my life as Delia, the doomed flapper I was in the 1920s. The song was a slow, jazzy riff on "It

Had to Be You," one of the songs Delia would
sing in the speakeasy while Sage played piano. It
was a favorite of theirs, and I smiled. I expected
to open my eyes and find myself lounging on the
baby grand, giving Sage a secret smile to show
I was singing just for him, not for the crowd of
admirers in the audience, and certainly not for
Eddie, the boyfriend who owned both me and the
bulk of Chicago . . . and who was destined to put
two bullets into the heads of both Sage and Delia,
killing her—*me*—instantly.

But this moment—me as Delia singing and
sneaking secret looks to Sage—happened long
before that, and I was eager to relive it. I already
had a knowing smile on my face when I opened
my eyes . . .

. . . but then my heart stopped.

I might as well have been hit by two bullets in
the head.

Not two feet away from me, Sage and Lila sat
on a thick bearskin carpet, lit by the glow of a
roaring fire in a massive stone hearth.

They were kissing, wrapped tightly together,
Lila's hands clutching Sage's shirtless back, his
hands embedded in her loose hair, slowly but
strongly pulling her mouth even closer to his. . . .

"Don't think I like showing you this," Petra's voice whispered in my ear, "but you deserve to know the truth."

I didn't know if she was in the room with me. I didn't look. I couldn't take my eyes off Sage and Lila.

Suddenly Lila pulled away, gasping for air. Her eyes glowed with a mix of desire and sadness, but Sage's eyes . . . I'd seen that look in his eyes before. I'd seen it when he looked at me.

He wanted her.

He reached for her.

"Lila . . ."

"No," she whispered, but she didn't pull her hand from his.

He entwined their fingers and whispered in her ear, "It's what you wanted. You told me. . . ."

"I know, and I do," she said. "So much . . . But it's not right, Sage. You don't love me. You love Clea."

"I . . ." Sage looked into the fire, thinking.

"Get me out of here," I whispered to Petra. I knew what Sage was about to say. He was going to say he didn't love me anymore, and I couldn't hear it. I couldn't. It would kill me.

"I do love her," Sage said. "She's my soulmate."

"I know," Lila said.

"But you . . ."

"I'm here," Lila said with a knowing smile.

"Lila, I can't do this." Sage looked pained, and moved closer to Lila, folding his body around hers. "I have real feelings for you. This isn't something I just do."

"You can't love us both," I said.

Lila said the same thing. Had she heard me?

"No," Petra said, guessing my thought, "she can't hear you. You're just playing out the oldest story in the universe. It's the same every time."

"I can't," Sage said, "but I do. I can't explain it. Being with you like this . . . you feel so good. . . ."

He pushed her long hair off her shoulder and bent to kiss her neck. I could feel the kiss in my fingertips and toes, but it wasn't mine. I wanted to disappear, I wanted to jump between them screaming . . . but I couldn't do anything. I couldn't even move.

"You're beautiful," he murmured.

Lila closed her eyes. Her resistance was weakening. Then she screwed her eyes tight and moved away from him so they were across from each other. The firelight flickered over their faces as her eyes bore into his.

"If you want this, there's a way, but you'd have to do something for me first."

"What is it?"

Lila closed her eyes, letting herself sink into his touch, then gave her head a shake.

"I told you how I came to the Saviors, right?"

Sage nodded. "They found you when you were in college."

"After my father died. I didn't know him well. He left early. And my mother and I . . . we didn't have much of a relationship. The Saviors became my family. There's a lot they do that I don't understand. And the way they've treated you . . . I can't understand that. But I've learned from them too. I've learned what love is, and I know real love isn't torture . . . like the torture you and Clea have put each other through."

"I didn't want to torture her."

"I know. That's my point. You're a good person, Sage. Clea must be too, or you wouldn't love her the way you do. You both deserve better. You deserve happiness."

Sage sighed, shifting away from Lila. "I don't know what I deserve. But Clea . . . she deserves everything. She does deserve happiness. It's all I wanted for her. Instead she gets me . . . and nothing but pain."

"I know. But, Sage . . . that can change."

"It can't. I've tried to keep away from her. I've tried everything. Travel, solitude, other women . . . it's deeper than you understand."

Lila flinched when he said it. I felt my whole body hollow out. I guess Rayna and I had our answer to that question.

"None of it worked," Sage said. "I always come back to her. I can't help it."

"You can," Lila said. "There's a ceremony. It will cut the tie that binds your soul to Clea's . . . but it won't work unless you go into it willingly, and ready to give her up."

"Give her up . . . forever?"

"You say you love her and want to protect her. If that's true, you can do it."

Sage was silent. The fire crackled.

"I don't know," he said finally. "I don't know if I can give her up."

"But if you love her . . ."

"You're right. If I love her, I should do it. But I don't think I can. I would die for Clea, but to cut her out when we're both alive and there's a chance, even the smallest chance, we could be together and be happy? . . ."

"Are you happy, Sage? Is Clea?"

"We have been. We've had moments of happiness more beautiful than anything else I've felt."

"And yet you're here with me."

"And yet I'm here with you."

He reached up to pull her close.

This time she didn't pull away.

eighteen

I WOKE TO PETRA clucking in my ear.

"Don't you love how he manages to seduce another woman by telling her how much he's in love with you? I'm not sure who's worse, him for being so manipulative, or her for buying it. Truth is, they deserve each other. And when he dumps her for the next thing, she'll have no right to be surprised."

"Get out," I said, climbing out of bed.

"No girlfriend-to-girlfriend postmortem?"

"*Leave!*"

With a bell-ring of laughter, she did.

I checked the clock. One a.m. Perfect.

In the dream, I'd been frozen in disbelief.

But now I was awake, and I was furious. I was ripping myself apart to find Sage and bring him back. I spent every single day tortured because I missed him so much. And what was he doing? Screwing around with someone else.

And not the first someone else. He'd said that himself. He used "other women" to distract himself from me. For my own good, of course. Because he loved me and wanted to protect me from the terrible horror of being monogamously tied to Sage.

Bullshit.

How many other women had there been? And over five hundred years! So if when you have sex with someone, you have sex with everyone they've ever had sex with . . .

Ugh. I felt like I needed a shower.

He was an asshole, and I was an idiot for believing in him. I'd been right from the start — soulmates were for fairy tales. In real life, people were just people, and they couldn't be trusted.

I took a shower and pulled on jeans and a low-cut T-shirt, but that wasn't good enough. I traded out for my favorite black sundress, the one I'd worn in Rio just a few months ago. It was chilly for it, but I could wear it with high boots and a leather jacket and it would be fine.

I dried my hair, leaving it loose, then spent time doing an expert job on my makeup. With purpose, I studied myself in front of the full-length mirror.

I was on a mission.

I'd done well. I looked good. Irresistible maybe? Even Suzanne would be impressed.

Suzanne.

She could put a wrench in things.

I'd worry about that later if I needed to. It was a work night. There was a good shot it wouldn't be an issue. I'd run with that.

I had taken my time getting ready. It was almost three in the morning when I left for New London, driving a solid eighty miles per hour. It took no time to get there. Glancing at the clock, I remembered this was around the same time it had been when I called here from Paris, panicked that Rayna had been hurt in a fire.

He was fine with it then; he'd be fine with it now. And if he wasn't fine with it at first, he would be soon enough.

The faculty housing at Connecticut College was a series of small, charming clapboard and rock-faced homes, arranged in a patchwork pattern along a road that wound through an endless green lawn. They looked very similar, and I had to count to make sure I went to the right one. His was the seventh house on the left, which he told me I could remember by thinking about his name. *B* was the second letter of the alphabet, *E* the fifth. That adds to seven. His house was on the left, which was the north side of the street, and *N* stood for north.

When he told me this system, I assured him he was the biggest dork in the universe. But it was the way I remembered.

There were no cars in front of his house or in the driveway. A good sign.

I knocked on the door.

No answer.

I pounded on the door.

No answer.

It *was* three in the morning. It would take more than pounding to get him up.

I rang the doorbell once . . . then twice . . . then three times in quick succession just to make sure he heard it.

I heard a roaring groan from inside the house.

I waited for him to answer, but no one came to

the door. I pulled out my cell phone and started dialing his number, but before I got halfway through, he appeared at the door.

"Clea? What the hell?"

He was wearing boxer shorts and no shirt. His front shock of hair was sticking straight up.

I put on my sliest smile. "Hi."

"Seriously?"

I rolled my eyes. He was going to make this difficult.

"I need to talk. Can you talk?"

"Now? It's . . ." He searched around for some kind of timepiece to help him finish his thought.

"Three in the morning . . . ish," I said. "Can you talk?"

I tried to read Ben's face. He was half asleep and looked like he wasn't sure how to respond. I waited. I wasn't going to accept a no, but I'd give him the time he needed.

"Yeah," he finally said. "Okay, yeah."

He fiddled with the doorknob so it wouldn't automatically lock, then stepped outside and closed the door behind him. "What's up?"

"Not here. I want to take you somewhere."

"Now?" He looked over his shoulder, as if he could see inside the house. It had to mean that someone was in there, waiting. She must have gotten a ride in his car, which was in the garage. It was an obstacle, sure, but I wasn't going to let it stop me.

"Now. Please. It's important."

"Why? You have another dream about Sage?"

I put my hand on his arm and moved closer, keeping my eyes on his. "Ben . . . I don't want to talk about Sage. I want to talk to *you*. I need to."

Ben met my gaze, and I didn't let it waver.

"Fine. I'll be right back," he said.

He slipped back inside and I waited.

Five minutes later he was back. He'd pulled jeans and a hoodie over his sleepwear and put on socks and sneakers, but his bangs were still sticking straight up.

"Where are we going?" he asked.

"You'll see," I said. "Come on."

"It's not far, is it? I mean, I can't be gone for a long time."

"It's not far."

He got in my car and we were silent as I drove. It was a ten-minute drive to Waterford, where I pulled into the Eugene O'Neill Theater Center. It was an enclave for theater people, with a conservatory school for college students, plus

devoted

showcases and retreats for playwrights and professional theater companies. None of that was my scene, but Rayna had dated a guy who was spending a semester of his junior year there, so we'd gone to visit several times. The center was pretty informal—just a group of rustic buildings set among the trees—but it was very close to a beautiful stretch of beach that the rest of the world ignored. When the conservatory was in session, students did tai chi every morning on the sand, but right now the beach would be completely empty.

I parked the car and we made our way to the beach, saying nothing.

The night was perfect. The moon was just over three-quarters full, and it reflected off the rolling waves. I kicked off my boots and sat on the sand, stretching out my legs until my feet were just inches from the water pulsing toward us.

"Come sit," I said.

Ben cocked his head, studying me. "Clea . . ."

"Come on. It's beautiful."

Ben shook his head, but he joined me on the sand.

I took off my coat and spread it behind us. I lay back on it.

"You have to lie back and look at the stars. They're amazing."

He did.

The night sparkled. With no other lights, it seemed like we could see the entire universe.

"It's incredible," I said. "It's like looking at eternity."

Ben nodded. "Kind of puts things in perspective. 'It doesn't take much to see that the problems of three little people don't amount to a hill of beans in this crazy world.'"

"*Casablanca*," I said. "And here I thought you'd go for Greek mythology."

"Because of the constellations?"

"Mm-hm."

"I can do that. I'm guessing you'd like Perseus and Andromeda. Star-crossed lovers so in love that after they died, the gods put them in the sky to be together for eternity."

"Eternity's a long time. I wonder if they ever wish the gods made a different choice."

"What's going on, Clea? Why did you bring me here?"

I let the question sit. I listened to the lapping of the water. I watched the stars. Looking up at them, I spoke.

"Do you ever think about what would have happened if things had been different?"

"Different?"

"Different."

"I used to."

I could feel the heat of Ben's arm, less than an inch from mine. We were so close, lying on my jacket in the moonlight. Nearly as close as Sage and Lila had been on the rug.

"It almost was, you know."

"Clea . . ."

"That night in Rio. It was just before sunrise. We'd been up all night. We were dancing together, and you were holding me, and the only thing I saw was you. And it was like everything in that moment changed, and more than anything I wanted . . ."

"Clea, don't. . . ."

I rolled over to face him. He needed to look at me.

"I wanted you, Ben. With everything I had, I wanted you."

I could tell he didn't want to look at me, but he rolled to his side and met my eyes. His were glassy, and when he spoke his voice cracked.

"Clea . . ."

I placed my hand on his cheek, just as I had that morning in Rio. Just like Sage had done to Lila.

"I think about that night," I said. "I think about it a lot. And I wonder . . . what would have happened if I'd . . . if we'd . . ."

I rolled closer to him, sliding my body next to his. I turned my head and pressed my lips gently against his. He recoiled for a second, then came back, his lips moving with mine. He pushed closer to me, wrapping his hands in my hair, just like Sage had done to Lila. I felt the hot rush of triumph and kissed Ben even harder, rolling on top of him. Bear rug by the fireside? Ha! Try sandy beach in the moonlight. I rolled us onto our sides and tugged at Ben's hoodie and shirt, sliding them up and feeling the heat of his bare skin. My sundress had slid up to my hips, and I could feel Ben's hands moving the fabric higher, freeing my skin to press against his. We rolled again and I was on the sand, my dress above my chest, the sand against my bare back. I wrapped my legs around Ben as we kissed, moving my hips against his. He was mine now; this was going to happen and Sage deserved every moment of it for what he was doing to me, what he had done to me over and over. . . .

"What the fuck?!"

Ben had sprung away from me. He was panting in sharp gasps, his eyes wild.

"What?"

He ran his fingers through his hair. "What are you doing? Jesus, Clea, what are you *doing*?"

His voice was breaking, and his hands clenched and unclenched. He kept darting forward, like he was about to run but didn't know if he could do it.

"If you have to ask, then I'm not doing it right," I said with a smile.

"Stop it! You don't want this! You don't want *me*. Why are you? . . ."

He grabbed his hair with both hands this time, wincing, his eyes shut tight. He took a long, broken breath and blew it out. When he opened his eyes, they were red and swollen.

"I think you should go," he said.

"How will you get home?"

"I can call someone. She'll come get me. Just go. Please."

He was immovable. I got up, not bothering to brush the sand off me. I grabbed my boots and jacket and turned back to Ben, but he was looking at the water.

"Ben?"

Nothing. He wouldn't even answer.

I trudged up the sand, then stuffed my feet into my boots for the walk along the gravel back to my car. I made it back out to the highway before I started to cry, but once I started I couldn't stop. I pulled over to the side of the road and freed the sobs that were buried so deep.

When I saw headlights coming the other way, I knew it was Suzanne. She whizzed by, and I started the car. I didn't want to be sitting there when she came back the other way with Ben.

Back in my room, I peeled off my clothes and climbed into bed, sandy grit and all. I didn't want to dream, I didn't want to think. I just wanted to stop.

I wasn't that lucky.

The minute I fell asleep, I was back in the Girly Room. I sat on a chair. Petra was there too. She sat cross-legged on the floor, a big grin on her face. I opened my mouth to ask her something, but she shook her head and pointed to Sage. He was there, pacing up and down like a lion. The comparison was apt. His eyes were wild, more agonized than they'd been during any horrible torture.

The door clicked open, and Lila padded in. She wore a long satiny slip, and was barefoot. She looked like she'd just rolled out of bed . . . except her hair was shiny from being brushed, and I could swear her lips shone with a coat of clear gloss.

"Lila!"

Sage pounced on her, his hands clinging to her upper arms.

"Sage? Are you okay? I heard you ringing for me, but it's so early, I thought I was dreaming."

Ringing for her? He couldn't just go get her? Was he locked in at night? Did that mean he'd tried to escape?

"*I* was dreaming . . . but it wasn't a dream. This woman . . . she took me somewhere . . . but it was real. What she showed me, it was *real.*"

My heart started thudding in my chest and I tried not to throw up. I turned to Petra, but she shrugged.

"What was it?" Lila asked. "What did she show you?"

I already knew, but he said it out loud anyway.

"It was Clea. Clea and . . ."

He couldn't even say it out loud. He looked like he was going to cry, but then he pulled himself upright and clenched his jaw.

"It's better this way. It's for the best. If she can

be with someone else . . ." His nostrils flared as he took a deep breath, then pushed it out through his mouth. "Maybe she can be happy this way."

"No," I said. "No, Sage, it's not like that! No, no, no, no, no!"

He didn't hear me, so I wheeled on Petra. "It's not like that! You didn't show him everything! You didn't show him what I saw! He doesn't know *why*! He doesn't know what happened! He thinks . . . what did you *do*?"

"It's not what I did, Clea. Honestly, if it's that awful to have someone see your behavior, maybe you shouldn't behave that way."

I lunged for her, absolutely prepared to wrap my hands around her throat and squeeze, but my hands clenched around nothing. She was across the room, sitting at the head of the bed.

I was helpless.

"I'm so sorry, Sage," Lila said. She took his hands and looked into his eyes with infinite understanding.

"Don't be," he said. "Like I said, it's for the best. It's over." He took another deep breath, then said, "I want to do the ceremony."

"Are you sure?"

"Positive."

"It's not reversible. It won't erase your memories or anything, but that tie that's kept your souls united . . . that will be gone . . . forever."

"Giving her a chance at a life. A real life. I want to do it."

Lila nodded and held out her hand. "Come."

Sage took her hand and they left the room. I tried to follow them, but I bounced back at the door. I turned to Petra, now lying on her side on the bed, her elbow propping up her head.

"Why can't I follow them? I want to follow them."

"You'd need me to take you, and I'm comfortable here. It's a nice room, don't you think?"

"Take me to them. *Now.*"

"Just let it go. He's letting *you* go. And if you want to know the truth, I think you're much better off for it. Plus, Ben's a good one. You'll be much happier with him."

"*Please!* I need to see what's happening!"

"You know what's happening. Sage is cutting his eternal ties to you. But fine, if you want to see, I guess I can show you."

Instantly I was back in the room by the fire. Again Sage and Lila were on the faux bearskin rug, but this time they were on their knees, and both looked solemn. The fire was raging as before, but sitting on the hearth was a small clay pot. It smelled like mulled cider. Between Sage and Lila was a basket. A cloth covered its contents, so I couldn't see them. A thick glove sat next to the basket.

"The pot on the hearth represents true love," Lila intoned. "Its contents are herbs that represent love: clove, cinnamon, cardamom, and apple blossom."

She removed two candles from the bag. Both were red and had plants tied around them.

"Two red candles," she said. "One wrapped in sage leaves, representing you, and one wrapped in iris petals, representing Clea."

She handed the candles to Sage, and gestured for him to hold them together, which he did. She wrapped the two candles together with a red ribbon.

"Two souls, tied together for eternity in love. Tonight we will poison that love, and break those eternal bonds. To do this, we take a symbol of the two of you and your lifetimes together."

She pulled something else out of the basket.

"My necklace!" I gasped.

Sage recoiled. "How did you get that?"

devoted

"I don't know. The others gave it to me for the ceremony, in case you decided you wanted to go through with it."

"How did they get it? Clea always wears that necklace. Is she okay?"

"Please don't think I'm being glib, but . . . did she *look* okay?"

Sage opened his mouth to reply, then closed it in a grim line.

"She looked fine. Continue."

Lila nodded. She placed my necklace into the clay pot filled with herbs. She tugged the thick glove onto her hand. "By melting down the symbol and mixing it with the herbs of love, we reduce your bond to its most elemental."

The glove was fireproof. With it on her hand, she placed the clay pot into the hottest part of the fire. I could see my silver necklace melting away to a puddle. It hurt me so badly, anger burned inside of me.

Lila pulled a capped tube from the basket.

"Sulfuric acid. Very corrosive—enough to corrode even the love bond held in this crucible. Be careful—this isn't something you want to breathe in."

Using her glove, she poured the acid over the melted silver-and-herb mixture.

"Should I be feeling anything different?" Sage asked softly.

I was wondering the same thing. I didn't feel different. I shouldn't have worried. If love bonds are real, then nothing can break them apart. Certainly not a few words intoned over a melted necklace.

"Not yet," Lila said. With her gloved hand, she pulled out another item from the basket. It was a thick black needle threaded not with yarn but with barbed wire. She held it up to show to Sage. "I'll coat this needle and wire with the mixture in the crucible, recite an ancient spell, then pierce the needle through the candles representing you and Clea. Once I do that, there's no going back. Your bond will be broken. Do you understand?"

"I do," Sage said with the solemnity of a bridegroom.

"We can stop right now, if you want. It's not too late."

"It's okay. You can continue."

Lila nodded, then reached into the flames, soaking the spiked needle and thread in the noxious mixture. She let the excess drip off, then gestured to Sage to raise the candles, which he did. Lila closed her eyes and intoned something in a language I didn't understand. She opened her eyes and locked them on Sage, who gave the smallest nod and moved the candles closer to her. She raised the needle to their side and pierced it through . . .

. . . and I bolted upright in my bed, gasping for air.

There was a hole in my body. A hole, right in the middle, and every breath I took escaped through it. I sucked in air, but it wouldn't stay. I reached my hand to my chest and felt it—a gaping hole in the middle of my body. Where my stomach and heart used to be was nothing. I could feel the sheets beneath me as my hand went through . . .

. . . and I bolted upright again.

I could breathe.

I felt my chest, my stomach.

Intact.

And yet part of me was missing.

There was no other way to describe it.

Physically I was whole. I looked in the mirror to check, because it seemed impossible. I felt like everything about me was different, the way I imagined someone would feel if they lost a limb. I was fundamentally not the person I was before, yet unlike someone who'd lost a physical part of them, I couldn't point to it and say *this is what I'm missing.*

It wasn't like I didn't remember Sage either. I remembered everything. And I loved him. That was the worst part. I loved him just as much as before, but it was our love that was different. Once we were tied together in an eternal bond. No matter what separated us, we would find each other. For at least a brief period of time, we were guaranteed to have each other. It was our destiny.

Now it wasn't.

The bond was broken.

We were just two people, floating separately along in a giant world. Maybe we'd find each other, maybe we wouldn't. And if we did, there'd be no eternal pull of destiny keeping us together. That was gone forever.

Sage may have been eternal, but our love was not. Not anymore. It was fleeting, and mortal, and human.

My stomach turned as I had a horrible realization.

I pulled out the overstuffed file full of my Sage pictures—the grainy, enlarged prints I'd made of his image hidden in my photos. I flipped through them, one by one. I didn't need to—I knew once I looked at the very first what I'd find in the others, but I had to look anyway.

They had become barren landscapes.

Sage wasn't in a single one.

nineteen

When I came back to myself, I didn't know how much time had passed, and I wasn't sure where I stood with Mother. Had she punished me because she knew what I'd done with Clea and Sage, or had she just sent a warning, and it was my weakness that made the effect so powerful? I wasn't sure.

What had happened while my consciousness was gone? Was I too late?

No. If I was too late, I'd have awakened in my body, in the glass-enclosed Snow White bed I'd been sealed into so very long ago.

There was time, but I didn't know how much.

I thought about Grandfather, and was quickly united

with his consciousness. He was in the last place I expected him—the secret room of our safe house, looking at our bodies in their four glass cases.

"Strange to see them, isn't it?" he said. I didn't have to say hello or announce myself—he knew I was there the minute I arrived.

I looked down at my own face, slack in its deathly repose. "Very."

"Even stranger to think how soon we'll be back inside them. I wonder if it will feel strange. Cramped, even."

"Will it be soon?"

Grandfather turned to face me, an inscrutable look on his face. "I haven't seen you lately, Amelia. Your mother was worried."

I lowered my head in obeisance. "She wasn't happy with me," I admitted. "But she was mistaken, Grandfather. I hadn't done anything."

"That's what I told her. The results bear it out. Nothing has upset our plans. You'll be happy to know that Sage is no longer tethered to the mortal realm."

"You mean . . . he agreed to cut his ties to Clea?"

Like magic, the minute I said the word "Clea," Mother appeared. I didn't hesitate. I ran to her like the eager, loving child I'd once been. "Did you hear, Mommy? Did you hear? He cut his ties to Clea! We can have our bodies back!"

"It's true, baby!" She scooped me into her arms and spun

me around, then peered down at her own face in her sealed bed. "You hear that? Get ready for me, 'cause I'm coming back!" She grimaced and recoiled. "My God I need a manicure. That's just frightening."

Grandfather laughed. "A haircut as well. Our nails and hair have been growing in our absence. I'm afraid we'll have a lot of grooming to do when we first come back."

"A spa day!" Mother crowed. "Maybe I should whisper in Lila's ear and have her set up appointments for us. I just hope we can find a place that schedules at the last minute."

"Last minute?" I asked.

"She'd be setting them up for tomorrow," Mother said with a smile. "The full moon comes out tonight."

twenty

I HAD BEEN STARING at my ceiling in a catatonic daze for several hours when Rayna pushed open the door.

Her arrival didn't stop me.

"Clea, come on! Nico and I are kidnapping you. We know you've been working hard on stuff, but it's a beautiful day and you deserve a break, so we're dragging you out for a ride."

"There's nothing to take a break from," I said dully to the ceiling. "I'm done."

Rayna picked her way past the ream of photo printouts thrown everywhere across the floor.

Nico stayed in the doorway. "You're done *cleaning,* that's for sure," Rayna said. "Come on, let's go."

"It's over," I said.

"Clea?"

I turned to face her and she got a good look in my eyes. Immediately she sat at the edge of my bed, her voice full of concern.

"My God . . . Clea, what's wrong?" She turned back to Nico. "Nico, I'm sorry, will you —"

"No," I said. "He can hear. He should know too."

Rayna looked confused but didn't press me about why. She just listened, and I told her everything.

She's a good friend. By the time I was done, she looked as stricken as I felt.

"Oh, Clea . . . But it can't —"

"He's not in the pictures anymore. None of them." I looked at Nico. "I'm sorry."

His head was bowed. Despite the complications, me leading the CV to Sage had been his best hope for a normal life.

"Not your fault," he said.

Rayna looked back and forth between us.

"I don't understand. . . ."

"Rayna," Nico said. "There's something I need to tell you."

twenty-one

No, no, no, no, no, no!

Tonight? The full moon was tonight?!

I had until midnight. That's it. But I couldn't do anything on my own. Mother had acted loving and happy to see me, but she also turned up the second I said Clea's name. I'd be a fool to think she wasn't on high alert and watching me.

If Clea and the CV were going to come, they had to come immediately. But after what Clea had seen, would she do it? Even if she would, how could I tell her where to go without Mother picking up on it?

I could go right to the CV and tell them, but they had no idea who I was, and I couldn't make it clear without being explicit enough to get Mother's attention.

My family was very busy that day, working with the Saviors to prepare and celebrate. I joined in wholeheartedly, but inwardly I racked my brains for something I could do.

It came to me in the late afternoon.

There was someone else in Clea's story.

I'd heard Mother talk about him. He'd been part of her plan, but she didn't see him as anything but a peripheral player, a planet in orbit around their twin stars.

He knew things though . . . enough that he could help. . . .

If he wanted to.

It was a big "if."

I couldn't try him right away, though. I had to wait for just the right moment, when I had the best chance of not being discovered.

It didn't happen until seven in the evening. Five hours before midnight. We were in the living room of the inn. It was large and cozy, with several couches, chairs, and tables surrounding a large fireplace. A bearskin rug draped the floor. Most of the Saviors were present. Lila was not. She was let go after Sage broke his bond with Clea. Lila had earned both her exorbitant fee and an extra bonus for her silence, and was quite happily long gone. She had no idea that several Saviors considered her a threat because she knew too much, and planned to hunt her down once they were immortal and free from human consequences.

devoted

The Saviors not in the living room were on security detail. Several had been dispatched to the roof with binoculars and guns. Several others were guarding Sage, waiting to drag him back to the rock altar and chain him up.

In the living room, my family gave the remaining Saviors what they needed most: encouragement and reassurance that immortality was just around the corner. We appeared in physical form and answered their endless questions.

When I saw that everyone—especially Mother—was deep in conversation and firmly tied to the spot, I finally split my consciousness.

A moment after the splintered part of me arrived, I heard a wicked laugh behind me. "Going somewhere?"

I spun around and smiled. "Mommy! You can do it now!"

She had ached to be able to split her consciousness like I could. Apparently she'd been determined enough to make it happen.

"Mm-hm," she said darkly. "And just in time, too."

"You're right. I'm so glad you're here with me!"

That's when Mother looked around and realized we were in our safe house, with our glass-encased bodies.

"I wanted to watch us," I said. "I wanted to see that last second before we come back."

A shadow passed over Mother's face. She was sure she'd catch me trying to stop the ceremony, but I was doing something completely innocent.

"That's a lovely idea, Amelia," she said. "How about I stay here and watch with you?"

"Will you?"

I asked like it would make me the happiest girl in the world.

It would.

It gave me the chance to do something she had no idea I could do.

Even as I stood in the living room of the inn and the secret room of the safe house . . . I split my consciousness a second time, and sent a part of myself to visit Clea's friend Ben.

I knew where he lived. The Saviors had a full dossier on Clea and everyone in her circle, and I'd helped myself to the information. I hoped he'd be home. If he wasn't, I'd be in trouble.

He was home. I found him wearing a towel, standing in front of his bedroom mirror. His hair was wet, and steam poured out of the bathroom from his just-finished shower.

"'Body of a superhero,' you say?" he said, flexing his pecs. "Oh, I don't know about that. I mean, sure, I work out, but I can't call myself a man of steel or anything." He turned and flexed his back, twisting his head so he could see the full effect in the mirror. "Maybe a man of bronze . . ."

"Hello," I said in his ear. I didn't want to say his name. Even split in two, Mother might have picked up on it and been pulled to me.

Ben jumped and nearly lost his towel. I probably could have made things easier by manifesting physically, but I was already in two other places, one of them in human form. If I did that here as well, I'd risk losing strength, and I had so much more to do.

"There's not much time. My name's Amelia. Someone — please don't say her name because people might be listening — might have told you about me. I appeared in a field with my family. I'm seven in mortal years . . . and about twenty-five hundred in immortal ones."

Ben's eyes grew wide and he sat on his bed, unable to keep his feet.

"You know who I am?" I asked.

"Yes," he said. "I mean, no . . . who *are* you?"

There was no time to explain, but I could try another way. It was something I'd never done before, but like many of our psychic skills when they first evolved, I suddenly had the sense I could do it.

I could tell Ben everything in an instant — at the speed of thought — "downloading" the relevant parts of my mind to his. I'd leave out the most sensitive information — anything that might be a beacon to Mother, in case she could tune in to this as well.

Ben was already sitting. As he understood everything that was happening, he fell back onto the bed and pulled the pillow over his face, completely overwhelmed.

I had chosen the wrong person. He couldn't help, and now it was too late to go to someone else.

Then he muttered, "You didn't tell me where to find him."

"What?"

"Him," he said. "I'm not supposed to say the name with you around, in case she's listening. I need to know where to find him."

"You are *going to help!"*

"I have to."

Well, no, technically, he didn't, but I didn't think he was talking about being compelled against his will. He had to because the world would go to hell if he didn't. Of course, that hadn't stopped other people from doing the wrong thing. Like my family, for example.

I also could tell there were deeper reasons he wanted to help. More personal. I had *chosen wisely. Ben was a good person.*

"I can't tell you where. For the same reason we can't say the name. You know that now, right?"

"Yes, but . . . if I can't do anything in time, why tell me?"

"You can. There's a connection there. Not like the one that was severed—it won't stop things—but if I strengthen it, it will lead you where you need to go."

"You can do that?"

"I believe I can."

"But then . . . why wouldn't you have done it before, with . . . her?"

"I didn't have the power. Or if I did, I didn't know it. That's how it works, being like this. We can't do things, or there are things we don't even consider possible . . . and then we get stronger and make more synaptic connections . . . and they're there. I believe I can do this, but I'll have to rest after, so you won't hear me. Oh, and it might hurt."

"How badly?"

"A pinch. Like getting a shot."

"I pass out when I get shots."

"Then maybe not like that. I've never had a shot, so it's hard to say. I've also never had this done to me, so . . . maybe just stay lying down, just in case."

He did, and even more than when I downloaded my thoughts into his, I moved my consciousness into his mind. I tried not to make any sudden movements in there. I remembered the squeezing sensation my mother created in my brain, and how long it took me to recover. I tiptoed gently until I found the connection I needed to enhance. Then I concentrated . . . enlarging it and strengthening it until the whimpering moans from the bed told me I had done as much as Ben could take.

It was just as well. I was exhausted. I needed to stay strong in my two other spots to keep my cover, and I had to be rested and ready for what would come later . . . if Ben could succeed.

It was time to go.

twenty-two

I LIKED NICO. I hoped he could avoid the curse long enough to find another way to end it.

After our conversation, he told Rayna everything, although I think she mainly heard the part about him being completely in love with her. He'd been living under a cloud his whole life, he said, and loving her gave him a reason to want a future.

It was tragic and beautiful. I felt happy for them. However long they had, they would make the most of it. Maybe even more than they would otherwise, because they *knew* there was a good shot it couldn't last. Their love would stay as intense as it was right now, and they'd squeeze every bit of rapture out of each second together, because they wouldn't take it for granted.

It reminded me of what I'd had with Sage . . . before.

Now he'd cut ties so he could be with Lila.

How was it affecting him? Did he think of me? Did he remember everything the way I did? Did I even matter to him anymore? Or since he was the one to make the choice, was it over for him . . . like an old girlfriend he'd maybe friend on Facebook one day but didn't matter in his new life?

After their conversation, Rayna and Nico went away. They invited me to come with them, but I didn't want to. Staying in bed seemed a much better option. Maybe forever. Rayna thought the occasion warranted the drama, so she left me to it . . . for a few hours. Around six thirty she and Nico came back with pizza, sodas, and a stack of DVDs. I might be taking to my bed, but I wouldn't be doing it alone.

About an hour into a perfectly absurd and blissfully *not* romantic comedy, my door opened.

It was Ben.

I wanted to pull the covers over my face and

disappear, but that wouldn't be fair. I'd messed up horribly, and I had to face him.

"Clea . . ."

That's when I noticed how pale he was.

"Ben?"

"It's Sage. I know where he is."

twenty-three

It was just about time.

The déjà vu was overwhelming.

There had been no grand celebration this time, just the group of us in the living room. Mother and I were also with our bodies at the safe house, but only the two of us knew that.

At exactly eleven thirty, the Saviors rose and trooped outside. We followed.

It was just like before. The large Stonehenge-like boulders. The tiki torches. The ceremonial fire. The display of tokens from the human world. The pure silver bowl.

Sage, shirtless, chained to the altar. Five men with Tasers flanked him now, not just two. This time he didn't struggle.

Mother told me that once the bond with Clea was broken, they stopped giving Sage the drugs that kept him open to suggestion. He was allowed to understand the enormity of the choice he had made, what would happen next, and how he had been fooled. Losing Clea didn't have the emotional impact it might have once had, but the knowledge that he'd been used and defeated by his own weakness . . . that shut him down.

I was so tired. Tired from separating into three, tired from enhancing Ben's mind, tired from keeping my truest thoughts tucked away from Mother.

I hoped Ben was on his way . . . and that I'd have some strength left to help him if he needed me.

twenty-four

BEN DROVE THE CAR.

I sat in the passenger seat. Nico rode in back.

Rayna had wanted to come, but Nico wouldn't let her. He said he'd rather die than see her in danger. No matter what happened, he said, he wanted any time he had left to be spent with her, and he couldn't guarantee that unless she waited for him at home.

Then he kissed her as if it were the last moment in both their lives.

Pretty powerful stuff. She agreed to stay behind.

Nico *had* invited another woman to come along, though. The minute we left, he called Sloane with an update. After my and Ben's visit, she and a battalion of around twenty CV members had apparently relocated from Cincinnati to a base closer to my house. That way they'd be ready to fall in and give chase at a moment's notice . . . which is what they were doing now.

They had to follow us, rather than just join us wherever we were going, because Ben didn't know what our destination was. The tweak that Amelia had made to his brain allowed him to lock in on Sage's location and be drawn there like a magnet, but he couldn't say where that location might be. He was running on pure instinct, but he was positive he was beelining us toward Sage.

Sage.

How had I gotten everything so wrong?

Time is short . . . , the message on my computer had said, and apparently it was shorter now than ever. Ben hadn't explained anything back at the house. He just said a young friend of mine had come and told him everything, nothing was what we'd thought it had been, and we had to leave immediately. He was surprised when Nico jumped up to come with us, but all I had to say was "Charlie Victor" and he understood.

After hours in the car, Ben had told me the whole story. About Amelia and her family. About the Saviors' quest for immortality and the terrible things they'd do once they had it.

And about Sage: tortured, drugged, his mind altered by suggestions he couldn't fight off, seduced by an actress playing a role. Yet he fought back . . . until he saw me with Ben.

I had been Sage's key to staying alive. The Saviors' plan couldn't have worked if he stayed tied to humanity.

I'd had the power to save him . . . and I threw it away. The bond between us had already paid the price. Now he'd pay with his life and his soul. He wouldn't be alone. The whole world would suffer because of my lack of faith.

The clock on the dashboard read 11:35. Twenty-five minutes until midnight, and not even Ben knew exactly how close or far we were from our destination.

I couldn't live with myself if we failed.

twenty-five

Ben was close.

I could feel it. It was a mortal feeling—not like the way it usually felt when I used my enhanced mental powers. This felt like intuition . . . which I suppose is the mortal form of what we do.

It had been several hours since I'd worked with Ben's mind. I'd had time to recover. I was still holding on to consciousness in two different places—the safe house with Mother and the ceremony site with everyone—but I was feeling stronger. Strong enough to go to the roof and do something about the guards. I needed them out of the way so Ben and whoever was with him would have safe passage.

I split off a third piece of my consciousness and sent it there.

Immediately I knew I'd made a huge mistake.

"So. I was right about you."

It was a voice I'd once loved more than life itself, but it now both sickened and terrified me.

Mother was there on the roof.

"Very clever, keeping me busy in the safe house so you could sneak up here. I'm sure you didn't imagine I could be in three places. You probably thought two was a stretch for me."

"Of course not, Mommy. I —"

"Don't even try it, Amelia. It's over. I've been waiting on this roof from the minute these guards were posted, knowing you'd try something like this.

I tried to give off waves of "terrified." It's what she'd expect and want. The truth, however, is I was relieved. If she'd been up here that long, she was already split in three when I went to see Ben. She might have more skills than I'd imagined, but there was no way she could have split in fourths. She caught me coming to check out the guards, yes, but she didn't know about Ben. He might have a chance.

I heard the wicked smile in her voice. "And now I can do what needs to be done . . . what's needed to be done for a long time now. Good-bye Amelia."

I felt her lunge to me, and my terror turned real. Even

rested, I was still so much weaker than normal. . . . Was I weak enough that she could destroy me?

"Wait!" I said. "What about Daddy and Grandfather?"

"Oh, right," she said. "They send their good-byes."

Mother shot herself like a bullet into my consciousness. The pain was more intense than anything I'd ever experienced.

"Whatever you see, shoot to kill," I heard her speak into the guards' ears.

Then she popped away, quickly. With my last thoughts before I disappeared I wondered: Did she leave because she trusted the guards to do their job . . . or because she was weak after everything she'd done?

I hoped it was the latter.

Maybe then Ben would have a chance.

twenty-six

BEN GRIPPED THE STEERING WHEEL when we saw the weather-beaten sign for the Arable Farms Inn.

"This is it," he said. "This is where they are."

The name was completely unfamiliar to me. We were in Vermont, but this was *not* one of the inns my research had turned up. From the looks of the sign, it had been abandoned for a long time. Had Amelia not reached out to Ben, I'd have led the CV on a hopeless wild-goose chase.

Eleven fifty. Did we even have time?

Behind me, Nico used his cell walkie to relay

Ben's information to Sloane. I heard her voice crackle back, "We take the lead from here. Military operation, no fucking around."

The CV members were in a fleet of five cars, which spread around us like a police escort as we made the turn into the long driveway.

We were halfway up the drive when the car in front of us started swerving madly. Nico's walkie crackled to life with a male voice: "High-powered rifle! Silencer! They got Damian! He's dead!"

And Sloane's voice in return: "Peel off! Take over the car if you can! Everyone else, keep moving, return fire, and shoot to kill! College boy, what the fuck?!"

The last part was for Ben. With the late Damian's car swerving in front of him, he was having a difficult time keeping our car on the road. We were swerving wildly and nearly knocked into the cars on either side of us.

"You're doing great, Ben," Nico said, leaning forward so his calming voice was close to Ben's ear. "Just hold that wheel tight."

The dead man's car peeled away. Sloane's took its place in front of us.

We could see the inn now, a white mansion that

in its heyday must have been the picture of New England tranquility.

Now gunshots rained down from its roof.

Thanks to the silencers and the sound of our own car, I didn't hear them, but I saw the muzzle flashes. Sloane's car and the others returned fire, using silencers as well. I watched a tall woman with long black hair lean out the front passenger window of the car to our left. She was inches from Ben. She couldn't have been much older than me. In another world she'd be carrying books across a college quad and laughing with friends instead of aiming a rifle, her muscled arms flexing as she took aim to fight for her life.

Her face exploded, struck by a hail of bullets.

I screamed and Ben jumped. He looked at me, then turned to follow my stare.

"No," Nico said softly but firmly in Ben's ear. "Don't look. Do. Not. Look."

Ben didn't look. He clenched his jaw, his lip twitching, and kept driving, his hands clutching the wheel.

He was lucky. I couldn't tear my eyes away. Two seconds ago the girl was alive; now her ruined body lolled out the window, bouncing with the movement of the car. I felt my gorge rise. I almost lost it entirely when her body slid out of the window and a boy just as young took her place, shooting up at the roof. I wouldn't let myself watch him.

A minute later, the flashes from the roof stopped.

"We got 'em," Sloane's voice came through the walkie. "Two casualties our side. If the Saviors are inside, they know they have company."

"They're not," Ben said, his eyes lighting up as he realized. "At least Sage isn't. There's a field in the back . . . then a clearing in the woods. That's where he is. That's it."

"It's eleven fifty-five," Sloane said. "Let's move it out. Now."

Ben took a deep breath and floored it. With the CV cars flanking and following us, we tore past the end of the drive, onto the grass that ran alongside the mansion, across the grassy field in its back, and as far into the woods as we could go.

We stopped short at the outer edge of a tornado. Projectiles spun in the air, making a wall ten feet high. It was impossible to see through: dirt mixed with branches mixed with rocks, all swirling madly. As I stared, I saw an entire bush whirl past, its roots intact. Then came a massive stump that must have weighed several hundred pounds.

"What the fuck?" Sloane gaped.

Pretty much my thoughts exactly. She just said them more eloquently.

"It's Amelia's family," Ben said. "They can move things with their minds. The tornado's protecting the ceremony to get the Elixir."

Nico used the walkie to relay the information to Sloane. She took only a moment to digest it.

"Eleven fifty-six," she said, her voice crackling over the walkie to the whole team. "This thing's going down in four minutes unless we stop it. There's some weird shit going on in there, and it's going to be messy, but this is our chance. I want Sage, and I want the dagger. You stab him at midnight, great. If not, just get him. This is the best chance we've had. Let's make the most of it."

It was surreal to hear Sloane give a pep talk about killing Sage but still feel she was on my side . . . for now. I needed her to stop the Saviors. I needed Sage alive for four more minutes, I'd figure everything else out from there.

"Face masks," Sloane ordered. "Now let's go!"

The CV pulled on face masks—they were prepared for anything. They piled out of their cars, guns blazing. Their bullets ricocheted off the flying debris. One grazed Sloane's leg.

"No guns!" Sloane screamed. "Not until we're inside!"

As the CV fought to get past the tornado wall, Nico put his hands on Ben's and my shoulders.

"You two stay back here. It's too dangerous."

He pulled on his mask, and stormed into the swirl of debris. Ben turned to me.

"Clea . . . ," he said.

"Not a chance."

I checked my watch: 11:57. Three more minutes. I raced after Nico, straight for the deadly storm.

I stood at the edge of the whirling madness, blinking the dirt out of my eyes. I heard thuds and screams as CV members who had jumped in ahead of me were pummeled by debris. I wished I had a face mask.

"Clea!"

I looked over. Ben had wrestled his arms out of his T-shirt, and pulled it up over his face. Smart idea. I did the same. The fabric of the tee I'd pulled under my hoodie was sheer enough that I could see, if only a little bit. With a final nod to Ben, I dove into the tornado.

Inside, I was practically blind. I was pelted from every direction, like a million bees were stinging me. Two feet in I tripped and fell, landing face-to-face on a dead body: the boy who had been shooting from the car next to us, impaled by a large branch.

No time to scream. I scrambled up and kept moving, dodging and ducking to avoid anything large. It was like running through an asteroid belt.

An eternity later, I emerged on the other side of the tornado wall. There was no calm in the eye of this storm. The CV who had made it through, bloodied and battered, had taken cover and pulled out their guns. They were shooting toward a clump of armed people shielding a large, flat rock. Tied to that rock was Sage. His mouth was gagged, his body wasted.

I needed to go to him . . . but how?

I scanned the gunmen around Sage. There had been more, I realized. Several were rolling on the ground, screaming from bloody wounds. As I watched, more were hit. The CV was outnumbered, but they were better shots.

Two more Saviors went down, opening a path to Sage. I ran for it, and almost made it to him when a wounded Savior grabbed me by the ankle. He raised his gun to my head, but a rock pummeled the side of his face before he could shoot.

I looked up to see who threw it. It was Ben, but

he still looked panicked. I turned. Next to Sage, the bloodred readout of a large digital clock read: 11:59:01.

Then I looked up and saw him: a single Savior. He ignored the gunfire and stood solidly, holding Magda's dagger high above his head, ready to plunge it into Sage's exposed chest.

I threw myself on top of Sage, blocking the path to his heart.

My face was inches from Sage's, his eyes staring into mine. He looked . . . confused. As if he had an idea of who I was but wasn't entirely sure.

"Clea," I said, choking back a sob. "It's me, Cle—"

A bolt of pain shot through me and I rolled off Sage, unable to control my muscles. I landed faceup in the dirt, next to a wild-eyed man. He was covered in blood but had reached up to blast me with his Taser. With a horrible smile, he pulled out a knife and lunged . . .

A bullet smacked into his chest. He landed on top of me, and though his knife fell uselessly to the side, his large body pinned me to the ground.

An electric buzz blared as the digital readout clicked to 12:00:00. The stroke of midnight. For exactly one minute Sage could be destroyed, and the Elixir delivered to the Saviors. The man with the dagger gave a mighty victory cry and hurled his arms toward his target.

"SAGE!" I screamed.

The dagger swung down, but a second before it hit its mark, Ben leaped out from the surrounding fray and tackled him.

"Ben!" I gasped.

The man was twice the size of Ben, but Ben was strong, and he wouldn't give up. They wrestled like bears, the only two not wounded or caught up in a gunfight.

A minute . . . if Ben could just keep the man engaged for one minute . . .

A giant tree branch flew out of nowhere, knocking into the side of Ben's head. Amelia's family. I couldn't see them, but I knew they were here, hurling rocks and roots and fighting to keep the CV from spoiling their plans. I knew their strength was limited, but not limited enough.

Ben clung tight to the Savior, even as he went down. The two fell together, Ben's full weight crunching onto the Savior's arm.

The dagger came loose, rolling away from them . . . and toward me.

I could practically grab it, but my muscles were

helpless from the Taser. I tried to reach out . . .

Nico lunged from the woods and grabbed it.

For a second his eyes met mine. I could see the agony there. He'd made me a promise, but now he had the chance to save the lives of himself and the others who were wrongly cursed.

"DO IT, NICO!" Sloane yelled from several feet away, where she was locked in battle with a Savior.

12:00:30.

He stood over Sage and held up the dagger. He tried to wield it like the Savior had, but his arms seemed weak. He lifted the dagger no higher than his own heart. Indecision plagued his face.

"DO IT *NOW*!" raged Sloane.

"NOOOO!"

It was Ben.

He had squirmed away from the Savior and dived for Nico, tackling him to the ground . . . and onto the dagger. It plunged into Nico's stomach.

Ben rolled off him immediately, his eyes filled with horror. "Oh my God . . . Oh my God . . . Oh my God . . ."

He rolled Nico onto his back to look at the wound. It was awful.

Nico smiled.

"Thank you," I heard him croak to Ben. "The choice . . . I couldn't . . ."

He winced.

"GODDAMN IT!" roared Sloane.

With a frenzied cry she threw a knife at her assailant. It hit its mark, lodging in his shoulder and throwing off his aim. Now out of the line of fire, Sloane raced to Nico's body, yanked the dagger out of it, and plunged the dagger into Sage's heart.

12:00:59.

I screamed.

The ceremony was complete. The gunfire ceased. The rocks and trees stopped flying. It was so quiet I could hear the blood bubbling like a fountain from the hole in Sage's chest, a hole far bigger than that dagger should have rightfully made. It flowed over Sage's side, pooling into a silver bowl mounted next to the rock altar. Sloane's eyes grew wide as she stared at the fluid.

"Elixir," she breathed. She laughed, a ragged insane giggle. "Elixir! Eternal life! Look!"

She held out the bowl, filled not with blood, but with a viscous silvery fluid, dancing with shapes and colors. The Elixir of Life.

Sloane lifted the bowl to her lips.

Summoning all my strength, I threw the dead body off me, pushing it into Sloane's legs. She lost her balance and didn't get her drink. Before she could recover, I dove into her. She fell back hard, her head cracking against a rock. She still held the silver bowl. I needed it. I needed to dump it out. I'd lost Sage, but I would *not* let Petra and the others win. *No one* would profit from his death.

I had almost reached the bowl when several vines looped and curled around me, stopping me cold. A lilting voice trilled in my ear.

"Bad idea, Clea. You lost."

Petra's unseen hand took the silver bowl and floated it toward the remaining Saviors.

It was over.

twenty–seven

I thought I was gone forever, I did. I wanted to be gone. The pain was unreal. Once, more than a thousand years ago, I had the unfortunate experience of seeing someone drawn and quartered—literally pulled apart in four directions. This felt like what I imagined that would be, except instead of four directions I was being ripped to shreds in a million directions at once, my consciousness sharp and feeling every bit of the excruciating pain. Disappearing forever would have ended the horror. Fighting it risked staying in a state where I was aware, but in this kind of pain, for eternity.

But I knew I was needed. So I fought.

By the time I had any awareness, most of it was over.

I took in the carnage quickly. Most of the Saviors and Cursed Vengeance members had been flung to the ground, dead or wounded. Sage was destroyed, the fountain of eternity bubbling from his pierced heart. Ben sat on the ground, clutching at the body of a blond-haired young man who was either dead or nearly so. I sensed Grandfather and Father, weak from their efforts. Mother was running on pure adrenaline, but I could feel her strength throbbing strongly through the air. Her energy was so strong, I was surprised she hadn't realized I'd returned.

Then I saw Clea, and I realized Mother's concentration was elsewhere. Clea was grasping for the silver bowl of Elixir, then was grabbed by thick vines controlled by Mother. As Clea struggled fruitlessly to escape, Mother moved the bowl toward the mortals in the area.

Mother let her voice echo into their minds.

"I hold the Elixir of Life. Drink it—your wounds will heal, and you will become immortal! Drink . . . and become one of us!"

She manifested. She looked like an angel, in the flowing white robes we wore in ancient Greece, her hair cascading to her shoulders in a halo of curls. Even after everything, she took my breath away. Among the remaining Saviors, she appeared nothing less than a goddess. Even the CV members, struggling for life against their painful wounds, forgot their dedication to destroying the Elixir in the face of possible immortality. They reached out to her, beseeching her.

I could feel my family's hunger for it to happen, to finally happen. I felt a surge in Father's and Grandfather's strength. Even if one of the mortals tried to stop them now, it wouldn't work. My family would overcome them. They had come this far, nothing would get in their way.

Except me.

I remembered the first time my family hurt me, when their horrible words and thoughts sliced into me and left me as battered and bruised as if I'd been beaten. I remembered realizing that they could destroy me if they wanted to . . . and that I could destroy them, too.

I felt their presence. My family. The people I'd trusted. The people I had loved most in the world.

I bid them a silent good-bye.

As Mother was about to lift the silver bowl to the lips of the first eager Savior, I concentrated every bit of energy I could summon. I imagined myself a sea of whirling weapons, chopping, lacerating, destroying.

Then I took everything I had, and threw it into their minds.

twenty-eight

I HEARD NOTHING BUT THE SOUND

of my own screams.

It couldn't be happening. I was trapped, unable to move . . . unable to do anything but watch as Petra held out the chalice to a Savior.

Then suddenly it was Petra who was screaming. The sound was so horrible it stopped me cold. It was the cry of a woman in the worst torture imaginable. She was flung backward as if she'd been shot. The bowl of Elixir flew out of her hands, the fluid spilling out and turning from the silvery Elixir back to blood as it hit the ground and dissolved back into the earth. Every one of the wounded gasped, and those who were able lunged or crawled after the bowl to try to catch whatever drops clung to its sides. Before the first Savior reached it, the bowl itself exploded into a million pieces.

No one but me even noticed Petra, whose throes of agony continued. She turned her face to me and opened her eyes . . . but they were blank inside, dark, vacant holes.

Then she disappeared, leaving the clearing in silence.

The vines released me.

"You!" one of the Saviors screamed as she pointed to me. "You destroyed everything!"

She reached for a gun.

"No!" Ben cried, leaping toward me, but one of the CV members grabbed a gun and trained it on him.

"What are you doing?" Ben asked, confused. "You *wanted* the Elixir destroyed!"

"We could have all lived forever!" he wailed.

I shot a look at Ben. This was it.

In the split second before they pulled the triggers, I tried to be brave. At least we'd stopped the Saviors from becoming immortal. And with the Elixir gone, the curse over the CV would be lifted. Ben, Sage, Nico, myself . . . none of us would die in vain.

But the bullets never came.

Instead the earth began to rumble and shake. The giant boulders surrounding the altar shattered and fell. The first hunks of broken rock knocked away the guns pointed at Ben and me, and the Saviors and CV members scrambled to get away from the chaos.

"Just stay low and covered," said Amelia's voice in my ear. "You'll be fine."

Amelia. I hadn't even known she was here. The earthquake was from her . . . her way of protecting us.

She must have spoken to Ben, too, because he hit the ground, curling into a ball and covering his head. I did the same, but I peeked out just enough to see the complete devastation of the ceremony site. Everything in a fifty-foot radius shook to the ground, and the earth itself opened into a bottomless crevasse, swallowing several CV and Saviors not smart enough to scramble away when they could.

Eventually the dust was so thick I couldn't watch anymore. I ducked my head and remained hidden until the shaking stopped.

Finally I looked up.

There was nothing but a circle of flattened ruin, with Sage's ragged, empty shell of a body strapped to the rock altar in its very center. It was too horrible. I couldn't even look at it.

Ben was already standing, looking down at Nico's lifeless body.

"I killed him, Clea," he said. "I killed a man."

I wanted to tell him he had no choice, but I didn't know. Would Nico have done it? Would he have held on to the dagger until after midnight and saved Sage? I had no idea.

I couldn't even imagine how I would explain everything to Rayna.

It was time. I had to face Sage. Carefully, I stepped to his side and knelt down. He had looked the same from the time I was born, but now I barely recognized him. The man I loved wasn't in this wrecked and ravaged body. He wasn't anywhere.

I put my hand on his sunken cheek. I remembered our last moment. He'd looked at me like he wasn't even sure who I was.

I started to cry. This was what I deserved. I had made him break the bond between us. Now I was doomed to remember everything, every second of our love and lives together . . . while he'd died with me meaning nothing to him.

No. He didn't die. He lost his soul. It was torn from his body. I remembered how Magda described it—Sage's soul had whirled around, suffering terrible pain until it ripped apart into nothingness.

"I'm so sorry, Sage." I sobbed, "I tried . . . I tried so hard." I looked into his unseeing eyes, reaching out to a soul that was no longer there. "I love you. I'll always love you."

"Clea!" Ben gasped.

I turned . . . and nearly collapsed in shock.

Nico . . . all but disemboweled by the dagger when he fell on it . . . was stirring.

I locked eyes with Ben, and I knew he was remembering too. Nico had been dying at the same time the dagger ripped away Sage's soul. Magda had said something else about the ceremony . . . something about a ripped-out soul searching for an empty vessel. . . .

Nico's body rose to its feet, unsteady but very much alive. He looked down at his stomach curiously, as if he'd felt a strange bug crawling on it. He lifted up his shirt . . . to reveal his unscathed skin.

He lowered his shirt, then looked around. He took in Ben, gazing at him from head to toe.

Then he turned to me. He cocked his head and furrowed his brow, as if searching for a piece of information he knew he should have but didn't.

"Clea?" he asked.

"Yes," I whispered.

"It's me."

acknowledgments

AN ARDENT THANK-YOU to my dedicated fans for their continued support and for making *Elixir* such a success! I wish I could express what your love means to me, and how it continues to shape the person that I am.

To my friend Elise Allen, you never cease to amaze me with your skill and passion for your craft. Thank you!

To my literary agents, Rob Weisbach and Fonda Snyder, thank you for your continued guidance and for taking the time to make everything run smoothly.

Thank you to my editor, Zareen Jaffery, and her assistant, Julia Maguire.

And thanks to the hard-working camp at Simon & Schuster, who have collectively made this effort an exciting endeavor: Carolyn Reidy, Jon Anderson, Justin Chanda, Anne Zafian, Paul Crichton, Nicole Russo, Elke Villa, Jenica Nasworthy, and Lizzy Bromley.

XXO
HD

Want another dose?

Keep reading for a

sneak peek of *true*,

The spellbinding
conclusion to the
series that began
with *New York Times*
bestseller *Elixir*
and *Devoted*

true

HILARY DUFF
an elixir novel

the exciting conclusion

to Hilary Duff's *elixir* series.

I'M FALLING IN LOVE WITH SAGE

all over again, a Sage who looks different, but who proves every day that he's still my soul mate. And while he no longer has the memories of our past lifetimes together, every day we make new memories, and grow even closer than before.

I'm so close to being blissfully happy. There are just a few things that stand in the way.

The first, of course, is Rayna. I feel terrible that she doesn't know the truth—that Sage's soul took Nico's body in order to live. And the closer Sage and I get, the more I feel like I'm betraying her. I try to reach her every day. I call, I e-mail, I text, I write her letters begging her to give me ten minutes to just talk to her. . . . I even knock on her door when I know Wanda's out with the horses, but Rayna never responds. I'm so frustrated that I fantasize about dragging Sage to her doorstep and shocking her so badly she'll have to listen, but I'd never actually do it. Much as I want to talk to her face-to-face, I know that if she keeps refusing to see me, I'll have to write everything in a letter and send it to her. It's not perfect, and if anyone else sees it they'll think I'm certifiable, but it's less unfair than letting her live with half the story.

Another problem is with Sage. The evening of the soul transfer he was nauseous all the time, then he became ravenous and always tired, but his latest quirk is more disturbing. When he tried to make the same breakfast twice I could chalk it up to stress, but the memory lapses keep happening. He doesn't forget anything major, like who or where he is or who I am, but it's a constant string of little things. He'll restart a conversation that we just had an hour ago. Or he'll say we should visit a museum we just saw the day before. When I ask if he remembers what happened before, he never does.

Ben, meanwhile, has been great. He spends hours each day either in Dad's studio or in the Yale library, going through the oldest books in their rare text archive, trying to find anything that might be relevant. I ask Ben what he thinks about the memory lapses, and he's not sure what to make of them. Sage and I meet him at a diner in New Haven one day, and he gives us a full update over burgers (Sage and me) and a bunless turkey patty on salad greens (Ben).

"What do you know about organ donation?" Ben asks.

"Why?" Sage asks. "Are you planning to give up a kidney?"

"Not at the moment," Ben says. "But when someone gets a new organ, the body can reject it. It does reject it, almost always, unless the patient takes drugs that stop the rejection."

"But Sage didn't get a new organ," I say.

"He didn't get a new organ," Ben says, "he got all new organs. And it almost didn't happen. Think about how many things had to line up for it to work. Sage had to be stabbed in the heart, at midnight, with a specific dagger that would rip his soul from his body."

Sage shifts uncomfortably. "Funny, it sounds so pleasant when you describe it."

"Sorry," Ben says. "I'm just laying it out so you understand. Even after all that, the purpose of the dagger and the ceremony you went through was to drain the Elixir of Life from your body, and wrench your soul away not just from your body, but from any kind of salvation. We heard all this from Magda, remember? Your soul was supposed to swirl around in eternal pain and agony until it dissolved into nothingness."

"You've really never considered a career as a poet?" Sage asks. "Maybe a grief counselor?"

"I swear I have a point," Ben says. "The Elixir is gone. That worked. We know that because of your cut. You're mortal now. What didn't work is your soul getting wrenched away, and that's because there happened to be a host body right there that had just lost its own soul."

"Nico," I say.

"Clearly." Ben nods. "Nico's body was there and empty, but it's not like it was planning to receive a new soul. It was dying. Sage arriving was a shock to the system. Like a body getting an organ transplant. Only for an organ transplant, doctors prepare the patient with antirejection medicine."

"To suppress the immune system," I say. My dad had been a surgeon, so I know a little about this. "The body doesn't recognize the new organ as its own. It thinks it's a threat, and attacks it."

"Exactly," Ben says. "But Nico's body wasn't prepped, so the same way it might try to reject a donated organ, it might be trying to reject the new soul."

"That's impossible," I say. "An organ is concrete. You can hold it and measure it. A soul is . . . it's ephemeral. You can't pin it down. The body can't attack it because there is no 'it' to attack."

Sage has been quiet, taking this in, but now he speaks in a measured voice. "Of course there is. The soul is its own entity. It has a life that goes beyond whatever body it's in. The three of us should know that better than anyone."

He's right, and I can tell Ben's diagnosis troubles him. I take Sage's hand and squeeze it.

"Are you sure?" I ask Ben. "You really think that's what's causing his memory lapses?"

"I'm not positive," Ben says. "It's not like there are medical journals on the topic. I'm extrapolating from stories and myths. But the symptoms are pretty consistent with everything Sage is going through: the sickness, the hunger, the blank spots. . . . I really think that's what's happening."

"So what can we do to change it?" I ask. "What's the spiritual equivalent of organ rejection drugs?"

"I haven't found one yet," Ben says. "That doesn't mean it isn't there, I just haven't found it yet. What I found so far is just about the things that can go wrong. I'll keep looking, though. I've found references to other texts, at other libraries. . . . I'll find something."

Sage watches as Ben pushes the last bits of turkey patty around his plate, and when he speaks, his voice is soothing.

"You already have," Sage says. "You know what comes next. If we don't find an antidote."

Ben pops his head up from his plate of food, as surprised as I am. "I —," he stammers, "I don't know anything for sure."

"But . . . ," Sage gently urges.

"They're old stories. And sometimes they're allegories; you can't take them literally."

I'm squeezing Sage's hand so hard my grip is going numb. "Ben, please, just tell us."

Ben gives a long exhale, then speaks to his plate in a single breath. "The stories describe a descent into madness by the new body/soul combination, often including violence against himself and others . . . and ending in death."

"His own death?" I ask, my voice tinny in my ear.

"The struggling soul rarely goes down alone," Ben says grimly. "There are usually other victims. Sometimes just one . . . sometimes many."

I feel like the air has been sucked out of the room, but Sage is calm. He leans back in the booth. "So now we know. How long do we have?"

"Not sure," Ben says.

"Then here's what we need to do, and I'm telling you both right now, because I won't be in a position to say it later, and because we've gotten into trouble with this kind of thing before. I don't want to be here if I'm a danger to the people around me. When things get bad, one of you needs to do something about it."

Sage says it calmly, like he's talking about catching a movie.

"What are you saying?" I ask. "You think I'm going to kill you?"

Sage's response is simple. "Do you love me?"

"What kind of a question is that? Of course I do! If I didn't, I—"

"If you love me, you won't let me become a monster."

My mouth is open, ready to scream back at him, but instead I just shake my head. "I can't."

"So it's up to you," Sage says to Ben, but Ben's already saying no.

"I won't. I can't. I already have blood on my hands. I can't do it again." His voice starts to crack, and Sage smiles sympathetically.

"Okay. How about this: Lock me up. When it gets to the point where I can't control myself, have me committed. Then I can't hurt anyone."

"I can do that," Ben says.

"Good." Sage extends his hand, and Ben shakes it. They're like boys making a trade in a school yard, and it nearly makes my head explode.

"Stop! What are you doing? You're not making some kind of bet! This is your life we're talking about!"

"Yes, it is," Sage says, as if that puts a period on the argument.

"But Ben even said he's basing this stuff on stories that aren't even real. He has no idea if this will actually happen."

"I have confidence you won't actually put me in a padded cell and straitjacket unless it's absolutely necessary."

"You're joking about this?" I gasp.

"No, I'm not," he says, so matter-of-fact that I want to smack him. He holds up his wrist. The bandages are gone now, but there's still a thick scar from where the beer bottle sliced him open. "When I got this, you know what it meant to me?"

"That you could die?"

"No. That I could live. This proves the Elixir is gone. I don't have eternal life. I don't have anything anyone else wants. When I look at it, I know no one's coming after us, and we can live like normal people. That's what I want, Clea. I want to live with you, and grow old with you, and one day, a long, long, long time from now, I want to die with you, knowing our souls will be together for whatever comes next."

He's turned toward me in the booth now, holding my hands, his eyes gazing into mine, and we're the only people in the world.

"That's what I want too," I say.

"Then we'll fight for it," he says, "and we'll hold on tight to every second we have. But if we can't have that future, if I can't have the life I want, I refuse to take you down with me. That would be worse than any death."

Tears fill my eyes, but I won't give in. "It won't happen," I say. "You won't get any worse."

"Ben?" he asks, not taking his eyes off mine.

"I'll take care of it," Ben says quietly. "If it comes to that."

When we leave the restaurant, Sage and Ben exchange a very formal handshake, then I hug Ben tightly. "Find a cure," I say in his ear. "We have to."

"We will," he assures me.

Several hours later, at dinner, Sage stops eating in the middle of his salad.

"Weren't we planning a lunch with Ben?" he asks. "When are we going to do that?"

I force a smile. "Sometime," I say. "We'll figure it out."

Ben's prognosis scares me, but I'm not convinced

it's inevitable. Old myths and stories aren't always true. Nico's body and Sage's soul have gone through serious trauma, and it only makes sense that they both need time to heal. The memory lapses aren't a sign of worse things to come, they're bumps on the road to health.

Still, they make me think of my own memories, and how they might fade. I don't dream about my past lives anymore, and while those dreams once confused and scared me, part of me mourns the loss of the women I used to be. I start writing down everything I remember about them, before it all disappears into distant memory, and I promise the memory of Olivia that one day, when Sage is healthy and Rayna knows the truth and has forgiven us, Sage and I will go to Italy and have the wedding she was promised, but never got to enjoy.

I also write about the way Sage used to look. After so much time with him, it's his new face and body that I see when I close my eyes and think about him. Sage's gestures, his posture, and his soulful eyes don't look like they're out of place on someone else's body anymore. They look like they belong.

I have the man I've always wanted, but I still wish I had some relic of the man he used to be.